TURN OF THE TIDE

TURN OF THE TIDE

Joan O'Neill

Hodder & Stoughton

British Library Cataloguing in Publication Data

O'Neill, Joan
    Turn of the tide
    I. Domestic fiction
    I. Title
    823.9'14[F]
    ISBN 0 340 69497 1

Typeset by Palimpsest Book Production Limited,
Polmont, Stirlingshire
Printed and bound in Great Britain by
Mackays of Chatham PLC, Chatham, Kent

Hodder and Stoughton
A division of Hodder Headline PLC
338 Euston Road
London NW1 3BH

To my sons, Gerard, Jonathan and Robert

ACKNOWLEDGEMENTS

I wish to thank my family; my friend Patricia O'Beirne for her help; Carolyn Caughey, my guardian angel; Jonathan Lloyd, my mentor.
Thanks also to Renata Aherns-Kramer, Sheila Barrett, Alison Dye, Catherine Phil McCarthy, Cecilia McGovern, Julie Parsons and to June Flanagan and Pat Kane.

My thanks to Anne Cooper, Jackie Dempsey, Mary Kirby, Maureen Keenan, Rita Stafford and all my friends in our literary group for their continued support. Thanks also to my staunch friend Anne O'Curry.

WISDOM AND DREAMS

I pray that I ever be weaving
An intellectual tune,
But weaving it out of threads
From the distaff of the moon.

Wisdom and dreams are one,
For dreams are the flowers ablow,
And Wisdom the fruit of the garden:
God planted him long ago.

W.B. Yeats.

Chapter One

'Will Daddy be coming to stay with us at Rathmore?' Katie Furlong asked, turning her head towards her mother, her voice apprehensive.

'I'm sure he will.' Eve gave her a reassuring smile.

'I hate it when he isn't with us.' Katie sighed. 'Why can't he come home, Mummy?'

The confusion in the child's tone caused Eve's heart to miss a beat. She did not know exactly what David's plans were so she couldn't really answer her small daughter – and although Eve was part of Katie's daily routine, as familiar as the air she breathed, David was her hero.

'Daddy'll be home as soon as he can get away,' Eve said gently. 'He loves us very much.'

'I know that,' Katie said brightening. 'Let's play "I spy".'

The game lasted until Katie fell asleep, stretched along the back seat of the car.

It was a sunny June morning in 1979, and Eve Furlong was driving her six-year-old daughter to the summer home of her parents-in-law, Jasper and Irene Furlong. Once out of Glencove, the landscape broadened into brighter fields of fresh growth. As they headed south Eve thought of her husband. David had been in New York on business for the past two months and although, at thirty-one, Eve knew all about compromise, she found life difficult without him. The worst time was waking up in the morning, when a wave of emptiness would sweep over her and she would burrow down into the soft warmth of her duvet, her loneliness keeping her there.

Later, standing in the kitchen, cup of tea in her hand, she would visualise David, in his dark suit and crisp white shirt, popping bread into the toaster. A few moments of comfortable silence would follow before Katie bounded down the stairs, her arrival always giving them a small surprise of happiness each time.

Once Katie was in bed, the evenings, too, were grim in the empty house. Wrapped in her solitude, Eve would sit in front of the television and watch anything at all. During the daytime she kept herself busy with her two coffee-shops, her mother, her friends, whatever helped to alleviate the flash of panic she felt when she thought about the empty house facing her.

Outside the village of Rathmore in County Wexford, she swung to the right, up a dirt track to Rathmore House, an eighteenth-century whitewashed farmhouse that loomed large and imposing on the landscape. First to arrive, she drove round to the front entrance and parked neatly to one side of the quadrangle, facing the spectacular views of sea and sand dunes. While Katie slept she sat at the wheel staring down at the jetty, her eyes on the small boats grazing the water, wishing she were thousands of miles away, with David. A quick glance in the rear-view mirror to check her appearance confirmed that her thick sandy hair was tied back neatly from her flawless features and that her eyes shone.

Eve knew that her father-in-law judged people by their appearance and what she saw in the mirror gave her confidence to face him. This visit to Rathmore, without David, was a further test of her strength. In Eve's opinion Jasper Furlong's family was incapable of sustaining a life separate from his and Jasper often enraged her with his tireless interfering and rigid views. She was always pleasant to him but he never got the better of her. Squinting against the glare of the sun, she realised that she was a little frightened of him, and desperately wished that she was not alone now, when she was about to face the biggest challenge of her life. David could always lighten his father's mood with a joke.

'Katie,' she said. 'We're here, lovey.'

Slowly Katie's head and shoulders appeared as she knelt up to look around her with the same startling blue eyes as her father. Eve kissed the blonde wispy hair that hung damp and soft into the nape of her neck. Katie hoisted herself to gaze out at a lone yacht in the distance, its stiff sails tipped towards the sun.

Eve got out and opened Katie's door. Wide awake now, the little girl jumped down and raced across the quadrangle to the long front porch, her sandals crunching noisily on the gravel, eager to ring the doorbell. The usual commotion ensued, of barking dog, Jasper Furlong's unmistakable voice, Irene's light tone. It was as familiar as the array of waders, abandoned fishing tackle and saddles hanging upside down on hooks from the wooden ceiling. Katie spent a good deal of the summer holidays at her grandparents' house, Eve and David joining her at weekends. The Christmas and Easter holidays meant family gatherings too, with everyone in residence.

The smell of cooking, lavender polish and damp wafted in the air as Jasper opened the door and Judy, his black Labrador, bounced out in front of him. A tall, broad-shouldered man, with a mop of woolly white hair and the florid complexion of a sailor, he had a dominating presence. Although he was seventy now he was still robust and vigorous. Dressed impeccably in grey slacks and blue sports shirt, he looked as elegant as he did in the three-piece suits he wore to the office.

'Welcome.' He greeted them both with an expansive smile,

and opened his arms wide to Katie. She jumped into them and smothered him with kisses.

Jasper Furlong was a successful businessman. He had come to Ireland from Wales as a young man to manage a small investment bank, which he had eventually bought. Over the years he had worked hard, building up his bank and branching out to compete with the international market. He was expecting the same success from his sons. Each one had been absorbed into the bank as soon as he graduated, and they all showed business promise. David, Eve's husband, now a top-level executive was the company's trouble-shooter. He showed the same single-minded determination as his father, and aimed to be just as successful.

It was Irene, Jasper's wife, though, whom Eve loved. She was a quiet woman with a sweet smile and the soft-spoken accent of her native Donegal, and Eve found in her the mother she had always wanted. But Irene lived in her husband's shadow. She hated the world trips and business functions that were often imposed upon her, and was overwhelmed by Jasper's colleagues. With her family, though, she was comfortable, assertive, and radiated warmth and confidence.

'Eve, my dear.' She stepped forward now, arms outstretched.

Katie, still in Jasper's arms and babbling with excitement, caught her grandmother's hands in her own small grubby ones. 'My new kitten's called Tabby and he's in a cage in the car,' she said. 'Can I bring him in?'

Irene kissed her and assured her that Tabby was welcome too. Jasper put her down, took her hand and they went off to the car, Katie pulling him forward, Judy the dog bounding ahead. Eve followed Irene downstairs to the kitchen.

For the rest of the morning she helped her mother-in-law prepare lunch, a captive audience for Irene's account of their latest trip to Japan. Eve moved around briskly, putting the finishing touches to the elaborate meal. Before the rest of the family arrived, she covered the long table in the bay window with a white damask tablecloth and set it with heavy silver, the best floral-patterned china, and a white napkin at each place.

When the doorbell rang again, Eve went to answer it. George, the youngest son, was there with his girlfriend, Marina, an attractive blonde with a light English accent, whom he whisked off to chat to his mother.

The rest of the family drifted in and Eve talked to Susan, Jason's wife, while her children, ten-year-old Ian and nine-year-old Samantha, ran around with Katie. Jasper held court at the drinks cabinet while Irene checked the oven and uncerked the wine and made sure there was Ballygowan for Eve.

Once everyone had arrived and they were seated around the table Jasper said grace. Katie was between Eve and Irene, enjoying being grown-up enough to sit at the big table.

'Soup?' Irene asked Katie, adding, 'Good girl,' as she served her from the tureen. Watching Irene, Eve was grateful that Katie was part of a real family such as she had never had. Her own mother had been too self-absorbed to notice her elder daughter and Eve had been hurt by her mother's rejection, especially after her sister Sarah's untimely death.

Bowls were passed down the table and everyone began to eat. Jasper poured wine and talked about his plans to take his sons on a fishing trip the next day, his firm voice and steely eyes brooking no argument.

He carved the roast ceremoniously and passed the plates of succulent beef to Irene, who served vegetables from a variety of dishes laid out before her. Eyes shining, diamond rings sparkling, she looked happy as she fed her family.

'The McCarthy's christening is next Sunday,' she said. 'Brenda doesn't know herself with a girl after all the boys. She'd given up hope.'

'What did she call the baby?' Samantha asked.

'Jane,' Irene said. 'After her own mother.'

'Ugh,' Ian said. 'I hate girls.'

'Jenny Whelan got engaged,' Irene continued. 'We met him after Mass last Sunday. He's a nice young man.'

'When's the wedding?' Jason asked.

'June,' Irene said.

'June's a lovely month for a wedding,' Marina said. 'I hope they'll be very happy.'

'Did you see *Kramer vs Kramer*?' George asked. 'It was enough to put anyone off the idea.'

'People have strange notions about marriage,' Jasper said, darting a look at Marina.

'It's no picnic,' Irene said.

'Don't I know!' Susan agreed. 'My new home help's fled, leaving me stranded.'

'What! Already?' Jasper said, amazed.

Susan nodded. 'Ran off with some hippie she'd been seeing. Even her mother has no idea where she's gone.'

Irene said, 'How are you managing, dear?'

'Mr Sterling wouldn't give me time off. I had to take holiday leave,' she said.

'You should come and work for a decent bank like ours,' Jasper chided.

When Ian and Samantha began to clear the table with their mother, Katie wanted to help, too. Irene gave her a large bowl of strawberry ice-cream to distract her and served apple pie and fresh cream to the adults. Suddenly, her mouth full, Katie asked, 'When will we be moving into the hotel, Mummy?' Everybody stopped talking, and looked up expectantly. Eve, eyes downcast, fiddled with her dessertspoon.

Jasper said, 'What's that, honey?'

'I heard that you're after the Glencove Hotel.' George looked at Eve. 'I thought it was just a rumour.'

'What!' Jasper almost leaped out of his seat.

'I'm hoping that Henrietta Ford Mathews will sell it to me.' She kept her voice casual.

'I didn't know it was for sale.' Jasper looked sharply at her.

'Only if I can persuade her to part with it.'

'Are you serious about this?' Jasper raised a quizzical eyebrow.

'Yes,' Eve said.

'My goodness!' There was disappointment in Irene's smile. 'I'm surprised. Why didn't you tell us?'

'There's nothing much to tell yet,' Eve said.

'Have you discussed it with David?' Jasper looked sideways at George, whose eyes were fixed on Eve.

Eve swallowed. 'No, because I've only just decided to go after it.'

'You've done financial forecasts, feasibility studies, that sort of thing?' Jasper asked.

Eve had not been anticipating an inquisition and ventured slowly, 'No, but I have a feel for the place. A hunch that I could make something of it.'

Jasper stared at her as he chewed. 'You won't make a living from a hunch, my dear. Not these days. The market's too competitive. You need cast-iron facts. Surely, as a businesswoman, you know that.' He wiped his mouth on his napkin.

'My hunches have worked for me in the past. I don't see why they shouldn't continue to do so.' Eve's tone was defensive.

Jasper took a deep breath. 'Quite,' he said. 'But for a venture as big as this you need accuracy.' He was shaking his head, her plans already doomed in his mind.

'I'm sure Eve knows what she's doing, dear. After all, her coffee-shops are thriving,' Irene said, and concluded the argument by urging Katie to finish the pink mess on her plate. The conversation resumed and, relieved, Eve finished her dessert. When the meal was over she helped stack plates on trays and washed up with Susan and George so that she could avoid Jasper.

＊   ＊   ＊

The reflection of afternoon sunlight danced in tiny ripples on the whitewashed wall of the verandah as Eve, glad of the quiet, sat in a deck-chair finishing a letter she was writing to David. Irene snoozed next to her, and everyone else had dispersed in different directions – Samantha, Ian and Katie to the beach. Eve ended by telling David that she was longing for him to return home. She worried about the time they spent apart. Sometimes she wondered what would happen if he were to meet someone else on his travels. The idea was unbearable. As she addressed the envelope to him Eve calculated the weeks until his return.

She really wanted the Glencove Hotel and she believed that, with careful planning and negotiating with her cousin, Henrietta Ford Mathews, she would get it. She sat back chewing the tip of her pen, and began to list the changes she intended to make. The dining room, a vast, ornate room with a chandelier, heavy red curtains and carved furniture, would be transformed to a bright white place with black satinwood tables, bentwood chairs to match, and light voile drapes. The oppressive shabbiness that had overwhelmed guests when they entered the lobby would go: comfortable easy-chairs and sofas would replace the existing threadbare ones. She just knew she could make a success of it.

Her conviction left her when Jasper asked if he could have a private word. She followed him into his study, a sunny room tucked away at the back of the house. 'Sit down,' he said, indicating a chair opposite his desk, which Eve took. 'Now,' Jasper said, settling back with an affable smile, 'I wanted to discuss with you your shares in Freeman's Enterprises.'

Puzzled, Eve leaned forward. 'Yes?'

'You weren't thinking of selling them to purchase the Glencove, were you?' he asked.

'No. I want to use them as collateral.'

'As you will have noticed from the increase in your dividend,

Freeman's shares are doing very well. I'd like to buy yours from you.'

'Why?'

'I want to streamline the company, expand world-wide. I'll make you a very good offer.'

And fire my father, or sell the business, she thought and said, 'No, thank you. Freeman's has been in my family since the thirties. I'd like to hold on to what's left to me.'

Jasper persisted, 'You wouldn't need collateral.' He was watching her closely.

She said pleasantly, 'As a matter of fact, I'm thinking of going to India to see the estates where it all began. Daddy has asked me out on numerous occasions.'

'You could still do that,' Jasper said.

'It wouldn't be the same.'

'Well, I'll give you time to think about it, of course,' he said. 'No need to make your mind up yet.'

Eve laughed. 'You never give up, do you, Jasper?' she said.

'No, I never do. That's what it's all about, isn't it.' He was laughing, too, defusing the awkwardness in the atmosphere.

Eve was thinking of the hope she cherished to buy back Freeman Enterprises some day. The trouble had started with Ron Freeman's bad management. Eve's father, unaccustomed to planting, had spent his time managing people and had neglected the crops. The tea bushes had suffered from drought and disease and had not yielded their quota.

After the takeover Jasper had gone to India to inspect the plantation. He had invested in improving the operation, starting with a new plantation of tea bushes. Gradually, under his management, Freeman's began to flourish, and he was now building up the business to sell it for a healthy profit, Eve was certain. As chairman of the board, and the majority shareholder, he could do as he wished, regardless of whether Eve sold her shares to him or not. She was aware of that.

Just as she had assumed that the meeting was over Jasper leaned forward. 'About this Glencove Hotel, Eve. I'm anxious.'

Eve's eyebrows shot up. 'There's no need to be.'

He raised his right hand. 'I know, I know,' he said. 'But with David away and you on your own with Katie, I'm not sure if this is a good time to be struggling with all the business of buying a place like that.'

Eve had to concentrate on the book-lined shelves until the danger of losing her temper passed. 'I'm perfectly capable of "struggling", as you put it, with my business, and taking care of Katie,' she said evenly.

'Yes, of course,' Jasper said, placatingly. 'But can't you see it from my point of view? It would be wrong of me to let you make a financial blunder. With David away I feel duty-bound to protect your interests.'

'You think I won't make a go of it?' Eve asked coolly.

He shrugged. 'I think you may not be aware of the pitfalls, that's all. You're going headlong into this thing without thought or consultation.'

'In other words, because I made a quick decision without getting your perspective, and didn't ask your permission, I'm being foolish.' Eve's voice was too loud.

Jasper met her eyes. 'Eve, I'm not deliberately trying to provoke you but there's no merit in hot-headedness,' he said. 'It only leads to bankruptcy.'

'I won't go bankrupt, I promise you that.' There was anger in Eve's voice now.

'No?' Jasper said, a smile tugging at the corners of his mouth. 'I'd like to be as sure as you are. But I have a proposal to reduce your financial strain. I shall take a share in the hotel myself.'

'No!' Eve rose from her chair abruptly.

'You won't do it on your own.' Jasper got up too.

'Yes, I will, and I still have my coffee-shops to fund me.'

Jasper stared at her, his true feelings hidden by a veneer of politeness. 'You seem to have a notion that somehow you're indestructible,' he said. 'Believe me, Eve, bigger and stronger businesses than yours have gone by the wayside. If the hotel proves to be a bad investment your money'll go down the drain, and your coffee-shops with it. It can happen in a flash. You know what I mean. You're no stranger to failure.' He was alluding to his takeover of her grandfather James Freeman's tea-importing business.

Eve said calmly, 'Don't worry about me, Jasper. I'll manage on my own.'

'If you insist, but as far as I'm concerned your attitude is nothing short of criminal.' He sat down again and began to toy with his paper-knife. 'Also, there's your drink problem.' His eyes were on hers.

Furious, Eve turned on him. 'I don't drink,' she said. 'You know how important my sobriety is to me. I never miss an A. A. meeting. Now I think this conversation is over.'

'Yes,' Jasper replied, a sudden smile on his face. 'Don't forget I'm here if you need to talk.'

'I won't,' Eve said, and swept towards the door.

'I'll say one thing for you,' Jasper called after her. She stopped. 'You may be stubborn but you've got guts, and that I do admire.'

'*Touché*,' Eve said, her hand on the doorknob.

'Eve, if you run into difficulties . . .' He was using his most flattering voice.

'When I fall flat on my face, you mean.'

Jasper laughed. 'Anytime.'

'Thanks, but no thanks.'

She slammed the door behind her and marched down the hallway, almost colliding with George, who was returning from a swim.

'Old man giving you a hard time?' he asked.

Eve did not wish to discuss with George what had happened, said, 'Fuck him,' and marched on.

She walked down to the beach. The sun was setting, a great orange ball rimmed with gold. Eve loved sunsets but this time she was thinking of Jasper and his infernal cheek, referring to her alcoholism in such a demeaning manner. She realised, more than anyone, that she was one drink away from becoming a drunk and didn't need him to remind her. That was why she stuck rigidly to her twelve step programme and never missed a meeting, no matter what the circumstances. She was on her way to one now. Of course she wouldn't tell him that. He didn't know the first thing about alcoholism and wouldn't understand.

Katie, Samantha and Ian were playing tig. Wild with excitement, Katie was racing around, shrieking, 'Caught you, caught you,' grabbing Ian by his T-shirt, swiping at Samantha's skirt, running off. 'I'm winning, Mummy,' she yelled to Eve.

'You're breaking all the rules,' Eve said, catching up with her. Katie stopped yelling and danced around her.

'It's OK. She's having fun,' Ian said.

Eve squatted down beside her daughter and took her in her arms. 'Calm down, sweetheart. You'll get overtired and you won't sleep tonight.'

Sand matted Katie's hair, and covered her body. She smelt of the sea. 'Don't care.' She wriggled out of Eve's grasp, her eyes bright, a red splodge on each cheek.

Eve looked anxiously at her watch. 'They'll never get her to bed tonight. She's far too excited.'

'I'll read her a story after supper,' Samantha said.

'Thanks, Sam. That should calm her down. I'm going back to Glencove, darling. Come and say goodbye.'

Katie ran to her and plonked a kiss on her lips. ''Bye, Mummy.'

'Be a good girl for Grandma. I'll phone you before you go to bed,' Eve said.

'I will.' Katie hopped up and down waving goodbye until Eve had left the beach.

Eve found Irene in the lounge, sitting with Susan and Marina. 'We were waiting for you,' Irene said. 'Would you like some tea?'

'I haven't time, I'm afraid,' Eve said, regretfully.

'Oh!' Susan said, disappointed. 'We haven't had a proper chat.'

'I know, and I'm sorry but I have to get back. I've lots to do.' She said goodbye to them all and walked out to the porch.

Irene followed her. 'Eve,' she whispered, smoothing the collar of Eve's jacket, 'take no notice of Jasper. He doesn't mean any harm.'

'Maybe not,' Eve conceded, 'but it's hard to take.'

'I know, dear, just don't let him get you down.'

'I'm trying not to.'

Jasper came out of his study and saw the exasperation in Eve's face. He took her arm and walked her to the car. 'Remember what I said. Come and see me if you need to talk.'

'Thank you,' she said politely, then got into her car and drove off.

On the way home she listened to the radio, letting the rhythm of Billy Joel's 'My Life' soothe her jangled nerves. Standing up to Jasper had probably confirmed his opinion that she was a woman who didn't know her place. Perhaps it would have been better if she'd held herself in check, but if David had been there she was sure that Jasper would have been subtler in his approach. Her father-in-law was a bully who enjoyed playing power games.

Driving fast along the deserted road, she thought of all the things she had to do before she could realise her dream. It would take energy and hard work — luck, too, would play a major part.

She smiled, imagining herself in charge of the magnificent

Glencove Hotel. She had always loved hotels. As a child she had found the sumptuous rooms and the elegant guests irresistible. When they stayed at their grandfather's favourite hotel, the Grange, in County Kerry, she and Sarah, who had died of scarlet fever at only twelve, used to dress for dinner, like grown-ups, wearing their best velvet frocks. Afterwards, they would play endless games of hide and seek among the shrubs that bordered the long avenue or, if it was raining, in the corridors.

The sadness of seeing the Glencove Hotel fall into disrepair through neglect was acute. With her special touch, Eve was certain she could transform it. And why confine herself to one hotel? Why not a second, or a third?

As the car moved steadily along the dual carriageway she relaxed, and by the time she turned right for Glencove, when familiar farms came into view and sheep and cows dotted the landscape towards the darkening mountains, she was herself again.

Chapter Two

Montauk had been all right in the beginning. Pauline was so happy with her baby that it didn't matter where she lived. Each day Seamie sat in his pushchair by her side while she smoothed the white linen sheets on the beds, dusted the old velvet curtains, swept and vacuumed, while the light caught the beads of perspiration on her forehead and the sheen of her dark hair. To keep Seamie amused she sang to him, patriot songs of Ireland and lullabies, in her low, sweet voice. In the same half-whisper she told him fairy stories, and stories about his father. His father had been a handsome young man with merry blue eyes and a dazzling smile, she would tell him, her voice faltering. A young rebel from the North, who had died for the Cause.

On her days off she took him for walks, to the park, to the beach. Pauline had worked for her widowed aunt Mary in her boarding-house in Montauk, Long Island, as a chambermaid, ever since she had left Ireland in 1969. In return her aunt provided for her and Seamie, and gave her a small weekly wage. During the long, dull days of cleaning, Pauline planned and saved for a business of her own. Three evenings a week she attended business college. On her evenings off she did bookkeeping for her aunt. She would sit at a worn old desk in a corner of her bedroom surrounded by ledgers, her pencil flying up and down the columns of figures while Seamie slept beside her.

As time went by Aunt Mary put her in charge of Reception. She took all the business calls and bookings, speaking in clear, precise tones. Sometimes Aunt Mary rocked Seamie to sleep or sang to him, in her high crackling voice. Often she would fall asleep and snore, which woke him up and made him cry. Once or twice a month Pauline went to a movie or a show with another girl. She would bathe in hot, scented water, sweep her hair up and spray herself with perfume before putting on her good blue dress. These nights out were her special treats. She never went out on a date.

The letter that arrived at the end of May from Madge Kinsella, proprietor of Kinsella's Select Bar, changed the course of her life and Seamie's.

I'm getting on and not as healthy as I used to be. The work is too much for me, and my profit is going on wages to pay staff for the work I used to do single-handed. In view of the fact that neither of my brothers have any interest in the pub and because I love Seamie dearly, I have decided to leave the place to him. I propose that you come and live here with me and help run it until Seamie is old enough to take it over. You'll be your own boss, come and go as you please. I hope you'll take up this offer.

Aunt Mary trained her sharp blue eyes on Pauline as she read it to her, the corners of her mouth dropping in disapproval. 'Well,' she said, 'that's a nice how-do-you-do,' and waited for Pauline to say something.

Pauline stared back at her, noticing the deep scores on her aunt's sunken face. 'I hadn't planned on going back to Ireland,' she said, when she finally found her voice. 'I suppose I'll have to think about it now.'

'You'd give up a good job here to run back to Glencove? No one ever made a decent living in that Godforsaken hole.'

'But Seamie would have his own pub with me in charge,' Pauline exclaimed.

'Go on. Turn your back on them that's been good to you,' Aunt Mary said. 'I took you in good faith, trained you, gave you time off to study. That's the thanks I get. How do you think the guests are going to take it when I tell them that you're walking off? Some of them have been here as long as you have. They're used to having you around the place.' Her voice had risen.

Mary Quirk believed her boarding house to be one of the finest establishments in Montauk, and herself the dowager duchess of the Irish community there. Her manner of speech and the way she dressed were intended to suggest wealth and influence. She ignored the fact that in the early days of her employment Pauline had had to double as waitress and chambermaid for little more than her keep, contributing to her aunt's wealth. A reminder of that to Aunt Mary would have been received as an insult and was not worth the furore it would cause.

For a long time Pauline had been afraid to voice her half-formed desire to return to Ireland. Eve was the only person to whom she had mentioned it, and that had been in a letter in response to Eve's news about wanting to purchase the Glencove Hotel. But to go back to Kinsella's Select Bar? And what about the past?

When Pauline had first arrived in Montauk, Martin Dolan, her ex-boyfriend, had stalked her dreams, in which she was always escaping from the awful flat at the top of the building in the Divis where Martin had held her prisoner. He had taken her there ostensibly to protect her from the dangers of Belfast but really to keep her from discovering what had happened to her fiancé. And also because he wanted her for himself. Pauline would wake up crying, perspiration trickling down her face. Once she had been screaming, and Aunt Mary had come running up to her room to find her in with tears streaming down her face. Sometimes, after a nightmare, she would lie awake for hours, every night sound making her twitch.

Pauline had left the North of Ireland before the hunger strikes, internment, the H-blocks. In Montauk she never spoke of her Belfast experience, disclaiming all knowledge of the 'Ulster question', a favourite topic of conversation among the Irish community. For years she had felt secure in her aunt's boarding-house on the corner of the street. Its old white-painted walls rose three storeys to encompass Aunt Mary, her son Tom and the fifteen guests who resided there permanently. Until Madge's letter arrived, Pauline had decided not to leave Aunt Mary before she had completed her course and Seamie was ready for college.

Although Montauk was busy in the summer, its bars and hotels teeming with holidaymakers, Pauline had never felt that she belonged there. But the memory of her past troubles clouded the joy she felt at Madge's offer. 'I want to travel a bit,' she explained to her cousin Tom. 'See the world, get experience. If I go back to Glencove I might never get that opportunity.'

'You're a strange girl, Pauline Quirk,' he said, reading the letter. 'To even consider turning down an opportunity like this is crazy. I've had my nose to the grindstone all my life to make something out of this place with my mother, and you're getting it handed to you on a plate. There'll be plenty of opportunity for you to travel when Seamie's off your hands.'

Tom was anxious to take over the running of his mother's business and, seeing Pauline as an impediment, added, 'With a pub behind you, you'll be on the pig's back.' He went to the safe in his office and took out a wad of dollars. 'Here's your fare home.'

'I haven't made up my mind to go,' Pauline pointed out.

'Listen, Pauline, that son of yours needs to breathe his

native air, and spread his wings in his native space. That's the kind of chap he is.' He looked at Seamie's lively face and mischievous eyes.

Tom was right. Madge Kinsella's offer had left Pauline with no choice if she was to do right by her son. She wrote to Madge, accepting, and knowing that the course of her life would change for ever.

After she had posted her letter she walked along the shadowy path that led to the beach. A warm breeze was blowing, ruffling the pine trees, mingling the tang of salt and seaweed with the smell of new-cut grass in the park. Pauline stood looking at the sea in the distance. The swirl of the incoming tide over the rocks reminded her of Glencove. She watched the gathering clouds and thought of the dark, rich land three thousand miles away that held her secret. Breathing in the scent of flowers in the well-tended park, she longed for home: the fresh hay in the hayrick, the rich soil after a shower of rain, the sweet smell of turf, the lacy pattern the trees made across the Wicklow fields. Yes, the time had come for her and Seamie to move on. Walking quickly, she retraced her steps, the moon hugging her shadow all the way home.

Chapter Three

Pauline flew to Dublin on a glorious June day, leaving Seamie with Aunt Mary in Montauk to finish the school year. As the plane descended she stared at the fields, marvelling at their green freshness, as if seeing them for the first time. Eve was at Arrivals, her mane of hair swinging as she came to meet her friend.

'Pauline! Oh, it's great to see you.' They hugged each other. 'How are you?' Eve was holding her friend at arm's length, amazed at the maturity in Pauline's beautiful, strong face.

Pauline laughed. 'I'm fine, but look at the state of me.' She gestured at her crumpled clothes.

'You look terrific. Come on. Let's get out of here.'

As they headed for the lifts, Pauline was thinking how impeccably groomed Eve was in her cream suit. 'It's so good to see you,' she said, squeezing her arm.

Before setting out for Glencove they stopped in Dublin city. Pauline looked out for signs of change over the last ten years, thrilled to hear again the Moore Street hawkers shouting out their bargains, the newspaper boys on the quays selling papers.

The city was alive with the hustle and bustle of mid-morning shoppers. Grafton Street glittered in the sunshine and reeked of prosperity. The shops were more exciting than Pauline remembered, with the heady scent of exotic perfume, the walls lined with expensive dresses, hats and hand-made shoes. Ten years on, everything cost more in Brown Thomas but on impulse, and with Eve's encouragement, Pauline bought a black cocktail dress.

'Let's have lunch,' Eve said, and led the way to her coffee-shop in Grafton Street. She strode in, Pauline in her wake. The air buzzed, cash registers rang and people queued for tables, foreigners among them.

'This is smashing.' Pauline looked around admiringly as the manager led them to a table marked RESERVED near the window. 'I didn't realise it was so big, and bright,' she added, taking in the pristine white tables, white walls decorated with posters of her favourite film stars: Meryl Streep, Julie Christie, Jane Fonda. 'And so busy!'

'I've no worries about this place,' Eve said. 'It runs itself now.'

'You look happy enough, anyway. How are things going with the hotel?' Pauline was surprised to see Eve's expression change from sunny to dismal.

'I was just scanning the accounts. If I'm to cash in on the summer season I'd want to get the deal closed soon. But Henrietta's still dithering.'

'You'll get round her.'

Eve frowned. 'I'm not so sure. This is a difficult one.'

'There'd be no fun if it were easy,' Pauline said. 'You thrive on challenges.'

Over prawns on home-made brown bread Eve told Pauline about her altercation with Jasper. 'He thinks that buying The Glencove is an act of lunacy on my part and has withdrawn my loan facilities. He referred to my alcoholism as one of the reasons. How I managed to curb my temper with him, I'll never know.'

'I'd have throttled the old fart,' Pauline laughed, 'and no

mistake. He'd like to see you fall flat on your face. Take care he doesn't slip you one himself when you least expect it.'

'He wouldn't!'

'You never know.'

'I'll make sure he doesn't,' Eve said. 'I'll keep out of his way and stick to the Ballygowan.'

'How did he find out about you being interested in the hotel, anyway?' Pauline asked.

'Katie let it slip,' Eve said, 'but George had heard the rumour.'

'Glencove hasn't changed, then,' Pauline said.

Eve turned her eyes to heaven. 'The hotel isn't even on the market. I just happened to say to Henrietta that if she ever thought of selling it to let me know.'

'Smart move. Do you think she will?'

'It's a millstone round her neck, and she's far too interested in her horses to bother with it.'

'Do you remember when Henrietta took over that place? She dressed Dermy McQuaid up in that ridiculous grey uniform with the red trim on his hat to match his nose, and put him outside the door. We used to howl every time we passed him by.'

'Will I ever forget!' They burst out laughing, and heads turned in their direction.

'If I can raise the money,' Eve confided, 'I'm sure she'll sell. I could get rid of the coffee-shops but I don't want to.'

'I've got a few thousand put by,' Pauline said. 'I was thinking of buying a guest-house at some stage. Maybe I'll take a share in your hotel instead.'

Eve was astonished. 'You're a dark horse, Pauline Quirk.'

Pauline was thinking aloud. 'I'll get a decent living from the pub so I won't really need to draw on my savings. And I could borrow a bit more from Aunt Bea. She's rotten with money.'

'Will she give you a loan?'

'She's using grazing land that belonged to my father. He

didn't make a will, so she might feel generously inclined towards me.'

'Are you prepared to take a big financial risk?' Eve looked at her.

'I don't consider you a risk, Eve. You're a good business-woman. Anyway, who cares? It's only a game. How much would I need?'

'I'm not sure.' Eve pulled out a notebook and wrote down some figures. 'I have enough capital if I can get the hotel at the right price. But I'll need finance for a decent function room, car-park and refurbishments. Let's go and look at the books.'

Eve took Pauline to her office above the coffee-shop and pulled out some ledgers. 'Take a look at these,' she said.

After a little while, Pauline said, 'There hasn't been much going on in the hotel for a long time.'

'I know, and I've got plans. But first I need to know how much money I can raise before I make a move. I'll go and talk to my old friend Mr Cummins — he'll put me in the picture about investors.' She stopped and her large blue eyes scanned Pauline's face. 'When will you talk to your Aunt Bea?'

'As soon as I can get to Ballingarret.'

'I was thinking of having a Saturday-night disco, with a bar extension. There's nothing in Glencove for the youngsters.'

'Good idea,' Pauline agreed.

At a garage in Ringsend, Pauline bought a second-hand Ford Fiesta for which Eve arranged temporary insurance with her broker. On the way to Glencove, Pauline drove along the coast road behind Eve's BMW, her happiness swelling each time she turned a corner to a see flash of sunlight on the water or the granite peak of the Sugar Loaf mountain above the trees in distant rolling Wicklow hills. When they arrived, a thrill of excitement shot through her.

Kinsella's Select Bar was the first surprise, its paint peeling and sign lacklustre over the door. Madge herself was the second.

She had been a large woman, raised among farmers, but her broad shoulders had narrowed and fallen and her chest was now shallow beneath her blouse. 'You took your own sweet time getting here,' she greeted them, and kissed Pauline. 'I was afraid you'd had an accident.'

'I bought a car,' Pauline said, pointing proudly to the Ford.

'What a good idea,' Madge said. 'We'll be able to go driving on Sundays.'

Eve left, promising to phone the next day, and Pauline followed Madge up to the flat. It hadn't changed. The same dingy sofa and chairs seemed to extinguish the brightness of the new modern prints of tall sailing ships. The spare bedroom was dark, too, crammed with a double bed and heavy Victorian furniture.

'You won't mind sharing this with Seamie until I do up the box-room for him?' Madge said.

Pauline said, 'Of course not,' making a mental note to get Madge to have it converted right away.

Over dinner Madge told Pauline the bits of gossip she'd omitted in her infrequent letters. It reminded her of the years when she had worked for Madge as a barmaid, and the closeness that had grown between them over other shared dinners. Perhaps it would never have developed, had Madge not taken charge of Seamie when Pauline went to Belfast to search for his vanished father.

'So, how do you feel about starting back behind the bar again?' Madge asked.

'To be honest I'm nervous,' Pauline said. 'I'm not sure how the customers will take to me.'

'You'll be grand.'

Though Madge sat upright and was as alert as ever, her thinness and the *papier-mâché* quality of her skin bespoke the new fragility in her. Pauline unpacked the gifts she had brought for her from Montauk: two chiffon blouses, a jacket from Aunt

Mary, chocolates from Seamie and perfume she'd purchased at the airport. Madge thanked her, then went to bed.

Pauline telephoned Montauk to let them know she had arrived safely, then decided to walk to the cove, cutting across the fields at the back of the pub. The wind hummed in the telegraph wires and dark clouds gathered over the horizon, their fleecy edges dipped in the gold light of the setting sun. As she stood gazing out over the sea and the distant dark grey woods, Pauline wondered what her customers would say when they saw her.

That night she slept fitfully in the strange bed and woke confused from a troubled dream, but the moment she remembered she was back in Glencove the excitement returned. She was among her own people. Everything would be all right.

She jumped out of bed and pulled the curtains. Sunlight streamed in to light up the dull walls and glance off the mirror of the dressing-table. Pulling on her dressing-gown, she tiptoed downstairs, afraid to make a sound that would wake Madge, knowing how much she needed her rest. Carefully she unlocked the back door and went out into the small garden. She walked barefoot through the long, wet grass, felt the earth beneath her feet, smelt its loamy smell. The last of the lilac, frosted with dew, lay heavy and purple against the pale pink clematis that smothered the old slate roof of the shed. Beyond the thick privet hedge, the neglected orchard was a profusion of dandelions and daisies. In the distance dogs barked and the church bell rang for morning Mass. Pauline vowed to keep this magical moment of her first day home treasured in her heart.

After breakfast Madge went out and returned some time later puffing up the stairs laden with carrier-bags. She looked harassed as she dumped her shopping unceremoniously on the kitchen counter and went into the sitting room to remove her shoes. 'I'm bunched,' she said, exposing her calfless legs and flat feet. 'That stairs is a killer.'

'Why didn't you tell me you were going out? I'd have given you a lift,' Pauline said, and went into the kitchen to make coffee. When she returned, Madge put her feet up and talked about the price of meat, the weather, then lapsed into a thoughtful silence.

After lunch she went for a rest and Pauline sat in her bedroom, looking out at the sloping grey roofs of the houses opposite, and the narrow spaces between them to the gable end of the gardai barracks.

That evening she went to work. The sunlight poured into the smoky bar highlighting the greasy fingerprints on the surface of the counter, the yellow walls and stained carpet. The ancient furniture had a bloom to its surface from the heavy wax Mrs Browne, the cleaner, used liberally. Pauline stood, in her neat black skirt and white blouse, refilling glasses for the few customers who were seated on high stools, hunched over their pints, strangers to her. A man in the corner, leaning forward in his shirtsleeves, followed her agile movements. 'Planning an attack or a retreat?' he asked.

'Welcome home,' Mrs Browne said, coming in the side door.

'Thanks.' Pauline smiled at her. 'It's good to be back.'

'I'd reserve me judgement if I were you,' Mrs Browne said, caustically. 'Things aren't the same since Madge got sick.'

'I've noticed,' Pauline said.

'If it isn't Pauline Quirk,' Jim Purcell, the postman, said, coming towards her with a bunch of letters, peeking at the tops of her breasts, just visible above the V of her blouse.

Pauline faced his toothless grin. 'What can I get you to drink?' she asked.

'A pint of stout. Come and talk to me,' he said. 'Tell me all about America.'

'Sure. In a few minutes.'

Manus Corrigan came in. 'Pauline, how are you?' he said,

extending his hand. 'It's good to see you again. And I'll have a whiskey, please. I wanted a word about Madge's will. I'd like to go over it with you. Discuss the legalities. Come over to the house tomorrow afternoon for a chat.'

'I will.' Pauline handed him his drink and moved off to serve more customers. She was beginning to relax.

The next evening, walking back through the rain-drenched streets of the town from Manus Corrigan's house, she passed people returning from work in the city. Children played hop-scotch over chalk squares on the pavement. A group of girls were skipping in and out of a rope.

She stopped at the towpath where the river widened, near the railway, to watch a family of ducks paddling downstream. In no hurry, Pauline sat under a willow tree to watch them glide by. Now and then one would dive down, then emerge to leave rippling pools widening in its wake. The river narrowed at the tow-bridge, babbling over the smooth stones. It seemed a lifetime since she had last gazed into it, Seamus Gilfoyle at her side. Who would have believed then, as they stood holding hands, young lovers, their future sealed, that Seamus would disappear and Pauline would emigrate, only to return as landlady of Kinsella's Select Bar? 'Life is only just beginning for you,' Manus had said. 'Building up the pub for Seamie is a real challenge.' But although Pauline had assured him that she was looking forward to it, she couldn't help feeling that she was returning to the prison from which she had once escaped.

As the days passed Madge let her do most of the work. Pauline was never in bed before midnight and up again next morning at seven. Madge worked in the mornings but soon complained of fatigue. She seemed to be growing weaker.

Missing Seamie, Pauline phoned him regularly. He listened politely while she talked, but his voice was distant as he answered her questions. Pauline knew he, too, was lonely. She wanted him here with her in Glencove, wanted to ruffle his hair, tease him about the girls in his class, and grab a quick kiss from him when he least expected it. They hadn't been separated since he was a baby and his awkwardness on the phone made her realise that he had not forgiven her for leaving him behind.

She got Liam Meaney, the local handyman, to begin the attic conversion. Standing back one evening to admire his handiwork, she caught her reflection in the mirror of the new white wardrobe she'd bought for the room. Her face was youthful, her eyes bright, skin elastic. The gentle roundness of adolescence was gone, replaced by harder lines, that accentuated her good bone structure and well-shaped breasts. She reminded herself that she was only thirty-one, too young for the weight of responsibility she had felt since her return. She promised herself that she would get out more and enjoy life.

The changes in Pauline's body were nothing compared to the changes in her mind. In Montauk, when Seamie was a toddler, she had joined a women's group. They spent whole evenings discussing women's rights in the workplace, assertiveness, marriage and sex. For a long time she had been too shy to speak out for she lacked the confidence education would have given her to join in. When she went to college, though, as well as learning about business she began to grasp the things about life that everyone else seemed to know.

Seamus, her fiancé, had been the first person since her mother had died to share her joy and pain. When he disappeared she had been alone again until she joined the group. Eventually she shared with them the intense pain of his disappearance, and after that, she had the women and they were enough for her. Although she was only thirty-one she didn't want to fall in love again; didn't want that rush of excitement when a certain someone phoned, or walked in the door, didn't want the awful fear of losing him again.

Chapter Four

The rain hopped off the pavement and ran along the gutters in a heavy downpour as Pauline drove through Ballingarret. Looking around, it struck her that she was driving into strange territory. New red-brick houses, clustered together, all the same, gave the town a different perspective.

Near Aunt Bea's farm the sun burst through the clouds and cast sharp shadows on the road, which stretched like a ribbon through the woods. She passed the grey haggard to the left, sagging on its metal frame. Rusting farm implements were strewn in the field where she had gathered buttercups.

Around the corner Aunt Bea's house still stood, large and threatening. Pauline parked her car, crossed the wide courtyard, passed the water-butt, and went in through the open hall door calling, 'Aunt Bea.' Everything was quiet except for the ticking of the clock on the mantelpiece and the snores of Aunt Bea's old dog Brute by the range. The same pine table sat in the middle of the floor surrounded by the same pine chairs. The same floral curtains were at the windows.

Out the back, bees buzzed in the tangle of wild honeysuckle that trailed its scent along the grassy bank to the heather and gorse bushes. Crows clamoured in the trees, sparrows chirped, and in the distance, cattle grazed on the sweet fresh grasses of the riverbank. Heavy with milk they moved slow and content, their tails flicking off flies. Somewhere Pauline could hear a tractor.

She walked to the edge of the bog, stopping on the way to examine the roses. The men were cutting turf with a triangular slane. As she watched a fresh-faced young boy piled the dripping sods, two at a time, into a wheelbarrow and pushed them across to the riverbank to dry, Pauline was reminded of Seamie and wondered how he would like the farm. Aunt Bea was coming towards her carrying a bucket, her knees bent with the effort, her jaw slack — she looked old, Pauline thought, but when she saw her niece she straightened, and the years fell away. ''Tis an ill wind that blew you in,' she called.

'Hello, Aunt Bea,' Pauline said.

The sun glanced off the rim of the bucket as Aunt Bea placed it on the ground, water spilling over its rim. 'I was at the well,' she said needlessly, gazing at Pauline. For a moment Pauline thought her aunt was going to shout at her but instead Aunt Bea crossed the space between them and kissed her. 'I knew you'd be coming to see me soon,' she said matter-of-factly. 'Where's Seamie?'

'He's back in the States finishing his school term,' Pauline said.

'You left him all by himself in America?' Aunt Bea looked shocked.

'Only till the end of term. Aunt Mary will take good care of him.'

'That's tough on the young lad, all the same,' Aunt Bea reflected. 'Still, now that you're here you'll have dinner with us. You can collect the eggs while I'm getting it ready.'

Pauline took the basket from the hook at the back of the shed door and collected the eggs from the nests in the corner of the haggard, by the old pump, under the eaves of the shed. When she returned Aunt Bea was putting scrubbed potatoes, whole in their jackets, into the skillet to boil. A joint of salted beef, a treat reserved for turf cutting, was ready to be carved. She called to Pauline to set the table, pointing to the good china in the glass cabinet. 'They'll be in soon,' she said, putting plates in the oven to warm. 'There's no feeding them when they're cutting turf. Same as the threshing or harvesting.'

'Where's Mary?' Pauline asked.

'She married Joe Byrne and moved into the village. Comes in of an evening to give me a hand sometimes.'

As Aunt Bea bent forward over the oven Pauline noticed that her face had coarsened, and that she was short of breath with the exertion of lifting out the bread. 'Well,' she said, 'how are things in Glencove?'

'Much the same. Madge is not well.'

'I heard that,' Aunt Bea said.

'I need to borrow some money,' Pauline said, her eyes on the window beyond her aunt's head.

'What?' Aunt Bea said. 'Haven't you just inherited a pub?' She moved around the kitchen, banging pots, clattering dishes. 'What do you want it for?' She was her old brusque self again.

'Eve Furlong is buying the Glencove Hotel and she's offered me a stake in it. I thought it would be a good investment.'

'The Glencove Hotel no less! Have you lost your mind?' Aunt Bea's eyes were intent as Pauline filled in all the details of Madge's will and finished, 'I want something for myself so as not to be dependent on Seamie when he takes over the pub.'

'What makes you think I'd lend it to you?'

Pauline shrugged. 'I thought that if you had it to spare you wouldn't see me stuck. I'll pay you back with interest.'

Aunt Bea gazed at her shrewdly. Before she could say any more, Mary Byrne came lumbering in the back door. She crossed the kitchen floor, in her milking boots, to greet Pauline shyly with a warm handshake of her work-roughened hand. ''Tis well you're looking,' she said, seating herself down at the table, stiff and uncomfortable in company. 'We haven't seen you for a long time. How's Seamie?'

'He's great thanks. Almost a teenager.'

'Doesn't time fly? Will you be staying long?' Mary asked, all in one breath.

Mary was peering at Pauline. 'I remember the day Seamie was born as if it were yesterday.' She flushed to the roots of her hair. 'How is he?'

'He's wonderful,' Pauline said, with pride.

'Will I ever forget that day!' Aunt Bea's eyes flashed to the Sacred Heart lamp and back to Pauline. 'The roaring and bawling out of you. And now it's money you want. Pauline has come to borrow money to buy into the Glencove Hotel. Can you beat that?' Aunt Bea asked. 'A girl who abandoned us, and hasn't spared us a thought for the past ten years.'

'You could do worse than invest your money in Pauline,' Mary said. 'She's a great little worker. Surely you wouldn't begrudge a bit of money to one of your own and it stagnating in the bank.'

'Ten to one I'll never see it again,' Aunt Bea said.

'Indeed an' you will. The Glencove Hotel is a good solid dwelling. Two storeyed with a slated roof. It's ideally situated and all,' Mary supplied, then retreated into her shell.

Aunt Bea's mouth dropped open. 'How do you know all that? You're beginning to sound like an auctioneer.'

'My Joe was over there doing repairs on the boiler less than six months ago. He said it was a shame that Henrietta let the place go. She's horse-mad like the rest of them with double-barrel names.'

'You need a man around the place to look after a hotel,' Aunt Bea said reflectively.

'There's plenty of able-bodied young fellas would be only

too glad to give a hand,' Pauline said. 'And Eve's husband will be home again soon.'

'I'm sure there's plenty that'd offer help to *you*, Pauline,' and Mary sniggered as Aunt Bea left the room.

Pauline could hear the bureau in the parlour being opened. 'That's that, then,' Aunt Bea said, when she returned, and handed Pauline a cheque. 'I want the same interest rates that I get from the bank.'

'You're a hard woman,' Mary said.

'Being soft gets you nowhere,' Aunt Bea said.

'Agreed,' Pauline said, as she folded the cheque and put it into her handbag, knowing that any display of affection would upset her aunt. 'Thank you,' she said. 'You won't regret it.'

'I suppose we won't see you again until you want something else,' Aunt Bea remarked.

'I'll be bringing Seamie to visit you soon,' Pauline said.

Aunt Bea smiled with sudden gentleness. 'Mind you do. We're dying to see him,' and walloped the pots on the table together with such vigour that Pauline was afraid something would get smashed.

Chapter Five

Harry Wise, Eve's accountant, put on his gold-rimmed spectacles and checked the rows of figures on the coffee-shops' balance sheets in front of him. Eve watched, outwardly calm, but her stomach was knotted with tension. Finally, he said, 'Everything seems to be in order.'

She sighed with relief.

Removing his glasses, Harry Wise said, 'As things stand, Eve, everything is negotiable. You have enough equity to get your mortgage from a building society. I've spoken to Miss Ford Mathews and she's willing to let you have the hotel at the agreed price. There's only one fly in the ointment.' He gave her a measuring look. 'And I'm afraid it's a big one.'

'What's that?' Eve's mouth was suddenly dry.

'The Glencove Hotel is already mortgaged to the hilt. Miss Ford Mathews hasn't been able to meet her repayments for over a year now and the hotel is about to be repossessed by her mortgage society.'

'Oh!'

Harry raised his hand. 'And Jasper Furlong is her banker.'

Eve turned pale. 'Oh!' she said. 'So he's waiting to take it from her.'

'Precisely.'

'What chance do I have, if that's the case?'

'Jasper specialises in buying up large properties at rock-bottom prices from individuals or commercial businesses who find themselves in trouble, thus alleviating their problems while safeguarding the bank's investment, and making a swift profit at the same time.' Mr Wise patted his paunch. 'You may have a trump card. I suggest you talk to her. Offer to pick up her mortgage and have it transferred to your name.'

'How can I afford that?'

'Reduce the original offer. She'll still be better off because what she gets will be hers rather than Jasper's.'

'What's to stop Jasper doing the same thing?'

Mr Wise shook his head. 'Jasper's waiting to repossess it so he can do it up and make a fast buck. He blocked your loan facilities because he was certain that you wouldn't be able to raise the capital anywhere else. My advice to you is to see Henrietta as soon as possible and get the deal clinched before Jasper closes on her.'

'I'll make an appointment with her right now. May I use your phone?' Eve said.

'Certainly.'

Poised and calm, Eve walked to the outer office, picked up the phone and dialled Henrietta's number. When she returned she said, 'I'm going over there now. Boy, is Jasper in for a surprise!'

'Good.' He nodded.

'I'll phone Manus Corrigan when I get home,' Eve continued. 'Tell him to draw up the necessary papers.'

'Keep it quiet until everything is signed, sealed and delivered.'

'Don't worry, I will,' Eve said.

'Go carefully with Henrietta. She can be a temperamental old bird.'

✳   ✳   ✳

Henrietta Ford Mathews showed Eve into her office and sat at her desk, sedate in a pinstriped man's suit and gold cufflinks, her greying hair up in a bun.

'I heard about your plight, Henrietta,' Eve said, getting straight to the point. 'I think we can sort something out.'

Henrietta took a cigarette from a gold box in front of her, lit it and sat back. Eve could see from the dark circles beneath her eyes how strained she was. 'I rather thought they'd have given me a bit more time,' she said, looking around sadly. 'Now I'm afraid I won't be able to sell to you.'

'I have a proposition for you,' Eve said. 'One that might solve your problems.'

Henrietta looked at her.

'I'm willing to take on the back payments of your outstanding mortgage, Henrietta, which means that the hotel will still be yours at the time of sale and that the money will go into your own pocket. We'll have to move quickly, though, because if the bank repossesses it now you stand to lose everything.'

Henrietta chewed her lip. 'What's the catch?'

'I'm reducing my offer to forty thousand pounds.'

A deep sigh escaped Henrietta's lips.

'The market has plunged and, judging by your books, the business is on the decline,' Eve continued. 'This place is a terrible drain on your resources. It needs extensive renovation and money is hard come by.'

'I realise that,' Henrietta said. 'The trouble is, I've had to make cutbacks. Let things drift. But with more staff and a bit of working capital you could do wonders with this place. It's a beautiful house, and there are the gardens.'

'I know and that's why I'm offering to pay off your mortgage arrears. That way you'll have enough to buy yourself a house. But if Jasper repossesses you'll end up with nothing.'

To Eve's surprise Henrietta said, 'By the time I pay off all my debts there won't be much left to get something suitable for the horses. They cost a fortune, you know.'

'I'll let you keep the gate lodge for yourself,' Eve said, 'and you can have the use of the stables. That way you won't really be leaving at all. That is my final offer.' She pushed back her chair and rose to her feet.

Henrietta smiled a smile of great dignity. 'I must say it's tempting,' she said. 'A couple of the horses are getting old and wouldn't adjust to change. And I always did want a more manageable place.'

Eve said, 'It wouldn't cost much to fix up the gate lodge. But I must have an answer within the next twenty-four hours so that Manus Corrigan can draw up the necessary papers before the banks foreclose.'

Henrietta sighed again, wearily. 'To tell you the truth, Eve, I'll be glad to let it go. All this responsibility has been telling on me. And I don't really have much choice.' Her voice broke. 'I accept your offer.'

'Wonderful,' Eve said. 'I'm sure you're doing the right thing.'

A week later Eve and Pauline wandered from room to room admiring the hotel. The hall was the central point of this old building, its oak-beamed ceiling a master stroke of *faux* medieval architecture. Smaller rooms led off it, but the drawing room was the finest of all, with its open hearth and view of the sloping lawns and terraces to the river and old boat-house beyond.

The place was full of old-world charm, the south-facing bedroom windows glinting in the sun. In the old days the water for the household had been drawn from a well in the yard. The Aga heated the kitchen and, though it belched and coughed, it made no great protest at the enormous task of cooking all the meals. The rest of the rooms were heated by electric fires. It had been Henrietta's great-grandfather's house, and had been handed down from generation to generation. Her father had turned it into a hotel to help defray the cost of its upkeep. Henrietta had taken it over in 1967.

Now, though, it belonged to Eve, with Pauline as her main shareholder. There was so much to be done and so little time to do it. The entire building would require redecorating. Eve left Pauline in the kitchen while she nipped round to the back, wanting to be alone for a while with her thoughts.

She approached the gardens slowly, listening to the birds as she inspected the square lawns and terraces. Down the cinder path the lower part was a wilderness of nettles and overhanging branches. Pigeons cooed from lofty nests, crows rummaged restlessly, and small startled birds flitted among the dense, interwoven canopy. Emerging from the green depths Eve stood on the lawn, gazing back at the creeper-clad walls of the house, the trailing honeysuckle around the back door, the Gothic windows that peered out from the ivy and gave the building a church-like appearance and a personality of its own.

The avenue was rutted, the gate lodge on the Sea Road half hidden behind the rough-hewn wall, its thatched roof long since overgrown with moss. Sitting on an old garden seat Eve's mind raced as she planned her next move.

She would transform the garden, grow flowers and plants to remind her of her childhood and her grandfather. She often thought of James Freeman: closing her eyes, she would conjure up pictures of him in his old gardening jacket, digging the soil to plant potatoes and vegetables, his unlit pipe in his breast pocket, the smell of tobacco clinging to him. Evenings reminded her of their walks together in the dappled light of the wood, listening to droning bees. Sometimes they went fishing together: they would sit on a rock, the tide washing over the coloured stones, while they waited for a bite. Eve recalled the rainy day they had buried him in the cold, grey churchyard, the loneliness of the house without him.

Eve and her mother had packed up his books and 'personal effects', as Manus Corrigan had called them. 'To think I lived here for all these years and none of it's mine,' Dorothy had wailed, surveying the ornaments and the china in the cabinet, familiar objects that were suddenly no part of their lives because Eve's father had insisted on having them shipped out to India.

'Thought I'd find you here.' Pauline's voice made her sit up with a start.

'I was daydreaming,' she said. 'What time is it?'

'Time for a nice cup of tea. I've asked Dermy to bring out a tray.'

'You are thoughtful,' Eve said, moving to make room for her on the seat.

'You've had a rough time lately,' Pauline said, sitting down.

'It was worth it. We pulled it off, Pauline. That's the main thing. And I wouldn't have managed without your help.' Eve was amazed to see tears in Pauline's eyes.

'Did we ever think we'd see this day?'

'It'll be worth it all to see this place come alive again. Mum says it used to be a great house in the old days. Lots of parties when the horsy set came down for hunting weekends.'

'You could open an equestrian centre. Put Henrietta in charge. Maybe advertise in the *British Tourist Guide Book*. They'd love eccentric old Henrietta.'

Eve laughed. 'First things first. I have to get a builder.'

'What about the company that's building the new apartments at the convent? Madge says that Mother Mary of the Angels was raving about them. Apparently they can gut an old building and rebuild it better than it was originally, and they're not too pricy.'

'They're exactly what we're looking for,' Eve said. 'I'll have to recruit more staff, too, before the season starts.'

'Tell you what, you recruit the staff and I'll find out about the builder.'

Dermy McQuaid came down the path, a large tray wobbling in his hands. 'A drop to wet your whistle, ma'am,' he said, placing the tray on the wrought-iron table between them.

Pauline poured. 'Here, drink up while it's hot,' she said, handing a delicate china cup to Eve.

'Here's to us,' Eve said, and they chinked cups. 'We'll celebrate properly when David and Seamie come home.'

Chapter Six

Dressed in a short denim skirt and skimpy white top that showed off her tan Pauline drove to the convent. The summer had arrived with a procession of brilliant, sunny days. She had made the most of it, sunbathing in the back yard, or cooling herself at the cove in the afternoons when the pub was shut, leaving Madge resting.

The fields around Glencove were brown, the lanes cracked and dry with dust. The convent occupied the whole of Church Street, a narrow street off Main Street. An eighteenth-century grey stone building it had wide, shallow steps up to a fan-lighted hall door. The cold, high-ceilinged rooms of the first two floors were unoccupied, the five remaining nuns preferring to live in the relative comfort of the smaller ones on the top floor.

Mother Portress answered the door. 'Pauline Quirk!' she said, gliding forward, taking her hand and clasping it. 'How nice to see you. What can I do for you?'

'Madge Kinsella sent this for Reverend Mother,' Pauline held out a bottle of whiskey in a brown paper bag.

Mother Portress took the proffered parcel, beaming, and Pauline watched it disappear into a capacious black sleeve. 'Madge says the new apartments are beautiful. I'd love to see them.'

'I'll take you out the back. You won't recognise it, it's such a mess.'

Pauline followed her down the damp, dark corridor, past the enormous dim parlours, out into the sunshine again. 'I'll leave you to look around.' Mother Portress withdrew.

Pauline emerged into the sunlight. Two workmen glanced at her over their shoulders, then resumed work. Stripped to the waist, they sweated as they raked the forecourt of the new apartments into shape. A stylish modern edifice of grey stone and immense plate-glass windows stood where the lawns, the rose garden and the sycamore tree had been. As she tilted her head back to gaze up at the new building, Pauline's nostrils were assailed by the smell of tar. At the end of the site a giant crane stood out in sharp relief against the blue sky.

'Anyone in particular you want to see?' a man called to her from the scaffolding above.

'Where's the boss?' she shouted, and almost choked at the dust that rose with a sudden gust of wind and blew into her face.

'That'll be Geoff Ryan. He's over there.' He pointed towards the crane now lifting its cargo towards the sky. 'You'll have to wait a few minutes.'

She watched the pallet of bricks ease itself against the scaffolding high above. Eventually the crane stopped and a man in a yellow hard hat got out. She walked over to him. 'Are you in charge?' she asked.

He turned and looked at her. Suddenly, she had the sensation of tumbling through space, of being caught and held by his hypnotic eyes. She stared back at this complete stranger, from his broad muscular chest to his narrow hips, belted into a pair of jeans.

'What can I do for you?' he said, removing his hat and running his hand over his close-cropped hair.

'I'm from the Glencove Hotel,' she said, unsteadily. 'I

heard about the apartments and was wondering if I could see inside.'

'Were you thinking of buying one?' he asked, with a tentative smile.

Looking up into his face she smiled back. 'You never know!'

'Watch your step, the stairs are muddy,' he said, and took her hand to lead her up. The pressure of his strong fingers burned into hers and she felt a sudden desire to touch him through his sweat-soaked vest. She wanted his hands to hold her against his powerful chest.

They stood at a corner of the second floor, where an L-shaped expanse of windows offered magnificent views of the sea.

'Would you be interested in giving us a quote for a new extension we're planning for the Glencove?' she asked.

'Where did you hear about us?' he asked.

'From the nuns.' Instinctively Pauline knew that he was equally aware of her, and wondered what was going on in his mind.

'So you came to see for yourself,' he said, stooping towards her slightly. 'Are you satisfied with what you see so far?' His eyes mocked her.

She looked around, her mind in a flurry.

'Well, are you?' he said, his voice low, insinuating.

'That depends on whether we can afford your prices or not,' Pauline said.

He leaned so close to her that she almost toppled backwards, and said, 'Just between the two of us, if you're looking for something for nothing, forget it.'

Furious, Pauline rounded on him. 'I've never looked for anything for nothing in my life. We're on a tight budget but we're not beggars!'

Their eyes locked. 'When did you want it done?' he asked.

'As soon as possible.'

'Sorry, I'm behind schedule here, as you can see.' He jerked his shoulder at the crane. 'I wouldn't want to take anything else on until we've finished.'

Pauline planted herself firmly in front of him. 'What do I have to do to persuade you?'

'Have dinner with me tonight.'

She took a step backwards. 'I don't admire your sense of humour,' she said.

'I'm not joking.'

In the ensuing silence, the sounds of the cement mixer, the workmen whistling and yelling to one another seemed to amplify.

'Think it over?' Geoff Ryan's languid eyes swept over her, a hungry look in them. 'Call me if you change your mind.'

'You think it over,' Pauline retorted. 'Phone the Glencove Hotel if you're interested in building the extension.' She started to walk back the way she had come.

His footsteps coming up behind made her stop. 'No need to get muddy.' He grinned, took her hand again and guided her along a plank raised slightly off the ground.

'Goodbye,' she said, as soon as they reached the back door.

'Wait. I don't know your name.' His eyes searched her soul.

A pulse beat in her temple. She looked down at their joined hands.

'What is it?' he coaxed.

'Pauline,' she said, letting go of his hand, and moving into the dark recess of the convent side-entrance.

'Pauline,' he repeated. 'I promise to think about your extension if you promise to have dinner with me.'

'I'll let you know,' she called back.

'It doesn't have to be tonight.'

That evening she kept an eye on the door of the pub, hoping that he would walk back into her life. During the night she couldn't sleep for thinking about him, his eyes, his hands, the air of sophistication about him, even in his working clothes. She knew she interested the men who frequented the pub and wondered from time to time if she would like any of them touching her. But now she knew that the only man she wanted was Geoff Ryan, and she didn't expect to see him again.

'My good friends,' Jasper Furlong said to his audience, the twenty businessmen and -women who comprised the Chamber of Commerce and who were sitting in the dining room of the sailing club, 'our greatest asset, you'll agree, is our dramatic coastline, which bestows on Glencove several miles of sandy beach, clear blue sea and a peaceful cove. By a stroke of good fortune I came to live in this lovely place over forty years ago, and I've seen various changes. But for all its assets it hasn't come together as a proper resort. It's time to address it as a tourist attraction.'

A burst of applause greeted his words. Jasper paused and looked around while waiters hovered in the background, anxious to serve more drinks. 'As you all know, times have changed radically. With an eye on the future and the leisure time it will bring, we must branch out, provide facilities for tourists as well as the young people of the town. I have ideas and plans that will move this town into the twenty-first century – and the money to implement them. All I need is your backing and co-operation.'

Everyone stood up and raised their glasses. 'Hear, hear,' they murmured, and toasted Jasper, who stood splendid in his evening suit as he smiled benevolently on them.

An impressive figure in the community, he held the towns-people in his grip: not one member of the Chamber dared ask a question.

'Good speech, Jasper.' Mr Cummins, the bank manager,

clapped him on the back as he returned to his seat at the top table.

'Thanks, old chap.'

'And what sort of plans do you have in mind?' Mr Cummins asked.

'Oh! This and that. As a matter of fact, I'm waiting for a deal to come off. Almost in the bag, actually. In fact, I was hoping to announce it tonight.' He drew Cummins closer and began to confide his plan for the Glencove Hotel when he repossessed it.

'If you look carefully at your post in the morning you'll see that the debt has been honoured,' Mr Cummins informed him.

'That's not possible. The woman's penniless.'

'Not any more,' Mr Cummins said, drawing on his cigar.

'Where did she get it?'

'Sold up, I presume.'

'She wouldn't do that, she couldn't!' Jasper rose from his chair in agitation. 'I have a lien on that property.'

'I'm afraid you've been pipped at the post.'

'What?' Jasper was rooted to the spot. Then, recovering himself, he left the room, not noticing Eve, who slipped into the cloakroom and waited there until she felt it was safe to emerge.

The next morning, Jasper was seething in his large, handsomely furnished office in Dame Street, Dublin, the cheque from Henrietta Ford Mathews in his hand. He sat at his huge mahogany desk, unlocked a drawer and pulled out a folder marked 'Freeman's Enterprises'. Opening it he scanned the figures. For several years now, Freeman's shares had been traded on the stock exchange, providing large quarterly dividends for its shareholders, Eve Furlong being one of them. He, as the major shareholder, had been supplying her coffee-shops with tea and coffee at special discount prices. He'd stop that immediately, and he'd thought of another way to thwart her plans. He closed the folder, put it back in the drawer, locked it and chuckled to himself as he lifted the phone to place a call to his friend Howey Swartz in New York.

Jasper had had luck on his side in his working life. He had a shrewd head for business but his expertise was in his timing. He recognised a good opportunity when it came his way, and since he had been in Ireland he'd plunged into business with courage and an eye for the main chance. He had wanted the Glencove Hotel for a long time: it was potentially the most lucrative holding in the town, which would give him even greater social prominence, and a strong foothold in local business. A logical place to start.

'Look at me!' Katie called over her shoulder as she leaped from boulder to boulder across the Blackwater river, her dress tucked into her knickers, the dark water swirling around her. Then she lost her balance and the dark water swirled around her. 'Ouch!' she cried, arms flailing. 'Ian!' she screamed to her cousin, who was climbing a nearby tree, 'I'm drowning! Save me!'

'Get out of there!' he yelled back.

'I *can't!*' she wailed.

'Don't be daft.' Swinging his legs over the tree trunk, he dangled from a branch before dropping to the ground and running to the riverbank. 'It's not deep. Turn around and wade in, and keep away from those boulders.'

Teeth chattering she began to move unsteadily towards him.

'Silly little fool,' he said, reaching out and grabbing her hand as soon as she got near to him.

Numb and mortified, her dress clinging to her legs, she hobbled over the gravelly shingle and sat on the grass verge, in the shelter of trees. 'I nearly drownded,' she snivelled.

'No, you didn't.' Ian laughed. 'It's too shallow. Now, stop moaning or I'll go off and leave you.'

Indignantly Katie turned away from him to examine the scratches on her legs. When she looked up again, Eve and Irene were coming towards her.

'We heard the screams from the garden. What happened to you?' Eve gathered up her daughter.

'Nothing.' Katie kept her eyes down.

'She was trying to cross the river,' Ian said.

'Why didn't you stick to the bridge?' Irene asked, pointing to the bockety wooden bridge to her left.

'It's boring,' Katie whimpered.

'You were supposed to be looking after her,' Jasper said to Ian, as he came into the clearing.

'I was. She was showing off,' Ian protested. 'Serves her right.'

'Meanie, meanie,' Katie chanted. 'I wasn't showing off.'

'Keep out of the woods in future,' Eve cautioned. 'It can be quite frightening for a small child.'

'But we were on an adventure,' Katie protested. 'Ian was a monkey and I was a crocodile. Only he ran off into the trees.' She burst into tears.

'Cry baby,' Ian said.

'Come on my brave girl,' Eve said, soothingly. 'It's over now. You're all right.'

They took the path to Rathmore House in slow procession, pushing their way through the wild yellow and blue irises that edged the meandering river. Irene stopped at the low garden wall to look at the back of the house with its high-pitched roof and sunny conservatory where Tabby lay basking in the sun, her mischievous eyes shut tight in slumber. 'I'll have to get Jimmy to tidy up the garden,' she said, pointing to the tall grass of the cottage garden that was threatening to swallow up the flower-beds and fruit bushes that led to the orchard.

'Don't let him cut down my roses.' Jasper's eyes were on

the fat climbing tea roses, which divided the garden from the gnarled apple trees.

'Of course not.' Irene smiled at him and continued on towards the house. In the kitchen she made tea while Eve cut slices of cake and apple tart.

'A word, when you're ready,' Jasper said to Eve, while Katie was eating her tart.

Eve followed him into his study. 'Sit down.' He pointed to the chair opposite his. 'I hear you bought the Glencove right out from under my nose.'

Eve was watching him closely. 'It was nothing personal,' she said. 'As I told you, Henrietta had promised me first option.'

'She had no right to do that. I wanted that hotel. I had plans for it.'

'And I have to expand if I'm to survive.'

'Well, this time I think you've bitten off more than you can chew. What has David said about it?'

'I haven't had a chance to tell him yet. It all happened so quickly.'

'I don't think he'll approve. You have enough to keep yourself busy as it is.'

'The coffee-shops are well organised and running smoothly.'

'I still say David won't like it.'

'He'll see the merit in it.'

'There's Katie to take into consideration. While you're manoeuvring your way around this new obstacle course, you're neglecting your responsibilities.'

Eve raised her eyebrows. 'In what way?' she enquired politely.

'Katie has hardly seen you since you bought the place. Who is going to take care of her in the school term when you're out at work all day?'

'I'll organise that.' Gazing into his bright eyes, under the shelves of heavy brows, she reminded herself not to be afraid of him.

Jasper was relentless. 'You don't realise what you're up against, and while you're fooling around with your daydreams the child is suffering.'

'No, she isn't.' Eve was exasperated.

'It's obvious. Look how insecure she is.'

'Let's keep things in perspective. I bought a hotel.' Eve kept her voice even. 'The management of it is well within my capabilities.'

Jasper opened a drawer and took out a folder. 'This is a copy of all the documents relevant to the hotel,' he said, his mouth tightening in disapproval. 'Believe me, you didn't just buy a hotel, you bought a pig in a poke. It will take someone with far more money and expertise than you have to make a go of it.'

'Let me be the judge of that.' Eve rose to go.

'It won't work, you know,' he said, following her to the door. 'The place is falling down. You'd be better off at home, minding your child. Women nowadays think they can do what they damn well please.' He was shouting. 'Irene was always there for our children. Poor Katie doesn't know whether she's coming or going.'

'So you'd rather I sat in all day watching television, smoking one cigarette after another out of sheer boredom,' Eve said, the rebellious fury of her teenage years rising in her.

'Your duty is to your child,' he said.

'I can take care of her. You don't need to worry.'

'You have a romantic notion of motherhood like your other romantic notion of being your own person. But I'll be keeping an eye on you – and Katie.' His eyes blazed.

Katie burst into the room. 'Mum, why is Grandpa shouting at you?' she said, running into Eve's arms and clinging to her. 'Is it because I fell into the water?'

'No, darling,' Eve said, lifting her up. 'He's just a bit tired.'

Upstairs in the bathroom Eve took off Katie's clothes. Her little body was brown and grubby as she stood naked while Eve applied Dettol to her scratches before putting her in the bath and soaping her gently.

'Why doesn't Grandpa like you, Mummy?' Katie asked.

'He does, darling. He's just anxious about you having a nice time, that's all.'

'I would have liked to go out in the boat but Ian wanted to climb trees,' she said, while Eve washed her. The warm soapy water was making her drowsy.

'We'll go out in Daddy's boat when he comes home,' Eve said consolingly.

'Will he be here soon?' Katie asked.

'He'll be phoning us tomorrow. You'll be able to ask him.'

Eve stayed away from Jasper for the rest of the weekend. He was furious with her for 'letting him down'. He would rant and rave at Irene as he paced up and down the kitchen, making everyone jittery. At night Eve could hear the murmur of voices as he plotted and planned with his cronies, then the sound of cars driving away and his footsteps on the stairs.

She spent the weekend playing with Katie on the beach or sprawled on the hammock in the porch, in shorts and bikini top, sunbathing, occasionally swimming, and wrote long letters to David as she listened to Katie's chatter.

Jasper shunned family meals and his silences created as much tension as the shouting. 'I can't understand why he's still so angry with me,' Eve said to Irene. 'Every time I walk into a room he leaves, slamming the door in my face.' Her lips trembled as she spoke.

The last evening of Eve's stay Jasper talked endlessly to Irene about his new business plans, and reminisced about his childhood. It was obvious as he talked that he was trying to undermine Eve. Irene responded with an occasional nod or a brief remark, her aloofness evident from her folded hands.

Suddenly Eve was shaken with a desire to kill him, to carve him up to discover what secret spell he wove over his family, which held them in thrall to him. What made his sons look at him with that possessive gentleness in their eyes?

When she was leaving, Eve went to Katie, stopped and knelt down beside her chair. The little girl swung into her arms and buried her face in her mother's shoulder. Eve hugged her tightly, then gently removed the child's arms. 'I have to go, sweetheart,' she said, kissing her and lowering her to the ground. 'I'll be back soon.'

'It's only for a few days. The time will fly,' Irene said. 'Katie'll enjoy herself.'

The cloying smell of furniture polish and the sharp odour of rashers cooking made Eve feel lonely as she walked out through the porch. Rathmore House never looked more beautiful than in the morning sunshine, its wide lawns sweeping down to the sea, the old elms and silver birch trees dappling the drive. In front of it the sea shimmered like a jewel. Eve's eyes misted over and the blues and greens of the landscape faded into a blur of sadness.

Chapter Seven

Pauline walked through the hotel gardens, marvelling at their transformation. With the lawns neatly cut and the flower-beds trimmed back, they looked magnificent. At the gate to the Sea Road, she stopped to admire the trees, before walking on, bypassing the woods for the path that led to the ridge. The bracken brushed against her legs as she climbed to the wider, bleaker landscape. Standing on a rise of ground, gazing over the fields and hedges to her left, the dark sloping woods to her right, she had a new sense of homecoming. So much had happened in the short time she was back that she had to pinch herself to believe it. She had bought a share in a hotel and met a gorgeous stranger called Geoff Ryan.

Thinking of him reminded her that she had accepted his invitation to the golf-club dinner. She was overcome with regret: in Montauk her life had been steady, unemotional, the way she had chosen to live it. The last thing she wanted was a quick fling with a devastatingly attractive man who was guaranteed to break her heart. It had been so long since she had experienced such feelings that she did not know how to control them. She turned her thoughts deliberately to her son. Seamie would be here soon and he would be her priority. She would devote all her spare time to him.

✻   ✻   ✻

She put on the black cocktail dress she'd bought in Grafton Street, and gold hoop earrings, with a sense of foreboding, then drove along the Sea Road. It was busy with groups of teenagers, joggers and people strolling along.

She saw him as soon as she entered the foyer of the Glencove Hotel. Tall and striking in a navy blazer, a pale blue shirt the colour of his eyes, matching tie and grey slacks, he came to meet her. 'You're looking lovely,' he said, eyeing her up and down.

Standing there in the middle of the foyer, people milling around, she tensed as she had when she had first met him, but he took her elbow and guided her to the dining room, his face tilted towards her.

It was busy with members of the golf club. Some stared at Pauline as she crossed the room.

'Relax,' Geoff said, as they took their seats. 'Enjoy yourself.'

At the next table Trish Lynam, glamorous in a blue satin dress, and her husband Morris said hello.

Pauline blushed. The waitress handed them each a menu, and Geoff ordered a bottle of Chardonnay, which they sipped while they waited for their meal to arrive. The murmur of conversation wafted around them and they could hear music from the ballroom.

Out of the corner of her eye, Pauline spotted Manus Corrigan sitting next to Ava Gregory, the doctor's wife. Myrtle Thompson was beside her husband, Ken, the local auctioneer who owned half of Goretti Terrace. Ken was a thin little man, with a face like a prune from too much drink, and shifty eyes; he was reputed to be one of the wealthiest men in Glencove and was a close friend of Jasper Furlong. Myrtle was laughing, her chins wobbling, her chest heaving as Dorothy Freeman, Eve's mother, took her seat further down the table, next to a debonair man Pauline had never seen before. She caught Pauline looking in her direction and waved over.

When the waitress came to clear their table, Pauline's plate was hardly touched. As they were sipping their coffee Manus Corrigan joined them. 'Pauline, good to see you,' he said, shaking her hand, his eyes fixed curiously on the stranger by her side.

'Hello, Manus. This is Geoff Ryan, the contractor on the apartment block at the convent.'

'How do you do?' Manus said. 'Are you thinking of joining the golf club?'

'You never know. I might be tempted.'

'We're recruiting new members. Great place for business. Can I buy you a drink in the bar before the dance begins?' Manus looked from Geoff to Pauline.

The new golf club had replaced the tennis club in the town's social calendar, with the same people in attendance, a generation older. Doctor Henry Joyce was there, arms folded, talking to Father McCarthy and Dr Gregory. The priest, beaming with bonhomie, his cunning eyes darting among his flock, greeted Pauline. 'I hear you're making a great go of the pub.'

'Thank you, Father,' Pauline said.

'It must be a consolation for Madge to have you back.'

'Yes, Father. I think it is.'

The Gaffneys, new to the town, joined the group. Jim Gaffney, the architect responsible for the new houses, reminded Pauline of a weasel as he talked to Henry out of the side of his mouth. In the years since she had been away, though, little had really changed among Glencove's inhabitants. Dr Gregory looked as youthful as ever, although the years had been less kind to his wife. Their eight-year-old twin boys had taken their toll on their mother's looks. She was talking to Lucy Joyce, Henry's wife, their heads close together, their faces averted, united in their shared confidences.

Pauline spotted Eve walking across to her. 'Come and meet

Geoff,' she said, and introduced them as the band struck up with the Boney M song 'Rivers of Babylon'. They chatted for a few moments, then Geoff led Pauline on to the dance floor. The music provoked an excitement in her that she had not felt since she was a teenager.

'You're good,' Geoff said into her ear as they danced.

She veered away from him, jiving to the beat. He followed, matching his steps to hers. Then he caught her and pulled her close.

The tempo slowed to Leo Sayer singing, 'When I Need You'. Geoff twirled her slowly and the air between them crackled with electricity. The other dancers swished around them, but Pauline, eyes closed, was lost in the music.

When the dance was over, Geoff drove her back to the pub. The light was on in Madge's bedroom. 'Let me lure you to my place for a nightcap,' he said.

A faint flush crept over Pauline's face. 'I'd better not. Madge is expecting me.'

'Come on.' He was pleading, his voice husky.

Pauline felt that everything had come to a standstill and they were the only two people in the whole world. 'I'm tempted,' she said, 'but I'd better go in.'

He kissed her, and a strange feeling came over her, a memory rising quickly only to be forgotten instantly. She pulled back, started to speak but faltered and bowed her head to hide her feelings. Eventually she said, 'Thank you for a lovely evening.'

'My pleasure.'

'I'll be seeing you.' She got out and walked quickly to the door of the pub.

'Wait!' Geoff jumped out and was beside her. 'Can I see you again?' he asked.

'I'd like that,' she said.

'I'll ring you,' he said, kissed her quickly on the lips and went back to his car. She watched him drive off into the night.

* * *

While Mrs Browne was away, visiting her sister in Dun Laoghaire, Pauline gave the bar a good cleaning. Now the long counter gleamed, the optics shone, the ashtrays had been washed, and she was scanning the advertisements in the *Evening Herald* for part-time bar staff, when the door opened and a man walked in. Dressed casually in jeans and a jumper, he looked smart and familiar. 'A pint of Guinness, please,' he said, propping himself against the counter.

Pauline looked at him from under her eyelashes as she poured his drink.

'You'll hardly remember me,' he said, in an unhurried lilting voice, his eyebrows raised in question.

'Have you been in here before?' Pauline asked.

'Aye,' he said. 'I have.' His eyes bored into hers.

Instinctively Pauline stepped back, the Northern accent jolting her into the terrible locked-away world of her past. His eyes were dark against the smooth white of his skin but it was the angle of his face as he turned sideways to lift his pint to his lips that she recognised. 'Scully,' she whispered, hardly believing her eyes.

She had never expected to see him again – anywhere. She had spent the last ten years trying to forget about him, and almost succeeding.

'I never thought ... we'd meet again,' she stammered.

'After all this time,' he said. 'I'd almost given up hope.' He smiled. 'We spent some time together, didn't we?' Lowering his voice he added, 'Through no fault of our own, of course. Must be ten years.' He shifted his weight from one foot to the other and stared at her over his Guinness. She opened the hatch and made to walk past him but he stepped in front of her, blocking her path, imperceptibly pushing her backwards. 'I used to wonder about you,' he said. 'Never expected this stroke of luck. You're looking well.' Gone was the round, youthful face, the dark stubble, and his eyes were sneering.

'How did you know where to find me?' Pauline was conscious of the customers listening yet she couldn't keep the tremor from her voice.

'Agnes Dolan told me that you were back from the States.'

'But Agnes is in France with Clare.'

'She wrote to me a while ago. You see, she knew I'd been searching for you.'

Pauline's heart lurched. Scully had visited the Dolans when Martin was alive. She had assumed that the connection had been severed once he was dead. She herself had avoided Agnes Dolan since her return, had even avoided the road behind the railway where she lived.

'How are you, anyway?' Scully asked.

Pauline had thought about this man so many times over the years, especially in that first year in Montauk. Now, ten years later, she was frightened, unready and unwilling for this encounter. Yet in some way she felt relief in seeing him again. It was as if she had always known he would turn up someday and, now that he had, the uncertainty was over. The silence between them was awkward. He sat down on a bar stool.

'How have you been?' he persisted, leaning close, con-spiratorial.

The scent of his aftershave hung in the air between them, haunting her with memories, and she was intensely aware of him physically. Watching him sip his drink slowly, savouring it, his steady brown eyes scrutinising her, she was taken back to the ghetto in Belfast where those same eyes had watched her when she was Martin's prisoner. He had rarely let her out of his sight then, had even accompanied her to the patch of wasteground below the flats where she had often gone for fresh air.

Madge came over. Pauline compressed her lips to hide her panic. 'This is Sc – Mr Scully,' she said.

'John Scully,' he corrected.

'Pleased to meet you,' Madge said, looking from one to the other, her eyes suspicious.

'Will you excuse me?' Pauline said, moving away.

'Wait!' Scully barred her path. 'Where are you going? We've lots to talk about.'

'I'm just getting you another drink,' Pauline said, fear creeping into her voice.

'Who's he?' Madge asked, following her, watching her pour his pint.

'Someone I met in the States.' Pauline shrugged to hide the lie.

'Take your time. Have a chat to him,' Madge said. 'I'll see to the other customers.'

'I've said enough,' Pauline replied, returning to him with his drink, leaving Madge to make out of it what she liked.

Pauline had told no one about her interlude in Belfast, confessed nothing. At first her secret had borne in upon her, in the middle of the night, every minute of the day. Often she thought she would burst with the longing to tell someone, if only to unburden her guilt. But the disastrous consequence of sharing something as horrific as that had stopped her. Although she could never erase the memory, time had blunted her pain. Now, all these years later, her secret intact, she wondered what had really brought Scully to this part of the country and how long he intended to stay.

It was not only strange to be sitting opposite him again it was also frightening. When they were together in Belfast, Scully had always stood around deferentially, awaiting orders from Martin, the boss. Now, even though she was on her own territory, a free woman, the power in his eyes threatened her. She answered his questions about Montauk, nervous of his rapt attention.

'What brought you to Glencove?' Madge asked Scully, when Pauline went again to refresh his pint.

'I move around,' he said. 'I'm working for Dwight's the builders at the moment. Saw Pauline over at the convent yesterday.'

'Nice apartments,' Madge said. 'Reverend Mother's a friend of mine. She showed me around.'

'A tough bird.' Scully smiled. 'Knows what she wants.'

'Could we have some drinks over here, please?' a customer called.

Pauline went to serve him, and Scully stood up to go. 'We need to meet,' he said urgently. 'We've a lot of catching up to do.'

Pauline felt her throat go dry. 'I don't think—'

'Here, give us a ring at that number.' He handed Pauline a card.

A couple came in. The woman looked from Pauline to Scully and back to Pauline. 'Are you serving?' she asked.

'See you later then,' Scully said, going out the door.

'A pint of Guinness and a gin and tonic,' the woman said. Pauline's heart thumped in her chest like a trapped bird.

It was only after the pub had closed, when she had cleared away the dirty glasses and stacked the dish-washer, that she let herself think about Scully. A long time ago she had closed a door on her past, had allowed herself no time to dwell on it. With the passage of time she had deluded herself into a false sense of security. Scully's reappearance had split her safety-net wide open. She locked the doors of the pub and went upstairs, glad to leave the intimidating world outside.

In the silence of her bedroom she hung up her working clothes, slipped on her dressing-gown, and went into the kitchen to make a cup of tea. The clock said twelve. Madge came in and stood barefoot on the cold lino. 'Are you all right?' She looked closely at Pauline.

'Yes. I'm fine, thanks.'

The kitchen was shrouded in shadows, and Pauline shivered.

'That friend of yours, what's his name?' Madge asked.

'Scully,' Pauline said.

'Know him well?' Madge threw her a glance.

'No, not very,' Pauline said, hoping the conversation would end there.

'Not your type.'

She didn't protest.

'I was thinking we might have a bit of a hooley when Seamie gets here. Celebrate your homecoming. Around the time of your birthday.'

Pauline brightened. 'That'd be lovely,' she said.

'I know you're missing him. But it won't be long now until you have him home.'

'No,' Pauline said, the thought bringing a smile to her face.

That night she dreamed she was back in that ghetto in Belfast. In her dream she could hear gunshots on the streets, and the drone of helicopter engines over the city, see the feet of soldiers running on pavements, their guns heavy.

She woke up panic-stricken, with the feeling that something sinister, a shape, not clearly defined, was hovering outside her window. She wished she could fly back to America, float in an unbroken, cloudless sky over the earth and never return.

Chapter Eight

Eve felt the tension the moment she stepped inside the door. Dermy McQuaid approached her, an anxious look on his face. 'I've everyone lined up in the drawing room like you said, ma'am,' he said politely.

The staff of the Glencove Hotel were all there, waiting: chambermaids, waitresses, kitchen help. Most of them had worked at the hotel for a very long time. Greta Murphy, the cook, stood apart, arms folded, a hostile look on her face. Eve guessed that she was the appointed spokesperson for the rest.

Shaking hands with each in turn, Eve greeted those she already knew, and memorised the names of the others: Eileen, the receptionist, Ivy, the telephonist, Peter, the night porter, Joe, the maintenance man.

Finally, she stood in front of them, took a deep breath and said, 'Good evening, everyone. As you know, I'm the new owner of this hotel and you are my staff.' She smiled. 'I know most of you, and I'll soon get acquainted with everyone else because I'll be around for a while as a member of staff. I also know how fond of Miss Ford Mathews you all were and I'm sure you'll miss her. She's happy with her new lifestyle and I hope you'll all be happy with the changes I plan for the Glencove.' She paused, her eyes flicking over their faces.

They waited warily for her next words.

'I intend to make a lot of changes,' she said. 'I want to make this place a landmark in the county with a reputation for excellence in food and service. To achieve this I need your co-operation, and I've no doubt that I'll get it. According to Henrietta, you are all hard workers.'

There was silence.

'First off, I'm going to make my way slowly around the various sections, meet you all individually, speak with each person in charge. Then I shall compile a report. I'll start in the kitchen with Greta, at the hub of things.' She inclined her head towards the cook. 'My hope is that by working together as a team our reputation will spread far and wide. I guarantee you that your efforts will be rewarded, starting with a pay rise all round as a gesture of my goodwill. I want you to remember that you are the pulse. The success of this business rests with you all.'

The clapping followed her out of the room as she went to the kitchen to discuss the catering. Greta presided over the kitchen with dogged devotion. She was responsible for the ordering of the food, its cooking and presentation. With Henrietta in charge, she had been her own boss and did not welcome interference from any quarter. She showed Eve reluctantly around her cavernous domain.

Greta spent most of the morning preparing lunch, shouting orders to Pearl Benson, the scullerymaid, whose hands were raw from peeling potatoes and vegetables. For such a large, plump person, her movements were surprisingly rapid.

From midday onwards Greta worked at the range, lifting huge, bubbling saucepans on and off the stove, stopping only to mop her perspiring brow with her apron, her haunches rippling under her white uniform, the soles of her sandals slapping off the red flagstones as she moved around. Greta loved the old kitchen, the steamed-up windows, the greasy, yellow-stained walls, where she clattered her pots, in her midday frenzy, shouting instructions over the clamour.

During the lunch-hour pandemonium, she spooned food on to plates as the orders came thick and fast. Girls ran to and fro with loaded trays, colliding with each other, swearing amid burns and spillage. At its peak Greta burst into song, wheezy as she tried to reach the high notes. When the rush-hour was over and Pearl had scoured the last pan, Greta sat Eve and Pearl down to spare ribs, cabbage and floury potatoes at a corner of the kitchen table, then brought a plate for herself. 'We're a happy little family down here,' she assured Eve. 'And you won't taste the likes of them anywhere else, I'll guarantee you that.'

'They're good,' Eve said, licking her fingers daintily. 'But we'll have to get a more efficient cooker for you, and an industrial dish-washer for Pearl.'

Pearl looked at her, eyes anxious. 'You won't be needing me so much if you get a dish-washer.'

'Of course we will. It'll have to be loaded and unloaded, and there's plenty of other things to be done.'

Pearl sighed with relief. 'I've a gang of kids at home, missus. The eldest is only eight, and my oul' fella not working.'

'Never gives you a minute's peace, does he?' Greta sighed, lifting a mug of scalding tea to her lips.

'Sure what's the use complaining?' Pearl said resignedly. 'When I suggested separate beds he went mad.'

'Separate beds, how are you!' Greta scoffed. 'A suit of armour is what you need to ward off that brute.' She laughed and, to Eve's relief, Pearl joined in.

'He has his usefulness,' she said defensively.

'Oh, we know. A child every year to keep you down,' Greta said.

'That's over and done with. The nuns had a chat with him, and Father McCarthy did too.'

'You think that'll stop him?' Greta boomed, her face reddening.

'I'll leave you to it,' Eve said, making for the door.

Then Eve climbed the narrow back stairs to the ground floor and Reception, wondering if she would ever get to know all the aspects of the business. People like Greta had years of experience.

The lobby was still busy with lunch-time customers filing into the bar and dining-room. Reception was noisy with the telephone ringing, a man making enquiries, voices raised in conversation. Eve decided that as soon as she had been round all the departments she would set about recruiting even more staff before the season got into full swing. At Reception Mary Dwyer, the housekeeper, came to inform her that two of the waitresses had phoned in sick, just as she was deciding to recruit more staff before the season got into full swing.

'Two!' Eve said in sudden panic. 'The busiest weekend so far and more bookings to come. We'll have to get someone to cover for them. Anyone.' She looked at the clock above the reception desk.

In another hour the dining room would be buzzing. Bedroom cleaning would have to wait.

'Send Betty McCabe into the dining room now, and Jenny when she comes in,' she said, then went straight to her office to phone the staff agency for replacements. As she put down the receiver there was a knock on her door. 'Come in.'

Dermy McQuaid was standing there. 'Excuse me, ma'am,' he said, removing his cap. 'I know who might be able to help us out.'

'*Who?*'

'Sergeant Enright's young ones got their school holidays last week. He won't want them hanging around the town all summer.'

'Might be the answer,' Eve said. 'I'll call in at the barracks this morning when I'm in town. Thanks, Dermy.'

At eleven o'clock Eve backed out of her parking space and drove into town. A queue of traffic was waiting at the entrance to the golf club, forcing her to stop too. As soon as it cleared she drove on, past Goretti Terrace, the row of Victorian terraced houses where Pauline had shared a basement flat with Seamus Gilfoyle. Outside the barracks she saw Delia Enright, in a hectic red dress. Eve pulled into the kerb and got out. 'Hello, Delia,' she said. 'Could I have a word?'

Delia turned. 'God, it's Eve Freeman! I wouldn't know you. You look terrific. I heard you'd bought the hotel.' She gazed admiringly at Eve.

'That's what I've come about. We're expecting a crowd from the golf club for a celebratory lunch, and we're short-staffed. There are two jobs there for your girls, if they want them.'

Delia's smile broadened. 'Of course they will! They're demented looking for work.'

'Can they start now?'

'Of course.'

'That's settled, then. Send them over to me as soon as possible and I'll fix them up with uniforms.'

'But you haven't interviewed them or anything.' Delia was aghast. 'You don't even know what they look like.'

'If they're anything like their mother, they'll do me fine,' Eve said, getting back into her car.

'I'll tell them,' Delia called after her. 'If one of them doesn't want the job I'll take it myself!'

Eve drove back to the hotel by the river, passing the towbridge and the station where summer tourists were getting off the train. Along the banks of the railway-track lovers walked hand in hand, and people sat on benches. Glencove was full of life. It was a good time to get started.

Chapter Nine

Pauline was in Lynam's, buying socks, underwear, shorts, T-shirts for Seamie for the summer, when she saw Scully crossing Main Street and realised how much she had dreaded him calling into the pub again, making a nuisance of himself and arousing Madge's suspicions. When she got home she phoned the number on his card. It was picked up on the second ring.

'Hello,' a female voice said.

'Hello, may I speak to Mr Scully?'

'Hold on, please.' The phone clicked, buzzed and clicked again.

'Hello,' Scully said.

'This is Pauline Quirk.'

'Pauline. I knew you'd ring.' She could hear the pleasure in his voice.

'You said we should meet, only I'd prefer it if you didn't call to the pub.' She held her breath.

'Where, then?' Scully asked.

'Murphy's tonight,' Pauline said quickly, before she changed her mind. 'It's my night off.'

'I'll be there at eight,' Scully said, and hung up.

He was waiting for her, his dark eyes staring at her, reminding her of the first time they'd met. She'd often asked him who he was and what his connections with Martin were, but he'd always refused to tell her. Now, as he took a seat opposite her, he said, 'You've changed,' and added, 'for the better.'

'Thanks.'

'You left Belfast very suddenly,' he said, as he perused the menu.

Pauline felt herself go cold.

The waitress brought the drinks, and Scully ordered food for both of them. 'Steak and chips, one rare, one medium, onion rings, don't forget the tomato ketchup,' looking at Pauline for approval. She nodded. 'See, I remembered how you like your steak,' he said, pleased with himself. Face thrust forward, he continued, in low, confiding tones, 'Of course, you knew Martin was killed, didn't you?' He sat stiffly, his eyes never leaving her face.

'Yes,' Pauline said, the word dying on her lips.

'The verdict at the inquest was murder.'

Pauline had trouble swallowing.

'I found him.' Scully looked at her. 'Luckily the IRA never discovered who did him in. But he had so many enemies it was anybody's guess. It was damn inconvenient for me, though. We were in the middle of a very important bit of business and, with Martin not around, the whole thing collapsed.'

'What did you do?' Pauline stammered.

The waitress hovered. Scully nodded to her and she put down their plates.

'Thank you,' Scully said, and waited until she was out of sight before he went on. 'I did jail. That's what I did,' he said, matter-of-factly. 'Some trumped-up charge about a taxi-driver. They were determined to keep me behind bars until they had something on me. When I got out I came looking for you but you'd disappeared off the face of the earth.'

Pauline squared her shoulders. 'My aunt wrote to me when I

was in Belfast, offering me a job. It was too good an opportunity to miss. Martin understood,' she lied.

'It turned out well, by the looks of things.'

'Very well.'

'You've no regrets, then.'

'About what?'

'About anything?'

'None. I got myself an education. Work experience.'

'Good for you.' He sat rigid, his eyes challenging.

Pauline was too scared to try to draw him out — he belonged to a powerful organisation. She preferred to think of him as having no past, no identity, except for the name of Scully. Yet, in Belfast with him, she had felt no fear.

As if reading her mind, he said, 'In jail I spent my time dreaming about getting out. Meeting up with you again. I escaped on day release. Shot the security guard.' He was staring at her, his eyes resigned and calm.

Pauline froze.

He continued eating, his hands relaxed. 'Got out barely in time. Before it destroyed me. My mates smuggled me over the border. Had a ticket at the airport for me. I can tell you, Pauline, I did the whole bit. Hunger strike, dirty protests, everything. I was glad to be away.'

'Where did you go?'

Scully shrugged. 'San Francisco. Worked on the buildings. But I always wanted to come home. I spent my time making plans to return and stage a revolution. Then, when the climate was right and with the mother going downhill, I came back.'

Bracing herself, Pauline asked, 'What got you involved in all of this the first day?'

'My father was killed by the enemy. My mother always said that her religion was a great comfort to her at that time but, as far as I could see, comfort was the one thing she was denied. Especially by her religion. She had no one to turn to but me.'

His hand shook as he raised his glass to his lips. 'That woman over there is staring at us. Do you know her?'

Pauline glanced over her shoulder to see Myrtle Thompson with another woman. 'I'd better get going,' she said. 'Madge'll be wondering where I am.'

Scully walked her to her car. 'We'll meet again soon,' he said. 'We've lots more to talk about.'

'Sure,' Pauline said, starting the engine.

'I'll ring you,' Scully said, as she drove off. She knew he would.

Eileen phoned through to Eve. 'Sorry to disturb you but there's a gentleman here asking to see you. A Mr Geoff Ryan.'

'I'll be right down.' She went to her cabinet and took out a file marked 'New Wing', then went to Reception.

'Hello.' She shook hands with Geoff. 'I'm glad you could come.'

'I thought I'd have a look around. See what's involved.'

They walked through the lobby, quiet after the lunch-hour, and along the corridor to the back of the hotel. 'As you can see the existing car-park is very small,' Eve said, as they stood facing the dining-room. 'The ballroom will be here.' She pointed to the left of the car-park. 'The conference room above it.'

Geoff strolled around the area, the plans in his hand. Occasionally he stopped to check them, make notes, discuss some detail with Eve. 'All done,' he said eventually. 'I'll put some figures together over the next few days, let you have them.'

'When do you think you can start?'

'End of the month, hopefully. The apartments are almost ready.'

'That's great. Let me buy you a drink,' Eve said.

Geoff looked at his watch. 'No, thanks, I'd better be getting back.'

'I'll wait to hear from you, then,' Eve said.

As he was leaving Pauline strode into the lobby.

'Hello,' he said. 'I'm glad to see you. You went off so fast that I didn't get a chance to say goodbye properly.'

'It was a great night,' Pauline said.

'So why did you run off like that?'

'Madge was waiting up for me,' Pauline lied.

'You were running away.' Geoff looked around. 'I'm walking back to the convent. Care to join me?'

'I'd love to.'

As they left the Glencove the sun was still shining. Pauline, in jeans and a white sweater, her hair tied back with a ribbon, walked beside Geoff feeling vulnerable. They stood at the harbour. Small boats shunted to and fro on the tide, and seagulls swooped down, scavenging for discarded morsels of food. 'I'm starting the extension at the end of the month,' Geoff said.

'That's wonderful,' Pauline said. 'Eve was getting anxious.'

They walked on. Nearer the convent she asked him how he had got into the building trade. 'I served my apprenticeship on massive building sites on the Costa del Sol,' he said, 'then took off to San Francisco. Built shopping centres, underground car-parks, hotels, roads. That's where I learned how to fight with banks, planners, contractors, sub-contractors.'

When they got back to the hotel he asked, 'Have dinner with me tomorrow night?'

'I'm sorry, I can't. My son's coming home.'

'Your son!' Geoff gasped.

She glanced at him as he stood, hands deep in his pockets, lips compressed, and realised how little he knew about her. She turned to him, the wind whipping her hair across her face. 'His name's Seamie and he's nearly twelve. I left him in the States to finish school.'

'I see. Well, I'd better get back to work,' Geoff said, off-handedly. 'I'll give you a call.'

Pauline retraced her steps, convinced, once again, that she had seen the last of him.

Chapter Ten

Upstairs in her private office on Grafton Street, Eve sat down at her desk. The last few weeks had been a nightmare: organising the builders, new staff, the tension between herself and Jasper at such a pitch that she had been almost at screaming point. The previous night she had been so exhausted that she had slept solidly for sixteen hours. And she was scared of the mounting debts. Taking a deep breath, she took some folders out of her filing cabinet and began work. The phone rang. 'Hello. Can Mrs Furlong take a call from New York?' the foreign voice rapped.

Eve frowned. 'Yes.'

'Eve.' David's voice floated down the wire, urgent, anxious.

'Darling. How are you? Is something wrong?'

'Does there have to be something wrong for me to phone my wife?'

Eve laughed with relief. 'I miss you so much. When are you coming home?'

'Listen, Eve. There's been a change of plan. I'm on my way to Paris.'

'Oh.'

'Catch the four o'clock flight to Charles de Gaulle this evening. I'll meet it.'

'But ...' Eve spluttered, thinking of her promise to Katie to spend the weekend with her at Rathmore.

'I thought it would be nice for us to spend a couple of days together.'

Eve collected herself. 'You're not the only one who works for a living. I've got my hands full right now,' she said.

'All the more reason why you should take a breather, enjoy yourself.'

Responsibility weighed heavily on Eve's shoulders. It was not a good time to be self-indulgent. On the other hand, how could she resist a couple of days in Paris, the city of romance, with the man she loved? She knew by the urgency in his voice that he needed her although he'd never admit it in so many words. She smiled with pleasure as he said, 'See you about five.'

Typical David, she thought, as the phone clicked off. He never took her work seriously.

As she lifted the receiver to phone home, a pang of regret shot through her at having to disappoint Katie once more. Katie, who resented any intrusion into her mother's precious time at the weekend. Another summer was slipping by with the pressure of work keeping her little family apart. She felt guilty about her child: she was letting her work encroach on her free time. But Eve liked being busy and had heaped more work into her already full schedule as if her world would fall apart otherwise. Now, she must go to David.

The anxiety in his voice had been unmistakable, and she wondered what could be amiss. There was no danger that Furlong Investment Bankers could be in trouble. She would have known from Jasper and Irene's demeanour the previous weekend. He's lonely, that's all, she told herself, as she made her reservation. Still, it was uncharacteristic of him to let his personal life intrude into his business world. Duty came first with David, regardless of the circumstances. That was the golden rule Jasper had instilled in his sons, reminding them regularly that the only things worth having, wealth and power, would be theirs if they abided by it.

The tragic death of David's and her baby son, two days after his birth, had left them both grief-stricken. Eve had consoled herself with her subsequent pregnancy but David had remained heartbroken. Even Katie's arrival did not erase his sadness. She decided that she would make a special effort this weekend to pamper him.

She checked the post for any urgent mail, then went through the week's purchases. Everything was in order. For the rest of the morning, she immersed herself in the business of the hotel. Jasper was right. She should have a master plan, and possibly an alternative in case it failed. She took out a jotter and began to work on figures for the coming year.

When she was satisfied with the result, she planned the refurbishment: sofas covered in chintz with matching curtains, pale Indian rugs on pine-panelled floors, big, bright, decorative lamps placed strategically here and there to give a soft light. A marble fireplace to be used on chilly days and the ornate over-mantel from her grandfather's drawing room above it would make the room warm and enticing.

She picked up the silver-framed photograph of him, which had been taken on his boat. As she gazed at his lined, gentle face, she realised how much she still missed him. James Freeman had started out with nothing, a youth with a dream and a bank loan of fifty pounds, and had built his tea-importing empire with courage and determination. The same courage Eve had shown when she opened her first coffee-shop. At the time, her grandfather had been the only one who believed in her. She must not fail him now. Oblivious to everything else going on around her she continued to work until lunch-time, convinced that the Glencove Hotel held the key to her future success.

At one o'clock sharp she gathered her papers together, put

them in her briefcase, then went to Arnott's a few doors down to buy some underwear for her trip — there was no time to go home and pack. She also tried on a dress that had caught her eye as she walked in: a simple style in cream, with classic lines and matching jacket.

At the airport she collected her ticket and made her way to the departure lounge thinking of David.

He was waiting for her at Arrivals. In his mid-thirties, he was tall, fair-haired, with penetrating blue eyes, and dressed impeccably in a pale grey suit, white shirt and floral silk tie. As Eve came through the barrier, he stepped forward, love and pleasure in his face as he went to greet her.

'Darling!' she exclaimed, hurrying to him. 'Were you waiting long?'

'Not long,' he said, taking her in his arms and hugging her tightly, before he held her at arm's length to look down into her face. 'You look gorgeous,' he said, kissing her full on the lips, oblivious to the crowds milling around them.

'Wow!' Eve was blushing when they pulled apart. 'This is too public.'

'You're right. Come on,' he said. 'Let's get out of here.'

He took her hand and led her out to a waiting car. 'Hôtel de Blanc,' he said to the driver, and ushered Eve into the back seat.

A thrill of excitement shot through her as they drove round the Arc de Triomphe, down the Champs Elysées, the names of the *haute couture* designers — Christian Dior, Yves Saint Laurent, Gucci — shining out from beautiful shops that displayed only a couple of garments in their windows. They stopped outside their hotel, near the floodlit Place de la Concorde. David spoke in rapid French to the driver, who helped him with his bags as far as the hotel steps. They registered and were escorted to their room on the sixth floor. From their bedroom window,

Eve could see the Eiffel Tower. 'What a good idea this was,' she said, surveying the elegant room, the fresh flowers.

David pulled off his tie and undid his shirt buttons, then held out his arms to her. 'I can't tell you how much I've missed you,' he said, clasping her to him and kissing her.

'I missed you too. And I promised Katie I'd phone her as soon as I arrived,' Eve said. She experienced a sudden tug at her heartstrings as she thought of Katie, so far away from her. David, seeing the anxiety in her face, went to the phone and dialled his parents' home.

Katie answered it. 'Daddy, I was waiting for Mummy to ring,' she exclaimed. 'Where is she?'

'Standing here beside me, poppet. How are you?'

'When are you coming home, Daddy?'

'As soon as I can. I'll have a big surprise for you. Here's Mummy.'

Eve took the receiver. 'Hello, Katie.' A smile flitted across her face as she listened to her little daughter recount the day's happenings. Before she handed the phone back to David she had a quick word with Irene, who assured her that Katie was happy.

While he talked to his mother Eve gazed at her husband from across the room and felt a thrill at the prospect of the next couple of days alone with him. Watching his lean, muscular body as he stripped to take his shower she felt the same physical attraction for him as she had when she was only a schoolgirl. David looked up suddenly and caught her eye. He was beside her instantly, kissing her with the same urgency and passion as he had all those years ago when they had finally met up again after his sojourn abroad. 'You're so beautiful,' he said. 'You'll never know how much I've missed you.'

She put her arms around him. 'I've missed you too,' she said, her head against his chest.

He was undoing the buttons of her blouse, then unhooking

her bra, slipping off her skirt, the pressure of his hands on her thighs drawing small moans from her.

Eve had always had a crush on David, her next-door neighbour in Glencove. After leaving school he had been sent abroad with the family firm and she had lost contact with him. Her brief marriage to Chris Winthrop had been a disaster, and it wasn't until she and David met again, in Glencove, during the takeover of her grandfather's business, that they had really fallen in love.

'My love,' David was saying into her ear. 'Oh! My love,' as he always did afterwards.

What struck Eve most about David as she looked at him across the table in the restaurant was his close resemblance to his father. It was in the sharpness of his eyes and his quick movements, as if there was no time for delay. After their long separation it seemed more pronounced than ever. Although he looked well, Eve could see in his eyes the strain she had detected in his voice on the telephone. The brilliant smile and cool reserve masked a deeply emotional man. David had been warm and fun-loving when she married him, but the loss of their son had almost destroyed him. He had allowed only Eve to see the more vulnerable side of his nature.

'It's so lovely to see you,' she said, clasping his hand. 'How have you really been?'

'Up to my eyes. I only managed to get away at the last minute. If Stuart Mitchell hadn't arrived I'd have been stuck there another week at least.'

Over dinner, Eve told David about her new acquisition. 'The Glencove Hotel!' David said, astounded.

'It's all thanks to Mr Wise,' she said hurriedly. 'Jasper wasn't pleased at the idea of being outmanoeuvred by me. He wanted it for himself.'

'Dad's a bully,' David said. 'I'm glad you hoodwinked him.' There was admiration in the look that he gave her.

'I feel a bit deflated after pulling off such a big deal,' she said. 'It's scary.'

'I know,' David reached across the table for her hand. 'It'll do Dad all the good in the world to have a slip of a thing like you outwit him. He would have wiped you out without a twinge of guilt if he could have.'

'What if I've taken on too much and it all goes wrong?'

'You took a risk, Eve. When the market picks up, that hotel will be worth a fortune and your investment will pay off. By then, it will have made a name for itself.' He picked up her hand and kissed it. 'We're in this together, my darling. I'll stand by you, no matter what.'

'Jasper's afraid I'm taking on too much too quickly. He's afraid that Katie will suffer because of it.'

For all her success with the coffee-shops and her outward sophistication, David knew that Eve was not as confident as she seemed. He had helped and supported her over the years, persuading his father to let her have the best terms available on her loans, and had always taken pride in her achievements. Now he said, 'You're brave, Eve. I admire your courage in taking on so much. That place was really in the doldrums.'

'What happens if it all goes wrong?'

'You'll sink without trace, Dad'll say 'I told you so', and I'll still love you.' Eve laughed. 'But that's not going to happen, because already the business gurus are forecasting a pick-up in the market.'

'I want to give value for money with prices people can afford.'

'Advertise. Go after the local market. Hit the town with everything you've got. Wipe out the competition. Don't forget your regular customers are your best ones.'

Eve began to relax. 'I'm afraid I'll have to spend a bit more than I thought on the décor.'

'You'll realise your money quickly enough.' David looked affectionately at her as he spoke. 'It's the only hotel for miles around and with your stamp on it it's bound to take off.'

'Do you really believe that?'

'Yes, I do. You have a flair for enterprise.'

'Thank you, darling. Now, tell me about your adventures.'

'Well, I think I've made an impression on a certain financial company on Wall Street.'

'Oh.' Eve looked at him in surprise.

'It's an old financial company with ageing management, stuck in the forties, struggling. Dad has his eye on it because it's close to the Chase Manhattan. My friend Lew Grey heard from a stockbroker friend on Wall Street that they're ripe for a takeover.'

'I see.'

'It's worth investigating, Eve. It's small, but their clients are rich. Old money, stocks and bonds. Perfect location. If I could get it at the right price ...' David's eyes shone.

'What will you do?'

'Make a few enquiries. Ask Lew to get me more information.'

The duck arrived, served with pommes frîtes and a crisp salad. David didn't speak again until the waiter had gone. 'If I do buy the business it would mean that I'd have to spend some time there. A year or so.'

'What?' Eve could hardly believe her ears. 'What about me? Us? We might have to uproot ourselves.'

'Only temporarily, darling. I'd hate to live in America for good.'

'But what about my coffee-shops? The hotel?'

'I haven't made any final decisions. And now you'd better eat up, your food's going cold and I've got plans for us for later on.'

Chapter Eleven

Pauline was amazed by Seamie's height. Dressed in shorts and a T-shirt, his legs were long and skinny.

'Mom!' he called, lumbering towards her, the weight of his kit-bag making it bump off his knees. He was nearly as tall as she was.

'You've grown so much.' She hugged him.

'I know,' he said, and Pauline had to walk fast through the car-park to keep up with him.

The noise of the city filtered into the car as they drove past cathedrals and churches, along rainwashed O'Connell Street, swarming with shoppers and raggy urchins begging on the bridge, along the Quays.

Seamie was fascinated by the huge white hulls of foreign ships, motionless in the docks, the swinging cranes next to them lifting their cargo high up over the grey water, to be guided by waiting men into blue and red freight trucks. When they got to Glencove Pauline took him straight into the bar to meet Madge.

'You're welcome home,' Madge said solemnly, her voice catching in her throat, her eyes misting at the sight of him. 'You're a prime boy, so you are,' she went on, after inspecting his blond hair and freckled face, which bore no resemblance to his mother's.

Seamie looked quizzically at her. 'Gee, thanks!' he said, and went with Madge to be introduced around the bar, where everyone was offered ham sandwiches and a drink on the house before Seamie was escorted upstairs to the kitchen. There a plate of cold meat, salad, hunks of delicious soda bread and a jug of lemonade were waiting for him.

'The life went out of the place when you left here as a little baby,' Madge told him, standing back to admire once more his silky hair and blue eyes. 'Having you back will liven us all up. We've been miserable long enough. And you won't be lonesome either. We'll find plenty for you to do.' She opened one of the drawers in the dresser and showed him packets of sweets, crisps and chocolate. 'In case you feel peckish,' she said.

'Thanks, Aunt Madge.'

Coming into the kitchen Pauline threw her eyes heavenwards. 'You're spoiling him already!'

After lunch Pauline showed him the newly converted attic bedroom.

'This is all mine?' he gasped, waving at the spacious room, the bunk beds, the rows of tubular shelves with games and books already on them.

'Sure,' Pauline said. 'And if you want to have a friend to stay there's plenty of room.'

'Cool!' Seamie said, then dumped his bag on the floor and rushed off to explore his new surroundings.

The welcome-home party for Pauline and Seamie Quirk, at Kinsella's Select Bar, was in full swing and the tight-packed pub was a frenzy of noise and hilarity. Sweating men and big-bosomed women sandwiched themselves together, knees touching, hips swaying, tongues wagging. Peter Brennan, the local fiddler, played hornpipes, jigs and reels, his throat working up and down in time to the rhythm as his right foot tapped frantically with the beat.

Madge, the sleeves of her crimson blouse pushed up over her elbows, held court behind the bar. Father McCarthy, chins wobbling over his dog-collar, drank his ball of whiskey watching Mrs Browne, whose gimlet eyes and sharp ears missed nothing. She stabbed him in the ribs with her index finger. 'And where's Pauline herself?' she asked.

Father McCarthy deferred to Madge.

'Upstairs getting ready,' Madge said, rolling her eyes. 'Wouldn't you know? Everything with her is a production.'

The faded wallpaper dripped with freshly spilled drink from the erratic dancers and landed on laps, sweaters and the tight dresses of giggling girls clustered together, eyes on the door, glasses in their hands.

Pauline appeared in her black dress, hair piled on top of her head, eyes dark with intensity, mouth curled in a distracted smile.

Geoff Ryan appeared as if from nowhere to claim her for a dance. The flashing movement of her body, the sway of her hips, the red nails against the white of his shirt caused consternation among the old women swilling gin in the corner. Over the music, their voices broke in outrage. Mrs Rooney nudged Mrs Browne. 'Would you look at the cut of her?' she said, wiping her lips with the back of her hand. 'I knew no good would ever come of her.'

'You're right,' Mrs Browne said, all ears, sipping her own pint slowly.

'God knows what she got up to in America,' Mrs Rooney continued, unabashed, her eyes on Seamie.

Madge heard this, jerked her head in their direction and, eyes blazing, shouted, 'I'll thank you to shut your trap, Mrs Rooney, if you want to stay drinking in my bar.'

'Can a decent poor widow woman not enjoy a drink in

peace?' Mrs Rooney moaned, and called for another round for the recently widowed Mrs Browne and herself.

'If you insist.' Mrs Browne tipped back her glass and mouthed to Madge that she'd keep an eye on Mrs Rooney.

'Did you know Pauline Quirk's mother?' Mrs Rooney continued, as a space was cleared in the centre of the pub for the dancers. 'A lovely God-fearing woman. I was terrible sorry when she died. If a child ever needed a mother that one did. Wild she was.'

'You're tellin' me.' Mrs Browne swigged her fresh pint with new energy and narrowed her eyes at the girls, who were laughing in gay abandon. 'I knew Tom well. He was lost without his poor wife. And a right useless eejit he was too, if my memory serves me cor-rectly.'

'Give us a song, Pauline,' someone called.

'My throat's out of condition.' Pauline laughed, embarrassed.

'Here, take a drop of this,' Geoff proffered his whiskey, caressing her arm coaxingly. 'That'll oil it.'

Pauline sat on a stool, the soft bare flesh of her thigh smooth against Geoff's trousers. After the call for silence she paused, then threw back her head and began 'Machushla'. Her singing brought sighs from the women and a deep intake of breath from the men, as they lifted their beer to their pursed lips.

Eve, observing her friend closely, felt her heart constrict with fear for Pauline. All those years ago Pauline had gone away to escape the hurt inflicted by Martin Dolan and Seamus Gilfoyle, and to find peace. She would have to be cautious with this new man in her life. And who was that strange man standing by the door, his eyes fixed on Pauline?

Pauline finished her song, the sweetness of her voice echoing through the pub. A long silence was followed by an eruption of applause. Cries of 'More! More!' snapped her back to the moment. Eyes wide, gazing at the crowd, she suddenly felt shy. She straightened her dress, and went behind the bar to help Madge.

It was a Tuesday in August when Pauline came up from the bar to find Madge sitting down, the table set for tea.

'I'll give you a hand,' she said.

'No need to trouble yourself, I can manage,' Madge assured her, putting rashers in the frying pan, enjoying her limited sovereignty over her own home. But she moved too quickly and had to sit down again to catch her breath. 'Think I'll put my feet up and watch telly. You'll know where to find me if you need me.'

Two days later she was taken ill with a pain in her chest. She had to clutch the kitchen table to prevent herself from falling. Pauline asked Seamie to sit with her while she phoned Dr Gregory.

When he arrived Madge told him that her legs were tired and that any exertion quickened her heartbeat. 'You're going to have to take things a bit easier,' Dr Gregory said, soothingly, as he packed away his stethoscope. 'Nothing serious. Plenty of rest.'

'I seem to rest a lot, Doctor,' Madge said, in a frail voice.

'You've worked yourself to the bone for years and you're not as young as you used to be.' He wrote out a prescription. 'What about taking a little holiday?'

'I might go and stay with my cousin Sadie in Wexford,' she said. 'As soon as we've found an apprentice barman.'

'Tommy Reilly's home from England. He worked in a bar in London.'

'I'll get Pauline to give him a ring.'

Dr Gregory said goodbye, then asked Pauline to show him out. 'Her heart is tired,' he said, when they were alone. 'Her condition is quite serious. I told her to take a holiday.'

'Is she going to die, Doctor?' Pauline asked, shakily.

'With a bit of care, she could last for years. Keep her quiet. Treat her like a visitor.'

Madge told Father McCarthy that she often contemplated death while saying her rosary at night and was not afraid of it. She'd done her duty and God had been good to her. Death, she explained, was something she thought of as a relief from the burden of her daily life – and wouldn't her parents be waiting for her at heaven's gates anyway? Father McCarthy laughed, and told her she was a long way from heaven's gates and that there was plenty of work still left for her to do on this earth before she could take herself off.

Pauline enlisted Mrs Browne to do the shopping and make a midday meal. Mrs Browne carried trays in to Madge if Madge didn't feel like getting up for her lunch. She sat by the bedside and gave her a litany of undiluted details about this fella and that woman who came into the pub. Her new responsibility gave her face a perky expression and brightened her eyes. Elevating herself to the status of housekeeper she dressed up in her best frock and pinned her good brooch at her skinny throat. In the bar she listened earnestly to the customers, her hat bobbing, her earrings swinging in anticipation of what she was about to hear. Everything was relayed back to Madge.

Freed from her duties Madge became more lively and laughed at the idea of Mrs Browne taking care of her, declaring that, for once, Dr Gregory had got his diagnosis wrong. 'There's nothing wrong with me. He's fussing too much,' she said.

For the first time in her life she lay in bed in the mornings and watched the sun filter through the curtains. She timed her day by the postman, cars driving to work, people hurrying to the ten o'clock Mass, children returning from school. For her there was no pub to run, no customers to distract her from her thoughts. Dr Gregory called to see her again and assured her that, with plenty of rest, she would get well enough to lead a quiet, inactive life. But Madge felt that if she couldn't work, or worry, or hope, or plan any more, she had no right to be a burden on those who could. She rested for a week then began preparing for her holiday.

Pauline found her helping Mrs Browne to hang out the washing. 'You should be taking it easy,' she said.

'It's doing me good to be up and about,' Madge replied, sitting on the garden seat, letting the sun warm her back. The day reminded her of similar mild days in Wexford when she was a young girl, helping her mother with the washing, hanging it out to dry with chapped, swollen hands, humming as she moved along the clothes-line.

Chapter Twelve

While Madge was away Pauline decided to decorate the flat and Seamie elected to help. Over the next few weeks, in paint-spattered overalls that Pauline had resurrected from the attic, they both worked night and day to have the place ready for Madge's return. With the steamer she'd hired Pauline removed the buff wallpaper from the hall, stairs and landing. It had been there for a hundred years, she reckoned, as she scraped vigorously, only to discover another layer of paper, with faded marigolds and bluebells, underneath.

'Probably the original,' she said to Seamie, pulling off a huge chunk of plaster with a strip of wallpaper. 'Damn,' she swore. 'It's more difficult than I thought.'

'It'll take ages for us to get anywhere,' Seamie lamented. Pauline continued scraping. 'What colour will we paint it?' he asked. 'I fancy something very bright, like orange, or red.'

'I'm not sure what Madge'll have to say to that,' Pauline said breathlessly. Her hair was damp, her face drained. 'I suppose anything's better than buff.'

When they were both too exhausted to continue Seamie took his shower and Pauline prepared supper, coating the steaks in mustard-seeds and peppercorns, the way Seamie liked them. She cut chips, set the table, made a salad, listening to Seamie singing in the shower. The thrum and shudder of the old pipes and his high-pitched rendition of Abba's 'Does Your Mother Know' gave her comfort.

He returned to the kitchen scrubbed and fresh-looking in a white Fred Perry T-shirt and blue jeans, and sat at the kitchen table. 'This is delicious, Mom,' he said, eating ravenously.

'Good.' Pauline was at her place by the window watching the rain pour down on the street below.

People were walking at a slower pace, their umbrellas flapping in the wind. The rain beat a steady tattoo on the corrugated roof opposite and hammered the pavement. Puddles formed on the road. Cars swooshed by. 'I'm glad we're not out in that,' Pauline said.

'I'm supposed to be going to the movies with Tom Rogers.'

'It's only a summer shower,' Pauline assured him. 'It'll soon be over.'

She cleared the table and washed up with the window open. The small kitchen was old-fashioned and dingy. She would have to get rid of the lino first, then clear all the junk out of the cupboards and replace the awful yellowing laminate with stripped pine or oak.

She caught her reflection in the mirror on the wall above her as she began to calculate the amount of money she'd need to do it. Her face, in the fluorescent light, looked calm, her eyes large and dark, and her hair curled in the damp. Seamie's homecoming had made her happy and had pushed all thought of Scully from her mind. Her sense of pleasure in ordinary, everyday things was returning. She felt good, glad to be alive.

Suddenly the rain stopped and a chink of blue sky appeared as the clouds dispersed. A gust of wind shook the drops off the trees and a shaft of sunlight struck the window-pane. 'Come on, Seamie,' Pauline called. 'I'll walk as far as Clem's with you.'

She watched her tall blond son sloshing through the

puddles, unconcerned about wetting his sneakers. As they walked along Goretti Terrace Pauline showed Seamie where she had once lived with his father, Seamus. Gone was the dilapidated terrace. The houses, recently painted in pastel shades of pink, green and blue, glistened in the sunshine. They had become fashionable now as private residences to professional people. Along by the railway Seamie insisted on seeing the small, clustered-together houses where Pauline's famous friend Clare Dolan had lived and where her mother, Agnes, was still to be found, when she wasn't in Clare's London or Paris home. They continued up the quiet, sloping street, past children skipping on the corner chanting, 'Policeman, policeman, don't take me, I have a wife and a fam-i-ly.' Pauline thought of Agnes Dolan, glad she wasn't there at the moment.

The familiar sight of the grocery shops in Main Street, some still as tacky as when she was a schoolgirl, always cheered Pauline. They stopped at various places in the town to introduce Seamie to whoever was around. Standing in one low-ceilinged shop after another, Pauline was conscious of their lack of distinction and antiquated wooden shelves. To her surprise the grubbiness she remembered from childhood excited Seamie and he poked around for hidden treasure.

The post office was a narrow section of Clem Rogers's corner shop where Tom, Seamie's first friend in Glencove, lived. It had wooden floors and pigeon-holes stuffed with papers, string, rubber bands and forms. When Seamie rang the bell it jangled through the shop and brought Mrs Rogers to her grille, her eyes squinting in the light. 'Hello,' she said. 'You're getting more like your father every time I see you, young Seamie.' Seamie smiled delightedly. 'Tom's gone to the wholesalers with his dad. They won't be long. You don't mind waiting, do you?'

He shook his head.

'I'll leave you to it, then,' Pauline said. 'Make your own way home after the pictures.'

'Sure.' Seamie was happy to rummage around in the shop.

Outside Rogers's, Pauline saw Scully in the distance, coming towards her. Confused and scared she walked away quickly, even though she wanted to go back into the post office and drag Seamie out and home to safety.

Once back at the pub the thought that something was terribly wrong came into her mind and wouldn't leave until Seamie returned home. Even Geoff's phone call, inviting her to dinner the following evening, didn't allay her fears.

Pauline saw him the moment he walked through the door. It had been a month since she'd seen him and as he came towards her Pauline tensed.

'Hello,' he said.

'Hello, Geoff.' She hesitated. 'Geoff, this is Seamie, my son.'

'Howdy.' Geoff shook hands with the boy. 'I hear you're taking over the bar tonight.'

'I wish I was,' Seamie said. 'I want to learn how to pull pints.'

'Soon enough,' Geoff said. 'You'll be learning how to drink them, too.' To Pauline he said, 'I've booked a table at Tyler's, a little restaurant in Wicklow. They have the freshest fish I've ever tasted.'

They took the coast road to Arklow, Pauline concentrating on the spectacular views of the sea. 'I haven't had time to get down to the hotel. How's the extension coming on?' she asked.

'It's frustrating. Delays and hold-up with the ordering.' He sounded nervous too.

'You work too hard,' she said, her anxiety easing.

Tyler's was an unpretentious farmhouse by the sea, the restaurant simply furnished with stripped-pine tables. Theirs was in a quiet corner overlooking the harbour and the sea. Geoff ordered gin and tonic and, while they sipped their drinks, she told him about Seamie's return and about her shares in the hotel, the plans Eve and she had for it. Before she realised it, the waiter was beside them pouring wine and serving the meal.

Afterwards he said, 'Come to my place for that drink you refused the other night.' His eyes devoured her.

Pauline sat silently looking at him, trying to make up her mind. Lifting her glass to her lips she ached to reach out to him, but she was afraid, tormented by thoughts of her past, her last encounter with love. While her sensible side urged her to resist him, the adventurous side, the one that had got her into trouble in the past, encouraged her to follow her heart. She had never been so confused in her life.

'Well?' he asked.

Here was this gorgeous man giving her his undivided attention and she was dithering. 'Just one drink,' she said. 'I don't want to leave Seamie on his own for too long. He's only getting used to the place now.'

They drove to a house in Bray that Geoff shared with a friend. He led her along the green-carpeted corridor, past a carved ornamental table, up the stairs. Pauline looked around the room as soon as he snapped on the light. 'Nice,' she said, noting the airiness, the double bed. Clothes were strewn on a chair, a suitcase flung open in a corner.

'As you can see, I haven't been spending much time here,' he said, taking a bottle of whiskey from the wardrobe and pouring it into two tumblers. He handed one to Pauline.

Standing by the window she gazed out at the moon surrounded by myriad stars. 'You'll have to teach me to dance properly,' he said, leaned towards a shelf above the bed and picked out a tape from a neat stack. He slotted it into a cassette player and the sound of Leif Garrett singing 'I Was Made For Dancin'' flooded the room.

Pauline put her hand to her lips, giggling. 'You'll disturb the neighbours.'

He turned down the volume. 'They're probably revving it up themselves,' he said. Then he held out his arms. 'Let's dance.'

They moved together for a few moments until Pauline pulled away to dance on her own, absorbed in the music. Then she remembered that she was supposed to be teaching Geoff the steps. 'Follow me,' she said, 'and don't look down.'

He followed her. When he drew close he reached for her, took her in his arms, holding her still. She tensed again. 'You're safe with me. Let yourself go,' he said.

She saw the longing in his eyes as he said softly, 'Pauline. Is there someone else?'

'No,' she said. 'I prefer to live without love.'

She looked into the strong, expressive planes of his face, studying him: the narrowed maturity of jaw, the sleek head, the gleaming eyes. In that gleam she saw what he intended, had known it all along, if she were honest with herself. Yet when he held her and whispered, 'My darling,' she was surprised at the gentle endearment and the strength of his arms.

He kissed her, his lips soft on hers, his fingers unzipping her dress, unbuttoning his trousers. They were on the bed, half naked.

'Pauline, you're so beautiful. You need love. I want to make love to you.'

His face was shadowed in the angle of the bedside lamp but Pauline could still see the blatant desire in his eyes. She jerked back her head. 'We don't know anything about one another,' she said.

Taken aback, he said, 'I'll tell you all about myself,' pulled her close and kissed her with such intensity that she forgot her fear, shut her eyes and hid her face in his neck.

Slowly he removed the rest of her clothes, holding her as if she were a rare and fragile object. 'I care for you, Pauline.'

His fingers moved over her body, and she shuddered with a pleasure she had not felt for a long time. She reached out to him, kissed him with a passion to match his own, his heat radiating through her. He rose above her on his hands and moved between her legs, looking at her all the time, his forehead damp with sweat. As soon as he entered her, he came. She pulled him close, felt his embarrassment. It allayed the charge of fear she had felt earlier.

For a while they slept in each other's arms until Pauline woke with a start. He stirred beside her and began to stroke the soft skin of her neck, then kissed the top of her head. 'You're beautiful,' he said, and reached out for her, his hands cool on her hot skin as they traced the outline of her breasts. Her senses reeled. If she had ever been touched this way before she couldn't remember it.

'I want to know everything about you,' he said, 'your every thought. Your dreams.'

'I'm Pauline Quirk from Ballingarret, a town not too far from here.'

'Did you love the father of your child?'

'Yes.'

'What went wrong?'

'He died,' Pauline said flatly.

'I'm sorry,' he said, watching her taut features in the lamplight.

'It was a long time ago,' Pauline said.

'You seem to have got over it.'

'It wasn't straightforward. I'm still vulnerable.' She stopped. He waited for her to continue, but she lay still, silent in his arms, until they drifted into sleep.

When Pauline woke again, she lay listening to the rhythm of Geoff's breathing. When she was satisfied that he was sound asleep she crept out of bed and gathered up her clothes. She dressed quickly and silently, hoping that the soft click of the bedroom door as she closed it behind her wouldn't wake him.

The faint white light of dawn was seeping through the sky as she swung out of the car-park and drove along the quiet, narrow street. The town was in darkness except for the lights from the lamp-posts that trailed off towards the harbour and faded into the distance. The pub loomed ahead, its windows shuttered. Switching off the headlights she sat in the gloom for a long time.

Eventually she went in, barred and bolted the door behind her, took off her shoes and crept upstairs. She fell into bed and lay there for a long time, waiting for the trembling to stop. As dawn broke she fell asleep.

Chapter Thirteen

'I've been so busy,' Dorothy said to Eve as soon as she arrived at her house. 'Collecting for the sale of work is time-consuming, and there's choir practice for the festival. Still, I know I'm better off out of the house filling my time with useful things to do.'

She was sitting at her dining-room table, a cardigan over her shoulders, her hand at the throat of her blouse. Her hair was in disarray, the blonde seeming almost white in the light from the window. She looked tired, Eve thought, and old. 'There's so much to be done.' Dorothy sighed.

'I've got some bits and pieces for the sale,' Eve said.

'Thanks, darling. Myrtle Thompson has been wonderful too, but I can't expect too much of her – she's got her own charities.'

The room filled with sunshine as Dorothy stood up, her face brightening as she inspected the contents of the bags Eve had brought.

Eve was staring out of the window at the large pots of geraniums lined along one side of the patio. Cabbage butterflies flew among the roses and the sweet, throaty song of a thrush filtered through the open window. She thought that now wasn't the best time to ask her mother to run the hotel boutique when it opened.

Dorothy, still sifting through the bags, said, 'Look at those sweet little pyjamas and nightdresses,' arranging the pretty colours together.

'I remember Sarah and I used to wear pyjamas like those,' Eve said. In a flash she saw her sister, a waif of a thing, drifting in a shadowy place, swathed in a long white nightdress.

'It's luxury compared to what we had to wear in that awful boarding-school in England,' Dorothy said, cringing at the memory.

Dorothy had always made sure that Eve and Sarah had beautiful clothes. She bought them bright cotton dresses, with smocked fronts and white collars. Their party frocks in taffeta or velvet with ballooning skirts were the envy of the other girls dressed in hand-me-downs. Later, at tennis-club dances Eve was always impeccable in the latest fashion, everything co-ordinated, nothing missing or out of place. In the early days in London, she wore casual clothes of which her mother would have disapproved: jeans or corduroy slacks with blouses. When she married Chris, Dorothy sent her a trousseau of Irish linen coat-dresses, fine wool suits and cocktail dresses to ensure that she was suitably attired for her new marital status.

'These remind me of Mr Rosen's pawn shop,' Eve said, going through items Irene had given her. 'Clare and I used to spend hours raking through the rails. Mr Rosen never minded how long we stayed.'

'That musty place.' Dorothy crinkled her nose at the memory.

'An Aladdin's cave,' Eve said.

'They're opening a flower shop where poor old Mr Rosen used to be. By the way, are you looking forward to Jasper's party?' Dorothy was surprised at the bleak look on Eve's face.

'Jasper and I had words about the hotel,' Eve said. 'I'm keeping well out of his sight.'

'That's just his way. He's ferocious in business, but family is very important to him. He'll expect you to be there.'

'Maybe.' Eve was sorry she'd said anything. It had taken years to break Dorothy's stranglehold on her life and she didn't want to tell her too much.

Dorothy had come a long way since James Freeman's death. Helpless with grief for the father-in-law who'd cared for her after she'd been abandoned by her husband, she had let Eve look after her until she recovered sufficiently to return to her job at Lynam's boutique. Agnes Dolan returned to clean for Dorothy, and could be relied upon to arrive each morning at ten o'clock sharp, except for the times she spent on holiday with her daughter. Eve had missed her grandfather desperately too.

Eve got ready for the party, trying on dress after dress, finally picking out a loose cream cotton sundress with a low back. She wore it with her long filigree earrings and sandals. The thought of meeting Jasper's business friends and acquaintances at his party without David at her side didn't appeal to her. And all that drink! She dreaded it.

The quadrangle outside Rathmore House was full of cars. Jasper, shirtsleeves rolled up, greeted her, masking the strain between them with proprietorial bonhomie as they walked out to the terrace at the back where the huge wooden picnic table was laid. Irene came to greet them, her face wrinkling in a smile. 'It's so good to see you, darling,' she said effusively. She talked on while she moved around with large platters covered in tin-foil, her steady stream of anecdotes punctuated by the odd comment from Jasper. Eve helped unwrap stuffed tomatoes, savoury eggs, salads of all kinds. Crisps and nuts were dumped into huge bowls and Jasper began to cook the hamburgers.

When the children returned from the beach Katie, a badminton racquet under her arm, engulfed Eve in a hug, wrapping her skinny arms around her, insisting on being carried around like a baby. The other children joined in, playing peek-a-boo with Katie every time she raised her head from her mother's neck, until Eve put her down. Plates were passed around the table and the conversation rose. Above the swirl of voices, Jasper's eyes, cool and measuring, were on Eve as she supervised the children's food. She wondered what he was thinking, what scheme he was hatching, knowing that behind his polite veneer he was up to something.

Irene was talking about the children's eating habits, then the junior-school system. Eve listened to the stream of babble, and heard Katie's yelp as tomato ketchup dripped down her white top. 'Blood,' she shouted, leaping down from her seat. Eve ran to clear it up as the terrace filled with people. Jasper put chicken breasts and lamb chops on the barbecue. Henry Joyce came towards Eve when she returned from the kitchen and put his arm around her shoulders. 'How are you?' he asked, his eyes on her glass of mineral water.

Before she could answer, Irene called, 'Come and eat. Everything's ready,' and led the way to the long trestle table under the floodlighting.

Henry Joyce, a local farmer's son, had been Clare's first boyfriend and a member of their group. Eve was thinking that Henry's marriage was still a delicate subject in Glencove. Strange, after all these years, that it had produced no children. Henry had married Lucy Grey, an American girl who had been visiting the Furlongs with her family. They had met at a local dance and he had taken to her instantly. The only daughter of Lew Grey, president of one of the oldest banking houses in America, she was twenty-five, but for all her money and social position Lucy was shy. It was evident in her high-pitched nasal voice as she greeted Eve, then turned to Irene.

'You look lovely Eve,' Henry said, across the table, his face deeply shadowed in the growing dusk, his eyes admiring her dress, travelling the length of her long golden arms, resting on her cleavage.

'Thank you,' she said, and gazed into the distance as if something had caught her attention.

'You've changed,' he said. He paused briefly then added, 'How's Clare?'

'Last I heard she was in the States preparing for a concert in the White House.'

'Good for her. She's got what she wanted.' He was thoughtful for a moment. 'Everything happened too fast with Clare and me. We didn't have time to get it together properly.' His voice was low and his eyes, in the candlelight, were as tawny as a cat's.

As it grew dark the children began to move into the house. Jasper was in the orchard engrossed in conversation with two other men. Eve shivered. Henry reached towards her, rested his hand on her shoulder. 'OK?' he asked.

'I'm fine,' she said, rising. 'It's getting cold.'

He rose with her, smiling that eager smile of his that she'd forgotten – it lit up his face. They walked towards the house.

'Clare and I went terribly wrong,' Henry said sadly.

'It was too intense,' Eve said, 'and we were all so young. None of us had a clue about all that romantic stuff. We were just experimenting.'

'I thought I was in love with her,' he said.

'I remember,' Eve said. 'You were always waiting around for her. Everywhere we went you were there.' They were reminiscing, teasing each other, laughing together, but Henry became serious. 'I never wanted her as much as I want you,' he said.

Eve gaped at him. Instantly conscious of his hand on her arm, she stepped back. Henry Joyce was her friend, and she must forget this extraordinary feeling he had suddenly aroused in her. She was married to David, and had no right to be interested in another man.

'What's the matter?' he asked, frowning. 'Have I offended you?'

'No. Not at all.' Eve smiled at him, endeavouring to see him as she always had, as a childhood friend. But Henry was acting differently towards her. His appearance was the same but there was a new perspective in his gaze. 'It's getting cold,' she said, abruptly. 'I'd better go and make sure Katie's asleep.'

'I'll see you again,' Henry said, his hand lingering on her arm.

'Yes,' she said. David's image loomed up before her as she ran upstairs. She must phone him, talk to him, if only briefly.

At Mass, Katie sat between Eve and Irene twisting in her seat this way and that to glance up at late arrivals who breezed up the aisle as Father Danaher, the parish priest, read the gospel. Irene, resplendent in a peacock blue coat and matching wide-brimmed hat, noticed that Katie was fidgeting, put her arm around her and whispered, 'Be still, my treasure. Say a prayer for your daddy so far away.'

Katie's eyes widened. 'Will that bring him back?' she asked, loudly.

'Yes,' Irene whispered.

Katie tucked her doll into the crook of her arm, knelt down, covered her eyes with her joined hands and bowed her head. The church grew hot and stuffy as the choir sang the last notes of the Ave Maria. People moved in reverent procession towards the altar to receive communion, and Katie eyed the pictures in the stained-glass windows, the stern faces of the statues of Joseph and Patrick. Money rattled into the collection boxes as they were passed around before the final blessing.

The congregation spilled out. Jasper took Katie's hand. Eve and Irene walked ahead, stopping to greet neighbours. Jasper, seeing Irene engrossed with a woman, caught Eve's attention. 'So, you're going to build the extension?' he said.

'Yes,' Eve said.

'You're determined, aren't you?' he sneered.

'Yes.'

The silence between them intensified.

'It's badly needed,' Eve said lightly.

Jasper's voice was edgy. 'You sure you know what you want? I remember a time when all you wanted was a drink.'

'I don't drink,' said Eve icily. 'The hotel is what I want.' These days she was in the habit of knowing what she wanted and going after it with dogged determination. She could remember a time, after her marriage to Chris Wintrop had fallen apart, when she was incapable of getting anything for herself. She had walked away from him empty-handed, her identity lost.

David had given it back to her – with the stamina to follow her instincts. He had rescued her from disintegration, and Jasper, grinning at her now through his even, crowned teeth, wasn't going to undermine her and get away with it.

Chapter Fourteen

The late-August afternoon was hot and Pauline was walking along the scorched brown towpath. Dogs lay panting under the shade of the trees, old men snoozed on benches. Outside the supermarket babies sprawled in prams, half naked under tilted sunshades, waiting while their mothers shopped in the stifling heat. Inside, piped music serenaded shoppers as they rummaged among the gaudy shelves that displayed everything from shampoo to garden gnomes. Pauline, dazzled by the fierce glare of the artificial lights, grabbed a chunk of steak from the long fridge in the meat section, a packet of rashers, sausages, cheese and eggs, weaving her way in and out of the aisles, hurrying to get back to her afternoon's sunbathing.

Out of the corner of her eye she spotted Geoff striding towards her. 'Hello,' he called, following her past shelves of biscuits, canned foods, fizzy drinks, his footsteps harsh on the tiles. He caught her by the elbow. She stopped. They faced one another. He was looking at her in such an intimate way that she blushed and turned towards the shampoos. 'You sneaked off on me,' he said.

'I had to get back before Seamie woke up.'

'That's not the only reason.'

'All right, I know.'

'What was it, then?'

'I didn't want us to wake up together.' Pauline blushed and looked away.

'Why?'

'Because I didn't want to have to leave your house in the full glare of daylight. Think of what the Glencove gossips would make of it.'

'I wanted to make love to you again.'

'Shh.' Pauline felt herself blush. She looked around to see if anyone was looking.

'You didn't want that, did you?'

'No.' She looked at him defiantly. 'And I didn't want you to see me first thing in the morning either. I guarantee you I'm not a pretty sight.'

'I could have lived with it.'

Pauline blazed, 'I don't want all that business of waking up beside someone, looking ugly, making small-talk over breakfast like an old married couple. I went through all that once before. Shared my life with someone and when he disappeared I was left to pick up the pieces on my own, put myself back together again. One person, suddenly alone, not a couple any more. That takes some getting used to.' She was shaking. Slowly she began to walk on.

'Hey, wait a minute.' Geoff was beside her. 'Aren't you jumping ahead here?'

'No. I don't want that kind of closeness again.' Realising that she had raised her voice, she looked around to see if anyone was watching.

Geoff leaned towards her. 'You didn't seem to object to us getting close the other night.'

'That meant nothing,' Pauline said. 'Anyone can do that.'

'Can they?' Geoff raised his eyebrows.

'You know what I mean.'

'I don't actually. Perhaps you'd like to explain.'

'That was just sex,' she said quietly, regretting the words as she said them, knowing how hurtful they were.

'I see. Thanks for letting me know.'

She was blushing again, thinking of how he had held her so tenderly, whispering endearments, raising himself above her while looking at her with such longing that she wanted to cry out to him to take hold of her for ever, never to let her go. She had risen to meet him with a passionate excitement that matched his own. With him she had opened up again, become aware of herself physically for the first time in ten years. In making her feel that she was the only woman on earth who could bring forth from him such a cry of ecstasy he had released her from imprisonment. And now she was afraid.

When she looked at him again his eyes were on her. 'So you don't want to see me any more,' he said.

'I didn't say that.'

'What did you say?' He searched her face.

She felt light-headed as if all the air was escaping from her lungs, knowing that she was boxing herself into a corner. 'I don't know.' She looked like a lost child.

He took her hands in his. 'Listen, Pauline. Forget the past. It's gone and there's nothing we can do about it. As for the other night—' He looked around then back at her. 'I got too excited, couldn't wait. Give me another chance. I'll prove to be the best lover you ever had. Let's start again from the beginning.'

Pauline stood bolt upright, shocked at the way he had laid bare their previous intimacy. He tightened his hold on her hands and drew her closer. 'Pauline,' he said, 'I want to make love to you again, slowly, for a very long time. I'd like that opportunity. Am I going to get a second chance?'

Her heart somersaulted in her chest. He was looking at her, his lips set, his eyes wary. 'Yes,' she whispered.

'Halleluya,' he exclaimed.

'Shh.' Pauline laughed, blushing.

'If we take it slowly, step by step.'

'If you don't mind waiting while I finish the shopping.'

He laughed. 'Let's get it over with and get out of here.'

In the fruit section, luscious raspberries and strawberries were heaped next to rich red plums and enormous watermelons, split in two, their pink flesh oozing with the ripeness of summer. Geoff looked longingly at her. 'Tempting,' he said.

'Would you like to have dinner with me?' she asked.

'I'd love to.'

She was loading fruit into her trolley. 'Madge will be home tomorrow so now's as good a time as any. Seamie'll be at a football match in Gorey.'

'So what army are you catering for?' he said, his eyes on the loaded trolley.

'I'll need some prawns,' she said, and set off to the fish counter.

'I'll buy the wine.'

'Coals to Newcastle.' Pauline giggled.

'No. I have a special one in mind and I'll help with the cooking.'

'Great.'

She finished her shopping and paid the bill while he went next door to the off-licence.

They drove back to the pub with the window down, the warm wind in Pauline's face.

Outside he unloaded her bags.

'The flat's up the stairs,' she said, turning the key in the hall door.

He carried the shopping up to the kitchen. As she began to fill the fridge he looked around, walked into the sitting room, noting the furniture, the carpet, before he went to gaze out of the window.

They drank gin and tonic while they prepared the meal

and had the cool Chardonnay with their prawn salad, and steak tartare. By the time the meal was over Pauline was more relaxed than she had been for a very long time.

As she stood up to clear the table he was beside her, caressing her. 'Leave it, I'll do it later. Come on, lead me to your den of iniquity,' he said into her ear, moving her towards the bedroom.

Once again as they lay on her bed a terrible shyness overcame her. Her legs felt like a ton weight as she turned to him.

'You're all right, Pauline,' he said, sensing her fear. 'You're safe with me.' He ran his fingers through her hair.

She watched him pull off his shirt, then his trousers. He was tanned all over except for his white buttocks. Lying beside her, he stroked her hair, then slowly, gently, removed her clothes as he told her how lovely she was, how desirable. He kissed her deeply, his tongue soft and warm inside her mouth, making her feel light-headed and dizzy. Gently he moved his hand down to her stomach, circling it slowly, then caressing her thighs. At last he opened her legs, stroked the insides of her thighs until she thought she would go mad with desire. 'Geoff ...' she whispered. 'It's hard for me to let myself go. To ...'

'Make love. Go on say it.'

'To make love,' she said.

He was holding her, his strength creeping into her as his warm breath fanned her face. He planted tiny kisses on her breasts, his tongue flicking against her erect nipples, teasing her, tracing a path of discovery down along her midriff. Her whole body shuddered as the familiar far-off sensation became a gentle pulsation that rose and spread all over her. He lifted himself between her legs, eyes shimmering, skin glowing. Kneeling over her he placed his hands under her buttocks. She arched her back to meet him, grasping him with her strong legs. He entered her, then stopped abruptly. 'Wait,' he said. 'Don't move.'

Closing her eyes, perfectly still, she waited until he began to move within her. A well of pleasure rose up in her, but as she moved with him, cried out his name, it floated away and evaporated.

She began to weep. Geoff held her, whispered words of tenderness, but nothing he said or did could console her. She wanted that elusive feeling again but she knew she would have to return to that place to seek it out. That was the most frightening thing of all. She didn't want to become a slave to a mindless, physical passion ever again.

Chapter Fifteen

Eve jumped out of bed and ran to the window of her bedroom, throwing it wide open. The air was moist and the sun was coming up in a cloudless sky. She leaned out to listen to the birds, letting the light wind blow warm in her face. Sighing with pleasure, she surveyed the dog roses massed along the parapet, their pink petals rambling into the tumble of starry white clematis. The garden was a riot of untamed plants and shrubs: geraniums, pinks, apricot and purple lupins, blue phlox, all merged with tall ornamental grasses. One of these days Jimmy, the gardener loaned to her by Irene without Jasper's knowledge, would arrive to cut back, tie up, clip and trim everything into shape and it wouldn't hold the same fascination for her. She lingered at the window, breathing in the deep fragrance, listening to the rustle of foliage, knowing that she would be late if she didn't hurry.

A few minutes later she made her way to the bathroom with little dancing steps and twirled before the mirror. Sweeping back her hair she tied it in a knot on top of her head then gazed critically at the round swell of her breast and her small waist.

Things were working out fine after all, she thought, as she slipped into the bath. If everything went according to plan the extension would be ready soon and she could start planning the winter schedule around it. Rummaging through her wardrobe she picked out one of her favourite outfits, a pale green linen suit, for her meeting with Harry Wise.

'You look lovely, Mummy,' Katie said, eyeing Eve solemnly, as her mother came into her bedroom.

'Thank you,' Eve said, giving her a hug. 'Come on, get up, lazy-bones. We're off to Rathmore. Grandma phoned. She's taking you to the carnival today.'

'Yippee.' Katie was out of bed in one leap. 'Are you coming with us?' she asked, following Eve downstairs.

'No. But I'll be back in time for supper.'

'Good,' Katie said, and helped herself to a large bowl of Rice Krispies.

Over lunch at Jury's, Harry Wise said, 'I think we'll just about get by. The bookings are up and fairly consistent. Yes, we'll cope.'

'The extension is going to cost more than we first anticipated.' Eve looked anxiously at him.

'I don't foresee any major difficulties with that. You're going to need the space at the rate your business is expanding.'

'As long as we can pay the interest on the new loan.'

'I don't see why not. I've reviewed every aspect of the business. We've accomplished more in the last couple of months than we ever expected to. Everything's in order. The new advertising campaign is good so I don't see why not. We've got the best terms available.'

'What about the plans for the boutique?'

'I've been looking at them and I have an idea. What about getting one of the leading fashion houses to rent it from you? That way they'll carry the stock and pay you a good rent. It'll take the worry off your shoulders. Not to mention the expense. But I don't think we're off the hook with Jasper.'

'What do you mean?'

'Well,' Harry said, 'I don't want to alarm you unduly but I think he's up to something.'

'Spit it out.'

'I've been watching Jasper's activities and thought I'd better put you on the alert. It seems he's buying up every available building site along the coast. Word has it that he's the owner of the new apartments at the convent and he wants to build a leisure complex close by. Your hotel is the ideal location.'

'I see,' Eve said.

'He's watching you like a hawk. One false move and he'll pounce.'

Eve laughed. 'You've just given me an idea, Harry.'

'What's that?'

'Why don't we build our own leisure complex, bigger and better than anything Jasper could envisage for Glencove?' Her eyes were sparkling as she saw herself truly beyond Jasper's reach.

'Hold on a second.' Harry sounded alarmed. 'We've borrowed already to the hilt.'

'I don't mean now this minute. I mean next year, as part of our forward planning,' Eve said, not stopping to consider the consequences of beating Jasper at his own game.

It was afterwards, at her desk, that she began to worry. If she succeeded in outwitting Jasper, how would it affect her relationship with David? But keeping one step ahead of him was the only way she could survive.

A few minutes later Pauline walked in. 'You look tired,' she said to Eve, and plonked herself down on the chair opposite the desk.

'I'm trying to coincide special events with our week-end breaks for our advertisements. The horse show. That sort of thing. And we're behind schedule on the exten-sion.'

Pauline blushed. 'It never dawned on me to ask Geoff when he'd be finished.'

'You've seen him!'

'Yes, last night.'

'You're not giving away any secrets.'

'Nothing to tell.'

'I don't believe that,' Eve said, putting away her files. 'Let's have a quick cup of coffee before I set out for Rathmore. You can tell me all about it.'

Through the shimmering haze from the artificial light Pauline and Seamie watched scarlet-ribboned ponies circling the inside of the big tent, their chestnut hides gleaming, the sequinned tops of the half-naked girls on their backs glowing. She spotted him in the distance and froze. The last thing she wanted was for him to meet Seamie. She got up, told Seamie she'd be back in a few minutes, and went outside.

She walked quickly past the whirling chairoplanes, the bumper cars, and jumped into the ghost train. It entered the dark tunnel with a rush of hot air.

'Hello.' His voice, coming from behind her, echoed in the tunnel.

She sat rigid, not answering. Outside again her face drained of colour as he joined her. People milled around, bumping into one another in their hurry to see the Fat Lady or queue for the rifle range.

'You've been avoiding me,' Scully said.

She walked on.

He grabbed her arm. 'When are we going to meet?'

Pauline's heart flipped.

'Why pretend I don't exist?' he insisted.

Pauline shrugged him off. 'I have to go.'

'Not until you tell me where we can meet. We have to talk.'

She wished for an open space where she could move right back from him and breathe properly.

He was watching her like a hawk.

'I know what's on your mind,' he said. 'You're hoping the ground will open up and swallow me.'

Pauline walked off into the crowd. He followed her across the grass to where she got caught up in a circle of men and boys whistling, howling and slapping their thighs as they watched a fat pair of wrestlers fighting it out. He caught her and shook her. 'If you want to buy my silence you'll pay for it and pay good. And not with money either. Do you understand?' He said, through bared teeth.

Pauline put her hands to her ears. 'I've heard enough. I'm going.'

'You're not going anywhere,' he said. 'We've ten years to catch up on. You know that, don't you?' He lit a cigarette, inhaled deeply, let it burn between his fingers while he waited.

'Please let me go,' she said, looking over her shoulder as a roar went up from the crowd and the whine of the music in the tent indicated that the show was coming to an end.

He released her suddenly. She tottered backwards, almost falling. 'I'll meet you tomorrow night in Murphy's. Wait for me I might be a bit late.'

He strode off, leaving Pauline paralysed with fear.

Slowly she walked towards the clear outline of the tent, its undulating walls billowing in the evening breeze as the audience stumbled out into the twilight.

Murphy's Lounge was dull and uninviting, its heavily shaded lamps casting a dim glow on the shabby tables and chairs. A well-dressed man stood at the bar, and a middle-aged couple sat together talking. She and Scully were huddled into a corner,

Pauline with her head bowed slightly, her eyes surreptitiously on the door.

'You see, Pauline,' Scully said, 'I always thought you murdered Martin Dolan.'

A searing pain gripped Pauline beneath her ribcage. 'I don't know what you mean,' she said.

'Oh, yes, you do.'

For the rest of her life she would remember that evening, and the inconsequential details of that moment of crisis: the plain woman dressed up in party clothes, her black patent shoes, and the little man perched beside her, looking around curiously.

Scully sat back and crossed his legs. 'Relax,' he sneered. 'I didn't want to drag all this up but you left me no choice.' He lowered his voice. 'The only reason you got away with it is because nobody, apart from me, knew where you were. When Martin hid you he made a good job of it.' He was shaking his head, laughing. 'Little did he know, poor sod, that his bright idea of having you with him would lead to his end.'

Pauline swallowed some of her drink.

'A lot of people in the organisation were very upset at the time. Martin was a high-ranking officer in the command.'

'What do you want from me?'

Scully ignored her. 'I know how you managed it. You waited for him, lured him into bed and then packed your bags and left.' His reptilian eyes had glazed over, full of loathing.

'I said, what do you want?'

'The pleasure of watching you pay the price. You thought you'd had the last laugh but you were wrong. When I lost Martin I didn't only lose a good friend, I lost a business partner. We had great deals going in Belfast. But with Martin not there to keep an eye on things whenever I was away, everything went bang. I was destitute when I got out of jail.

Now I want compensation and you're just the little lady that'll get it for me.'

Pauline sat like a dummy, heart pounding, eyes staring straight ahead at a small group of people gathered at the bar.

'I've very fond memories of our time together in Belfast, Pauline. You see, I, too, had plans. Dreams for when Martin would eventually take off and there would be just the two of us.' He threw back his drink. 'Pity it all went wrong.'

'You're talking rubbish,' Pauline said, her temper flaring.

'Oh, no, I'm not, and you know it.' He reached out for her. 'You relied on me then and I didn't let you down. Looking back, I was asking for a lot. You and me together. Me strong, you dependent.'

The door opened and Pauline looked up in dread of seeing someone she knew. It was the barman. 'Telephone for you, sir,' he said to Scully.

Pauline glanced at Scully, who was standing up, nodding, the veneer of politeness back on his face.

'I'd better be going,' she said, getting to her feet too.

'Don't go far,' Scully said. 'A girl like you could be very useful to a fellow like me. You know about things.' He spoke pleasantly into her ear. She shuddered. 'Pack your bags. You're going on a little trip with me. I'll give you the details later.'

Early the following morning Pauline woke Seamie. 'Get up and get dressed quickly,' she said. 'We're going to Aunt Bea's.'

'Wow!' Seamie said, leaping out of bed. 'Did she phone?'

'I phoned her. She's expecting us.'

Driving through Arklow the clouds dispersed and the sun broke through and rose high in the heavens. Pauline drove quickly, relieved to be getting Seamie away from Glencove. Scully was a dangerous man, of that there was no doubt. Where he intended taking her she had no idea. Of one thing she was certain. She daren't refuse to go. But whatever about herself, she would not risk Seamie's safety. It would be awful to be without him again but perhaps the sacrifice was necessary.

Aunt Bea was alone in the kitchen, rolling out pastry for apple tarts. 'Where's Seamie?' she asked, looking past Pauline.

'Hello, Aunt Bea,' Seamie said, standing patiently while her scrawny arms grasped him in a tight embrace.

'Seamie,' she said. 'After all these years. Look at the size of you. How are you?'

'Very well, thanks.' Seamie stood still while she inspected him.

'You're a fine lad,' she said admiringly. 'A true Connelly with those eyes and that lovely mop of hair. And the height of you! Come on inside. Nothing's changed since you left, though you'll hardly remember the place.'

Bruce came to meet Seamie, his tail wagging delightedly.

'Dinny'll be here any minute to take you down to the cattle in the meadow, Seamie.' Aunt Bea went on. 'It's good for you to get acquainted with the land and he'll be glad of the help. He's not as strong as he used to be. None of us are.'

After Seamie had gone, she said, 'It's great to see the boy so interested in everything. Your father hadn't the love for this place that your mother had, even though he was born on a farm. They'd come over to help with the threshing but whenever he could escape your da would be off, hidden somewhere reading a book, or cycling around the countryside, visiting old ruins. Didn't matter how busy we were. Believe me, there wasn't much affection between him and me.'

'He was a good father to me,' Pauline said.

'He did his best, I'll grant you. But things would have been different if your mother had lived. You'd never have left school at fifteen for one thing.'

'If my mother had lived everything would have been different,' Pauline said, drying her hands. 'For one thing I'd have had a much happier childhood.'

'Granted,' Aunt Bea said. 'Only God had other ideas. Your poor mother didn't want to die. She put up a great fight.'

Pauline was desperate to bring the conversation to an end. 'I'll go and see how Seamie's getting on,' she said.

The grass was damp as she crossed the fields and went down the straight, narrow lane to the meadow. Twigs snapped under her feet, and the long grass brushed against her legs. She sat on the gate and listened to birds calling as they flitted about in the overhanging branches of ash and rowan trees. Bees buzzed and flies hummed around the wild dog-roses. Across the meadow, cows moved towards the shed. Dinny, a milk bucket in each hand appeared, calling, 'Here, suckie, suckie,' to the calves.

Seamie, clad in waders, followed him, calling, 'Come on, tea-time. Here, suckie, suckie.'

The sight of him reminded Pauline of the early-morning milking with her father: sitting under Betsy, the Friesian, she had coaxed her with soothing words as the milk sloshed into the galvanised bucket, while further down young calves noisily suckled their mothers, necks outstretched, tails swishing in contentment.

Lulled by the rustle of the wind, Pauline wished she could stay in that spot for ever, watching her son safe and happy, surrounded by the familiar fields of home. As a little girl she had spent her summers climbing trees, running wild through the fields, safe in the knowledge that her mother was in the kitchen with Aunt Bea and that her father was not far away. She knew the names of every bush and tree, every flower and bird. Before her mother died she hadn't known the meaning of the word fear: nothing had intruded on her childhood to threaten her peace. The countryside had given her the strength that had enabled her to explore further afield as she got older.

Dinny came to meet her, doffing his cap, praising God for the glorious day. 'This young lad here is very useful,' he said, his eyes on Seamie. 'He's the makings of a good farmer, no doubt about it. I think we'll keep him.'

'I'm staying for a while, aren't I, Mom?' Seamie said.

'As long as you like.' Pauline smiled.

'Oh, a sensible young lad, this fellow,' Dinny said. 'He won't raise the roof and scald the heart out of you. You're blessed.'

That evening Aunt Bea insisted on them all going into the village for the harvest festival dance at the crossroads. Pauline danced set dances with toothless farmers, their beer bellies jiggling with each hard step of their hob-nailed boots, their Sunday suits reeking of hay. Seamie pranced around, imitating her, encouraged by Aunt Bea's clapping.

Later, in the local pub, women talked among themselves and men, encouraged by their companions, told stories, their pipes laid to one side, their eyes bright. Through a haze of smoke Pauline saw Scully at the door. Horrified, she got up and went across to him.

'What are you doing here?' she muttered, moving to one side to let someone pass.

'Never mind that. It took me ages to find the place, only to discover that no one was in. Then I remembered seeing the notice for the festival.'

With him came the events of the last few days, to haunt her and refresh her fear. His strange accent and city clothes made him stand out among the shrewd farmers, whose only interests were land and weather.

'Who's your friend?' Aunt Bea asked.

'This is Scully,' Pauline said.

'You'll come back and have a bite of supper with us,' Aunt Bea said, insinuating herself between them.

Scully shot a glance at Pauline. She looked away. 'I've eaten, thank you,' he said.

'A plate of pig's crubeens, just off the boil, go down very nice after the Guinness.'

The conversation broke while drinks were bought and distributed, then resumed and rippled through the bar as the men took up their fresh pints. Pauline felt afraid Scully would say something to alert her astute aunt. He didn't.

Back at the farmhouse, Aunt Bea put a skillet of potatoes and a pot of cabbage on the range to cook while she set the table. Dinny poured four bottles of Guinness into four pint glasses, and pushed the sleeping Bruce out from under the table so they could stretch their legs when they sat down.

'Tell me about yourself,' Aunt Bea said to Scully. She had put out the good knives and forks and the linen napkins reserved for visitors.

'What do you want to know?' Tension brought out the Northern tones that had been erased with travel and time from Scully's accent.

'Where did you meet Pauline?' Aunt Bea asked relentlessly.

'In the States,' Scully lied smoothly.

Pauline, ill at ease, told Seamie, in response to his question, that no, he could not put on the telly, but Aunt Bea, who laid down the rules, nodded consent.

The sudden burst of sound into the room was the late-night bulletin: 'Lord Mountbatten's boat was blown up by the IRA and Lord Mountbatten, his fifteen-year-old grandson and a fifteen-year-old friend were killed, as well as a seventeen-year-old boatman and the Dowager Lady Brabourne,' the announcer said evenly. 'Also today a Provisional IRA landmine killed eighteen British soldiers at Carlingford Lough.'

The screen showed the tranquil lake in Classeybawn, Sligo, near Mullaghmore and a smiling Lord Mountbatten in his boat, then switched to the jetsam on the shore, surrounded by deep-sea divers, reporters and photographers. The wreckage of Land Rovers and rubble in Carlingford Lough made Scully sit up straight. He was gazing at the screen with feverish excitement.

'Murdering bastards,' Aunt Bea stated, putting down her knife and fork.

'Where will it all end?' Dinny shook his head in dismay. 'Lord Mountbatten was a decent man.'

'Don't underestimate the problems,' Scully said, suddenly tense.

'You come from a queer part of the country.' Aunt Bea eyed him.

'I do,' he said, sipping the glass of stout Dinny put before him.

'Too many Protestants,' she said.

'We can't judge from this backwater,' Dinny said, looking meaningfully at Aunt Bea.

'It's an alien way of life up there,' Aunt Bea said, shaking her head. 'Murderers wandering around scot-free. All sorts of queer things going on.'

Pauline choked into her beer.

'I'd better be going.' Scully stood up abruptly and pulled back his chair. 'Thank you for supper.' He shook hands with Aunt Bea and Dinny.

'Any friend of Pauline's is a friend of ours,' Aunt Bea said. 'Come over any time.'

'I'll see you out.' Pauline wiped her mouth on her napkin and followed him.

Outside heavy rainclouds massed above the yard, and Pauline felt cold through the thin material of her dress. Scully stood beside his car, his hands deep in his pockets, his shoulders broad and menacing. 'I'm going away for a few days,' he said. 'Business.'

'So?'

'You're coming with me. I need your help. There's a job to be done and you're the one to do it.'

'What do you mean?'

'You're familiar with the lie of the land – to a certain extent anyway – and Seamie'll be safe here until you get back.'

'I'm not going.' She folded her arms.

He shrugged. 'It's up to you but I'd advise you to think seriously about what you're saying. You do this one job with me and no harm will come to Seamie.' He lit a cigarette and blew smoke into the air.

'When?'

'Have a bag packed by tomorrow evening. I'll call for you at the pub.' He walked to his car, his shoulders swinging.

Chapter Sixteen

David was away from home longer than he had expected to be.

'I think he'd better get back before you forget what he looks like,' Irene said to Eve.

'Before he learns that I can live without him,' Eve agreed.

David had told Eve that he was staying with friends in Cape Cod but would be flying home at the end of the week, and they arranged to meet at their home in Glencove. He told her he would take a taxi from the airport.

Later that day, as she was walking along by the harbour, she met Henry Joyce. 'I wasn't expecting to bump into you,' she said.

Henry took her arm. 'I saw you pass by and thought what the heck? This is the best part of the day for a walk. Come on, let's get to the top of the cove before the sun sets.'

Fingers of light spread from the last rays of the dying sun, and the wind blew colder. Henry walked further up into the shelter of the cove, where they had swum as youngsters, Eve following him. The sea was a lonely stretch of grey now, merging with a violet sky, and she couldn't help feeling sad as she looked out over the dark hills to her left and listened to the long, deep sigh of the waves washing into the shore. 'You never know,' she mused, 'I might persuade David to stay at home this time.'

'He's been travelling all his life. It's second nature to him.'

They sat for a long time, watching the sunset, then slowly retraced their steps, comfortable with one another in their renewed friendship.

Eve spent the rest of the week reviewing her marriage: her relationship with David, the life they had together, whether she would go with him to New York or not. Their separation made her realise how unhappy she'd been since he left, how lonely and cut off she felt. There was little she could say to him now on the telephone without a row ensuing.

As the day of their reunion drew nearer she began to dread it. Would things have changed between them? But the house had been so big and lonely without him and Katie, who was still in Rathmore at Jasper and Irene's insistence. Eve recalled all the things about her husband that she loved and realised how much she wanted to see him.

The day he was due home she returned from work early, changed into her tracksuit and went out, crossing the street to the tow-bridge. The rain had swollen the river and left a rivulet of water running along the side of the grassy bank. The swans were sheltering under a willow tree. A young couple passed her, talking, laughing, untroubled by the damp. Everywhere was fresh and green from the rain.

She walked quickly as far as the harbour and was back at the house to shower and change before he arrived. Carefully she did her makeup and hair. Then she called the airport. His plane had landed. She went across to the window, and waited there, watching. The wind rose, shaking the last of the rain from the trees opposite. Cars drove by, the sibilance of their wheels on the wet road breaking the silence. At last, David's taxi rounded the corner and came to a halt outside. By the time he knocked, Eve was already opening the door.

He stood in the hall, his blond hair combed neatly back, his eyes dark and glinting.

'How was your trip?' Eve asked formally, wishing for the ease they used to have with one another.

He shrugged, a helpless gesture. 'Fine,' he said. 'I missed you.'

The way he looked as he said those words made her rush into his arms, wondering why she had been worried in the first place. He swept her off her feet and carried her upstairs. She'd forgotten his strength, the feel of his solid muscular body, the length of his legs as he put her down beside him.

'I'm so glad you're home.' Her voice stuck in her throat so she kissed him, and he pulled her closer, murmuring words of love between kisses, on her lips, her neck, her breasts as his fingers worked at the buttons of her blouse. She was clutching at his shirt, then undoing the belt of his trousers, helping him remove out of them, climbing on top of him, easing herself down.

'Take it easy, I'm here, darling,' he said softly. 'I'm not going anywhere.'

But she couldn't stop. He held her hips to slow her down, and as he pushed up into her gently, she grew calm, transported to a magical place.

Afterwards, they lay still for a long time. Finally David fell asleep, his arms wrapped around Eve, his breath fanning her face. When he woke up she confided, 'I was scared.' Her voice was full of love.

'There's no need,' he said, pulling her closer. 'I'm here now. Everything's all right.'

Chapter Seventeen

Scully was waiting in a strange car outside the pub, two other men with him. Clean-shaven, dressed in a business suit, he looked sleek, like a well-oiled millionaire. Pauline saw that one of the other men was smoking a cigarette, listening intently to Scully, who sat with his arms across his chest, talking. There was something official about his pose. Suddenly the car door opened and Scully stepped out. The other two followed and stood either side of him like sentinels. Scully knocked on the door.

'You going to introduce us?' a tall, skinny man said, as Pauline opened it.

'This is Pauline,' Scully said. 'She's a good friend.'

The stocky man to the left of Scully laughed softly. 'How good?'

'Take my word for it,' Scully said.

'Hello.' Pauline looked from one to the other.

'You ready?' Scully asked her.

'Yes.'

'Excuse us,' the tall man said. 'We've got to be going.'

Scully nodded as they walked towards a waiting car. He waved them off before following Pauline upstairs.

'What's going on?' she asked, when they were alone. 'Who were those men?'

'Business acquaintances. Nothing for you to concern yourself with. Here's your passport. We're taking the five o'clock flight to Paris.'

'Paris!' Pauline wished she could tell him to go to hell, that she had responsibilities, a child to take care of, a pub to run.

'We're travelling as husband and wife. For this trip I'll be known as Jack Cribbins, your husband.'

Her photograph was on the passport, 'Mary Cribbins' written underneath it.

Scully threw several canvas money bags across her bed. 'You're in charge of these. Hide them under your clothes. I'll be downstairs waiting. Look sharp.' He left the room, banging the door behind him.

She opened one of the bags. It was full of Irish ten- and twenty-pound notes. She strapped two around her waist, hid one in each of her boots, stuffed another into her bra. Finally she put on a big grey jumper and her denim jacket over it.

'Come on,' Scully shouted up the stairs. 'What's keeping you? We've a plane to catch.'

'Keep your hair on,' she said to herself, feeling like an overstuffed goose, ready for the Christmas table.

She followed him outside, almost colliding with Mrs Browne who was on her way in.

'What's the big hurry?' Mrs Browne asked, staggering back.

'I'm going away for a few days. Tommy Reilly's taking over. Keep an eye on things.'

'Where are you off to?'

'Oh! Just a bit of a break.'

'This is sudden,' Mrs Browne said, shooting a glance at Scully who was putting the bags into his car.

'Come on,' he called.

'You certainly know how to pick them,' Mrs Browne said, but Pauline was already getting into the car and did not hear her.

✳   ✳   ✳

That night they met Scully's contact in the Hôtel Victor in Paris. A tall man, he stood at the bar, staring fixedly ahead as if in a trance, his face pale, his eyes sharp.

Pauline was at a corner table watching Scully and the other man. Eventually they left together. She waited. Presently Scully reappeared and signalled to her from the entrance to the bar. After a few minutes she left, to find him waiting for her near the lifts.

'I've managed to get us a room.'

'Just one?'

'I was lucky to get it. We're husband and wife, remember?'

They took the lift to the top floor. Scully led her down a corridor to the last door, which he unlocked. It led into a large room with a big bed and a sofa. There was a television in the corner.

'What do we do now?' she asked.

'Relax,' Scully said. 'Get some sleep. We're off to Zürich tomorrow.'

'Zürich! But you said we'd only be away for a couple of days!'

'There's a slight hitch.'

'Are we being followed?'

'No. Nothing like that. We wouldn't be staying here if we were.'

Pauline dropped down on to the bed and unfastened the money-belts. 'I hope I haven't carried all this lot around for nothing,' she said, flinging them on the bed. 'God! I'm boiling.'

Scully went to the mini-bar and took out two little bottles of gin and a can of tonic water. He poured the drinks, handed her a glass. 'Order something from room service if you're hungry.'

'No, thanks.'

She sipped her drink, but Scully finished his quickly. 'I'm going downstairs to make some calls. You take the bed. I'll sleep on the sofa.'

In the bathroom she prepared for bed. For a while she sat in her dressing-gown by the window, watching pools of light from the street-lamps reflect on the wet surface of the road, thinking of Geoff, wondering if he'd phone. She should have let him know she was going away for a few days.

What was it about Geoff Ryan that drew such instant reaction from her? It was different, that's all she knew. With Seamus she had loved his looks, had taken pride in being publicly acknowledged as his woman. With Geoff it went deeper than that, and here was Scully keeping them apart. If it wasn't for her fear of her past being exposed, and Scully's obsession with danger and self-deceit, she could be with Geoff at this very moment.

Who was Scully, anyway? And what was he up to? She couldn't bring herself to think about the risks and danger he was exposing her to.

Finally, she crept into bed, where she lay on her side for a long time before she fell asleep . . .

'Wake up.' Scully was shaking her. 'We have to leave now.'

'What time is it?'

'Eleven.'

'I've only just fallen asleep.'

'Get dressed,' he said. 'We're getting out of here. You can sleep on the train. I'll meet you outside in ten minutes. And make sure those money-belts are well secured.'

Pauline had slept for less than an hour. Dressing quickly, she thought how glad she'd be to reach Zürich and get rid of them.

Scully was waiting outside in the dark and showed no sign of recognition as she approached. She walked slowly towards him, wishing the notes were in larger denominations and the money-bags less cumbersome.

'Get a move on,' he said, from the side of his mouth, almost pushing her towards a waiting cab, looking right and left before getting in and directing the driver to the Paris Est railway station.

The train raced through the dark countryside, stopping at Belfort, Mulhouse, then screeching through tunnels. In her cold bunk, Pauline's mind raced with the wheels and the swaying carriages over the dark flat fields, but eventually she slept.

Sudden stillness woke her to bright dawn light streaming through her carriage window. Outside voices were calling to one another. Bewildered she leaned over and lifted up the blind, shielding her eyes from the light.

The train was at a brightly painted station, and the sign on the platform read Basel. They had arrived at the Swiss border. She opened the window and leaned out. The chill of the mountain air surprised her. Security guards were standing outside her window checking the passports of the alighting passengers.

Scully put his head round the door. 'We change here,' he said. 'Come on.'

The sky was pale, the rising sun dissolving the mist as, wearily, Pauline joined Scully in the queue to disembark. The customs official, smudges of tiredness beneath his eyes, checked their passports and tickets, nodded at Scully, and gave Pauline a cursory glance. Scared, she kept her eyes fixed on the customs official's face, with a smile that took all her courage. Scully, behind her, maintained a nonchalant air.

After an hour's wait, the train to Zürich arrived. In the dining car, Scully ordered breakfast. As the train picked up speed through the magnificent Swiss landscape, Pauline smothered a croissant in strawberry jam and sipped lukewarm bitter coffee, her eyes on the mountain farms that sprawled for miles. Scully sat staring out the window, brooding. 'Did you sleep?' he asked suddenly.

'A little,' she said. 'Will there be another passport check when we get to Zürich?'

Scully shrugged. 'Don't worry about it. Get some more rest. We've a long day ahead of us.' He seemed unconcerned but every time the train stopped she could tell that he was on tenterhooks. She made no further attempt at conversation but lay back against the headrest, watching the dappled light play tricks on the landscape as the train rushed along.

She would never tell anyone about this, not even Eve. Gazing at the majestic Alps rising into the mist, their peaks lost in swirls of clouds, she shuddered at the real significance of what was happening. She wasn't a tourist like the other passengers on the train. She was playing an important part in a scheme that had nothing to do with her.

That evening, when they arrived in Zürich they had their tickets punched before they left the train. They took a taxi into the city, booked into an hotel and went up to their bedroom, where Pauline divested herself of the money-belts and fell on the bed, exhausted. Scully removed the notes from them and put them into his briefcase.

'Get some sleep,' he said. 'We're out of here first thing in the morning. We'll be rid of this lot as soon as the place opens.'

Pauline got into bed, too tired to care where Scully was going to sleep. When she woke up next morning he was standing over her. 'Come on,' he said, 'we've no time to waste. The money has to be handed over before noon.'

They left the hotel and walked through a labyrinth of narrow streets to the centre of the city, Pauline carrying the briefcase. Up a narrow flight of stairs, in a dingy office, a man was waiting for them.

'Hand over the briefcase,' Scully said, making no attempt to introduce them.

Pauline gave it to him, relieved to be rid of it, and went back downstairs to wait for Scully. A white police car sped past, lights flashing.

Scully came down a few minutes later, took her elbow and steered her across a busy street. 'Wait,' he said, stopping at a news-stand, the headline on the front of the *International Herald Tribune* catching his eye. 'Arms Shipment Found at Dublin Docks,' Pauline read.

Scully scanned the rest of the page. 'A routine search of the cargo ship *Maeve* revealed a haul of IRA weapons, including ten AK-47 assault rifles (or Kalashnikovs) and 200 rounds of ammunition, was intercepted at Dublin docks last night. The commissioner of the Gardai said it was a very significant find and was the result of close co-operation between the Gardai and Interpol.'

People were passing them as they stood transfixed. A car pulled up with a jerk, and disgorged several passengers. In the distance police sirens wailed.

'Come on,' Scully said, elbowing his way through the stream of people coming towards him. 'We've got to get out of here.'

Pauline stopped. 'That money I've been carrying was for guns, wasn't it?'

'Shut it,' Scully snarled. 'Look happy, in love, happier than you've ever been in your whole life.'

The idea made Pauline want to laugh.

Back in the hotel lounge, Scully ordered sandwiches and coffee. 'My boss is going to ring here, so we'll have to wait.'

Time ticked by. Scully paced up and down, checking his watch every few minutes.

'Who's your boss?' Pauline asked.

'Never mind.'

'This is getting too dangerous for me.'

'It'd be more dangerous if you tried to get away. They'd follow you over there. Anyway, you won't get rid of me that easily,' he said, standing up, going to the phone, lifting it. He got through to someone, spoke for a few minutes.

'Come on,' he said to her, replacing the receiver. 'We're off.'

They drove to a large hotel on the outskirts of the town. Scully jumped out, paid the driver, grabbed her hand, ran up the steps and pushed his way through the revolving doors.

Across the lobby a tall, rugged man casually dressed in a tracksuit and sneakers was reading a newspaper. Scully went to him swiftly, Pauline following.

'This is my boss,' Scully said, by way of introduction.

'We're transferring you,' the man said to Scully.

'What?'

'Here's the keys of the green Citroën parked outside. Go to Berne, wait there. I'll contact you later when the coast is clear.' He glanced at his watch.

'Who blew the whistle?' Scully asked.

'I don't know but I'll find out.'

The expression on Scully's face betrayed his anger. Pauline imagined that his vision of himself as a Chief of Staff was draining away.

As they were leaving a police car pulled up in front of the hotel.

'Hurry!' Scully said, walking quickly to the car, Pauline at his heels.

They drove through winding country roads to Berne. Despite her terror, Pauline was filled with wonder at the beauty of the landscape. Villages, their neat houses clustered around tiny churches, dotted the mountainside. The woods were deep green against the snowy peaks, the road ribboning up hills and down valleys.

Scully braked. 'Don't turn round. I think we're being followed.' He pulled over to the grass verge to let the other car pass him.

In their hotel room in Berne Pauline sat at the window looking over the city while Scully waited for orders, cursing the organisation for their lack of efficiency. When he tired of ranting he took a shower, then locked the door, lay on the bed and read the newspaper until he fell asleep, snoring gently, his muscular body turned towards the window.

A police siren sounded outside and Pauline was reminded of her Belfast ghetto, she the prisoner, gazing over the rooftops, police cars flying up and down the road.

When the sound of Scully's breathing deepened, she inched her way from the window and moved stealthily towards his clothes on the chair beside the bed. Fumbling in the pocket of his trousers she found the hotel-room key and gripped it so tightly it nearly bruised the palm of her hand. She tiptoed to the door, put the key in the lock and coaxed it slowly with one hand, holding the handle rigid with the other. The lock clicked and Pauline held her breath as Scully twisted sideways and burrowed down into the pillow. She was overtaken by the temptation to strangle him and barely stopped herself from lunging at him.

Light from the corridor streamed into the room as she carefully opened the door. Damn, she swore under her breath, sliding out into the corridor, pulling the door after her as quickly and soundlessly as she could. Outside, she took a deep breath and tiptoed down the stairs, her rapid breathing slicing the air. The ticking of the grandfather clock in the lobby made her jump, reminding her of a bomb or a booby trap.

'Who's there?' The night porter, rubbing the sleep from his eyes, scrabbled to his feet.

But Pauline was gone, out of the door and away up the road, losing herself in the darkness.

Chapter Eighteen

Post skittered across the floor when Pauline pushed open the heavy door of the pub. As she bent to pick up the letters, she noticed several large muddy footprints crisscrossing the hall to end at the stair carpet. She shut the door and stood looking around. Everywhere was quiet. Upstairs, everything seemed the same. A jar of pickles and an empty Coke can sat in the middle of the kitchen table. The ladder was in the corner of the half-decorated sitting room where she'd left it. In Seamie's room, the bed was unmade, his clothes tumbling out of the wardrobe just as he'd left it.

She looked out of the kitchen window. There was no traffic on the road, just a man standing motionless at the side wall, his arms hanging loosely by his sides, his hair dishevelled. Going from room to room, pulling the curtains, she read the letter from Madge telling her that she was having blood tests but that the rest was doing her good. Pauline made a cup of tea and went to bed, looking forward to seeing Seamie the following day.

The tinkling of glass breaking woke her. She jumped out of bed, and stood listening on the landing. Silence. She stole into Seamie's room and looked around the back garden, trying to make out the shapes of trees and plants. Plucking up courage, she opened the window and put her head out. The night was warm and airless. Everywhere was still.

A crash made her jump. She ran downstairs, crossed the bar, fumbled in the dark hall, until she found the telephone. She pressed her back to the wall, and dialled the number of the Garda Station.

'Glencove Garda Station. Hello!' It was Sergeant Enright.

'Hello.' Pauline could hear the fright in her own voice. 'This is—'

The receiver was whipped from her hand and smashed against the wall. She opened her mouth to scream but a hand was clamped over it with such force that she fell backwards. Caught in a vice-like grip, she struggled.

'If you know what's good for you, you'll be quiet,' a male voice said, as light from a torch shone into her face.

Blinded she couldn't see her assailant until he moved the torch and she saw a tall, hooded figure, the iridiscent flash of his eyes through the woollen balaclava he wore, and the steel of the revolver he was pointing at her. Behind him stood another hooded figure.

'Where's Scully?' the man holding her asked.

'I don't know what you're talking about,' Pauline shrieked.

'Shut up,' he said, clamping his hand over her mouth.

The other man was making for the stairs. She knew, by his familiarity with the place and his enormous shoes, that it was he who had left muddy footprints in the hall. He turned round. 'Sorry, I was forgetting my manners. Ladies first.' He waited on the staircase for her and her captor to pass him.

'You go outside, keep nix,' Pauline's captor said to him.

Pauline climbed the stairs, the nozzle of a gun in her spine.

On the landing the masked man caught her hair, jerking her head backwards. 'Get dressed,' he said, and snapped on the landing light.

Pauline stumbled into her bedroom and put on the jeans and paint-spattered T-shirt that were flung across a chair.

'Hurry,' the clipped voice called.

Out again on the landing she stood cowering.

'Come on,' he rasped, and bundled her into the sitting room, the soles of his sneakers squeaking on the lino as he moved. 'Sit down there and don't move,' he said. 'We're going to wait here together for your friend.'

'I'm not expecting anyone.'

'We'll soon find out.' He flicked on the lamp.

Pauline clasped her hands together to stop them from shaking and forced herself to look into the eyes behind the mask. Meeting her gaze, he straightened and sat bolt upright, his head tilted to one side tense, alert, listening. His eyes were bright and dangerous.

He caught her sneaking a glance at her watch and said, 'You could save yourself a lot of time.'

'If I knew where he was I'd tell you,' Pauline said.

'My information is that Scully's on his way here to see you. I don't usually get it wrong.'

'If he is, nobody's told me,' Pauline said, defiantly.

He gave a deep sigh. 'Listen, I didn't come here to hurt you. Understand?' he said, more gently.

Pauline nodded.

'You just sit there quietly and you'll come to no harm. If Scully turns up we'll be off and no more. If he doesn't ... well ...' He didn't finish the sentence, just stared at her.

If Scully didn't show up, she'd be killed. Was that what he was implying? That she knew too much and her knowledge would be the destruction of her? Scully was proving to be more dangerous than she had ever imagined. She sat with her eyes closed to prevent herself from looking at the man in the balaclava because he reminded her of Martin. In the recesses of her mind she could see him, dressed in black, a skull and crossbones emblazoned on his chest. He was staring at her through holes in his gleaming skull. 'You always knew I'd come back to see justice done. You thought you'd get away with it. You murdered me, Pauline,' his voice whined. 'You're a killer. Scully has killed plenty of people in his time. He'll have no compunction about killing you.'

Loud knocking on the hall door brought her back to reality.

'Who the hell are you expecting at this hour of the night?' her captor said, raising his revolver, jolting Pauline out of her chair.

She followed him to the window, watched him lift a chink of the curtain to peep out, caught a glimpse of a snake tattoo slithering up his arm.

'Hey, it's the cops,' he hissed. 'Answer it. Keep them talking and don't try any funny business or you'll get this in your back.' He followed her downstairs, his revolver nudging her spine. As she opened the hall door he slithered behind it, gun poised, finger on the trigger.

Sergeant Enright peered at her. 'Pauline,' he said. Her initial relief at seeing him was replaced by fear as she remembered that the masked man's gun was now pointing straight at her face.

'Hello, Sergeant,' she said.

'Everything all right?' he asked.

'Fine, Sergeant.' Pauline went to close the door.

He pushed it back. 'Who's in there with you?' he said, his eyes darting to the staircase and back again.

'Nobody, Sergeant,' she said. 'Seamie's in Aunt Bea's for a few days. I'm on my own.'

'You expecting visitors?'

'No, Sergeant. I was fast asleep.'

'Fully dressed?' Sergeant Enright leaned against the wall and let his shoulders droop.

'I dozed off watching the telly.' Pauline yawned.

'Mm. There was a report of strange noises coming from your flat upstairs.' The statement hung in the air between them as he waited for a reply.

Pauline looked blankly at him. 'Must have been something on the telly.'

Sergeant Enright stood back from the door and shone his torch towards the roof, swivelling it in all directions, before returning the beam to Pauline's face.

'You didn't ring the station earlier, did you? One a.m. approximately?'

'No, Sergeant.' She could feel the fear of the gunman crouched beside her, only the door between him and the policeman.

'Well, goodnight, Sergeant, thanks for calling round,' she said, as cheerfully as she could, trying to close the door. But Sergeant Enright took out his cigarettes, lit one, and puffed away as if this was a social call. He was biding his time, not believing a word she had uttered.

'You'll forgive me if I sound personal,' he said, leaning into the door and letting his shoulders droop, 'but how well do you know John Scully?'

'Not well at all,' Pauline said.

'Does he have a key to your flat?'

'No, Sergeant, he does not.'

'You wouldn't happen to know if he has financial problems?'

'I told you, I hardly know the man.'

'You wouldn't happen to know where he is at this present moment?' Again Sergeant Enright's eyes swept the stairs.

'I've no idea.'

Sergeant Enright smiled a tight smile. 'I can see I'm getting nowhere,' he said. 'If you happen to see him, tell him to contact me. It's vital. Oh, and don't go off anywhere with him when he does get back. He's under surveillance.'

'Under surveillance?' Pauline blurted out.

'Yes, we're making enquiries and I expect your co-operation. If you hear anything let me know.' He turned on his heel and left.

The masked man lowered the gun and breathed a sigh of relief. The other man appeared out of the shadows and made sure the door was locked.

'Someone must have tipped Scully off,' one said to the other. Turning to Pauline her captor said, 'We'd better get going and you better get Scully here on whatever pretext you like. We'll be waiting for him. Only you don't tell him about us. Do ya hear? There's a little matter we have to sort out with him.'

'S-supposing he's g-gone off somewhere?' Pauline stammered.

'We'll be waiting for him no matter how long it takes. Now, you go on about your business as if nothing happened. One wrong move or one word out of place and your wee boy might find himself in serious trouble.'

Pauline's hands flew to her mouth.

'And remember, the longer you take to find him, the greater the danger for your wee boy.'

Chapter Nineteen

In the mirror of her dressing-table, Pauline stared at her reflection hardly recognising it. She applied makeup to her white face and ran a comb through her hair. Then she put on a warm sweater, went into the kitchen and looked round at the walls, the cupboards, the table and chairs, half expecting to find the hooded men sitting there waiting for her. The clock ticking reminded her that she was due to go to Ballingarret, but first she would search for Scully. Hurriedly she drank a cup of tea and left the pub, locking the door after her. She threw her bag into the car, and drove off without noticing the man who stood close to the trees, watching her.

She passed the hotel and took the road that veered left. The large dwellings at the end of the road where Scully's flat was looked dark and foreboding. She parked outside and stared up at his windows for a few minutes. Then she approached the house cautiously, mounted the broad, stone steps that were shared with the neighbouring house, and went in through the open door. The hall was dark. On the second-floor landing she turned left and went up another flight of stairs. She knocked at his door and waited, listening. Silence. She tried the handle. To her amazement it swung open.

The enormous room was high-ceilinged and ornamented, its tall windows overlooking a long narrow back garden. It was comfortably furnished with a large sofa, matching chairs, a sideboard, a table and chair. A photograph of a young woman in a gilt frame stood on the mantelpiece. In the bedroom the bed was unmade and clothes were tossed in a corner. Scully had left in a hurry.

On the bedside table there were papers, letters and maps. She rummaged through them feeling like a thief and thinking that she wasn't the only one to have rifled through his personal possessions. She was astonished at how quickly he had eased himself into her world, Glencove. The more she looked the more intimidated she felt. There was another photograph beside his bed, of a group of people sitting at a table, a birthday cake in front of them, Scully smiling as he blew out the candles, and she found another of a woman she took to be his mother. Where was he? What would she tell him when she saw him? The thought of him returning terrified her.

She continued her search until she was certain that there was nothing to indicate his whereabouts, then left. On the staircase she heard footsteps and a voice floated out from a room off the hall. She stopped to listen – a television. As she left the building her heart was pounding.

In the street she looked right then left before getting into her car. She sat in it for several minutes trying to calm herself before she drove back along the Sea Road towards the hotel.

Next morning coming round the back of the hotel Pauline saw four men, waiting, their yellow hard-hats glinting in the sun. They looked strong, healthy, impatient for action.

'Hello,' she said. 'Is Geoff around?'

'We're waiting for him,' the tallest man said, leaning back on his heels, surveying Pauline under the rim of his hat.

'Can I be of help?' another asked.

'It's personal.' She held her breath.

'If you wait over there, he'll be here in a few minutes.' The tall man pointed to the newly erected site hut at the end of the car-park.

'Thanks.' She was on her way there when Geoff rounded the corner, a clipboard under his arm. She followed him into the makeshift office amid wolf-whistles from the watching men.

'What can I do for you?' He stood drumming his fingers on the table where site maps were strewn.

'I had to see you,' she began. 'I want to explain why—'

'There's no need,' he said, looking at his watch, then out towards the men. 'We're behind schedule. We'd better get started.'

'Geoff, listen ...'

He took out a packet of cigarettes, and said, 'Shouldn't you be interested in this extension too?'

'I am,' Pauline snapped. 'But this is personal.'

'It'll have to wait until I'm off duty.' Sidestepping her he walked towards the men.

Eve was in her office. 'Pauline!' she said. 'You're back. Where were you?'

'The weather was so good I decided to take an extra couple of days,' Pauline lied.

Eve looked at her curiously. 'You should have phoned. We were getting anxious.'

'I only expected to be away for a couple of days. Sorry,' Pauline said feebly. 'Is everything all right?'

'Yes, of course. Aunt Bea was worried and Geoff Ryan asked for you several times ... Is something wrong?'

'I'm tired, that's all.'

'Have a coffee.' Eve picked up the phone on her desk.

'Two coffees, please, Marie,' she said. 'Well, what do you think of the idea of using that extra space for a new bar?' she asked.

'You may be biting off more than you can chew,' Pauline said.

'I don't think so.' Eve was full of enthusiasm, but as Pauline listened to her she wished she could tell her the truth about Scully, instead of fobbing her off with a lie. There was so much she had to keep to herself that sometimes she thought she would burst.

The talk faded and she was alone, removed from the scene. There was no getting away from Scully. Although she had no idea where he was or what had happened to him her every thought was centred on him and her past. 'You are a murderer. You killed Martin Dolan,' a voice in her head repeated, until she thought she was going mad.

'Are you worrying about Madge, Pauline?'

Pauline jolted back to the present.

'Yes, I am. I'm going to see her later on my way back from Ballingarret.'

'That's good. Give her my love. What do you think of the idea of putting another car-park underneath the ballroom?'

'I think you'll need to at this rate,' Pauline said.

Here she was, a shareholder of a hotel, surrounded by friends, full of hopes for the future. She should be happy. Everything she had ever wished for was within her grasp. But the fear Scully's return had invoked, and the guilt she had managed to control over the past few years would stay now to cast a shadow over everything. But hadn't she been waiting for it to happen?

Pauline thought of herself as two people. The Pauline who worked hard, looked after Madge and Seamie, had lunch with Eve, and the secret, frightened Pauline, who waited with dread for Scully's next move. She wondered if her eyes looked wild, if the craziness she felt showed in her face. But Eve was treating her normally. 'I'd best be going,' she said. 'Mustn't keep Seamie waiting any longer.'

Chapter Twenty

The telegram delivered to Dorothy stated that her husband, Ron Freeman, had died of a cerebral haemorrhage, and that the funeral had already taken place. She flew into a rage because the message had been signed by Sue Hope, the woman for whom he had deserted his wife and daughter.

Eve couldn't believe that he was dead – her daddy, always full of life, always keen for a new adventure, was gone for good. She wondered what upset her more: that he had died so far away from home, or that she hadn't seen him for over ten years.

Several relatives and friends attended the Mass Father McCarthy said for him the following week.

Dorothy wept at the service but Eve remained dry-eyed. She tried to pray for him but could no longer believe in a God who had left her prayers unanswered when she had asked him to send her father home.

Afterwards Dorothy continued to rage against Sue Hope, but Eve realised that her mother's anger was pitched against her own husband for leaving her. To Eve and Agnes Dolan she swore undying revenge against Sue, for stealing him from her.

Eve talked about Ron to Pauline. 'I wish he'd been ordinary, like everyone else's father, always at home in the evenings, mowing the lawn on Saturday afternoon,' she said.

'He was different,' Pauline agreed. 'Sort of aloof and distinguished. The neighbours didn't always know what to say to him, but he was a lovely man.'

With Pauline's approval, Eve wrote to Sue asking if they could meet. She felt she would like to see her again to hear all about her father. Sue wrote back by return of post: she would look forward to seeing Eve, perhaps they could speak on the phone to arrange something. They agreed to meet the following month at the Ritz Hotel in London.

Pauline was woken suddenly by a strange sound outside. She got up, went to the bedroom window. Everything looked peaceful yet she was sure someone was out there. Grabbing her dressing-gown she went downstairs and out into the back garden.

It was cool outside. A damp wind touched her face as she sat in the dark watching the silver moon and stars, the sheen on the grass. She pulled her nightdress tightly to her. After all these years, the walls she had built around herself were tumbling down about her and she was frightened. It would be better when Scully turned up. She'd find out what was going on, why everyone was looking for him. Her biggest fear was for Seamie's safety. The only way to guarantee it, she felt, was to send him to boarding-school in Wexford. She'd write to Father Raphael to arrange a meeting. For the moment, though, he was safe in Ballingarret.

Her eyes were on the apple trees that Madge had planted years ago, their outline barely visible. Suddenly she felt a movement in the hedge behind her. She whirled around in terror and saw a shape the size of a person moving near the gate. A shadow fell across the grass in front of her.

'Hello,' she croaked.

Her heart was hammering in her ribcage. The outline of the shed loomed up before her. Her eyes shifted from the house to the garden, her chest heaving. No one was there.

Back in bed she lay awake for a long time in the dark listening to the silence on the street below. When she slept she dreamed of Scully, walking with her through the endless rooms of a house she didn't know.

The next night she took the bus to Bray. A cold puff of wind slapped her face as she alighted and ran down the street.

'Geoff?' she called, and rang the bell.

Slowly the door opened and he stepped forward tying the belt of a bathrobe around his waist. 'What are you doing here?' he asked, making no attempt to disguise his surprise.

'Can I come in?'

In the dim landing light his face was shadowed, his profile sharp against the bare white wall as he motioned her in. 'I didn't hear a car,' he said.

'I got the bus.'

'Bit late for a social call.'

'I had to see you. I wanted to explain why I was away so long.'

He lit a cigarette, blew out the match and leaned on the mantelpiece. 'You don't have to. It's none of my business.'

'I want everything to be all right between us,' Pauline said.

Geoff took a couple of puffs of his cigarette then stubbed it out. 'I know why you went off, Pauline,' he said.

Pauline's heart leaped into her mouth.

'Scully broke your heart once. When you met him again you had to go off together to resolve it. That business of your lover being dead was a lie.'

'You've got it all wrong!' Pauline protested.

Geoff was shaking his head. 'No, I haven't. I knew it the minute I set eyes on you. The hunted look in your eyes screamed, "Broken heart."'

Pauline took a deep breath. 'It wasn't Scully.'

Geoff wasn't listening. 'So,' he continued, 'it didn't work out between you and you're back.' His breath was on her neck, his lips almost touching hers. 'I'm the man for you, Pauline, and you know it.'

She stood motionless, as if what he was saying was either of no consequence, or she didn't hear it. But she knew that he could sense the power he had over her body. Slowly he began to undress her.

Together on his bed they made love. 'This is what you came for,' he said in a hoarse whisper. 'You came sneaking here to me for this. Nothing else.'

Tears trickled down her face and she knew that she would keep coming back as long as he wanted her. Still inside her, his arms tight around her, he said nothing more until finally he turned away from her, and got out of bed. 'I think you'd better go now that you've got what you want. But I'll tell you this. When I make love, I want something more than that. I thought I had it with you but I was wrong. Go back to your lover boy. I want someone I can settle down with and you, Miss Quirk, are the kiss of death.'

He left the room. Pauline dressed quickly, took her coat and handbag from the chair and walked to the front door. She hesitated a moment then went out. It is over, she repeated to herself. It's over, it's over, it's over.

Half-way home she decided to go to the hotel, find Eve, talk to her, but then she realised there was no sense in confiding in Eve unless she told her everything. Which she could not do.

Chapter Twenty-One

Eve looked into the mirror, replenished her lipstick, combed her hair, and then went into the foyer of the Ritz Hotel. No sooner had she found herself a niche by Reception with a good view of the door, than a taxi pulled up and a large woman stepped out. She caught sight of Eve as she mounted the steps and waved frantically, like someone drowning.

'Eve.' Sue grabbed her. 'Look at you! You're gorgeous.' She patted down her blonde hair and looked around. 'I should have worn something more glamorous.'

When they were seated in the lounge and Eve asked her old friend how she was, Sue began to weep. 'I miss Ron so much,' she wailed.

Eve held her hand, forgetting for the moment that this woman had stolen her father. Sue pulled a handkerchief out of her handbag. 'I'll be right as rain in a minute.' She took a sweeping look around, like a child at a party. 'I've missed London so much. We had some good times here.'

'Great times,' Eve said. 'If it hadn't been for my mother insisting I came home I'd probably still be here.' But if she had thought she was going to get a word in about her mother she was wrong.

'Ron was the whole world to me,' Sue went on, as if Eve

hadn't spoken. 'He was everything I wanted. Amazing, isn't it? Me falling for such a conservative man! He was so beautiful.' She sniffed again, her eyes brimming as she looked at Eve. 'Silly me,' she said. 'I must stop this.'

Eve smiled sympathetically at her. At least Sue had loved her father. 'I can't imagine him getting old,' she said.

Sue's eyes were blank as she said, 'His hair had gone grey, he'd slowed down a bit and sometimes he drank too much, but he certainly wasn't old.' Then she paused. 'He was wonderful. I'll never go back to India again. It wouldn't be the same without him.'

They were escorted to the dining-room by a waiter, who led them to a table and signalled to another to take their order. The young man handed them menus and offered them an aperitif.

'A dry martini,' Sue said. 'I must look like hell, especially after making a show of myself crying like that.'

Eve ordered a mineral water, then said soothingly, 'You're fine.'

'You don't have to be polite. I know I'm a mess. Look at my hair. It's so fine that my hairdresser can't do a thing with it.' She pushed a strand behind her ear. 'Yours always looks wonderful.'

'Thank you.' Eve picked up the menu.

Sue gulped down her drink as soon as the waiter brought it, and told him they were ready to order. Pen poised he explained the day's specialities as Sue stared at him shamelessly, making him blush. Eve chose the duck à l'orange while Sue settled for calves' liver.

When the food arrived, Sue dived into it, stopping every now and then, knife and fork poised in mid-air, to relate an anecdote loudly. When Eve told her that Jasper Furlong was compiling notes about the progress of Freeman's Tea Imports since its foundation and was hoping that Sue might contribute anything she knew about Ron's input, Sue exploded. 'That shit.

I wouldn't lift my little finger to help him. He made Ron's life hell.' Her voice had risen an octave and she shook with rage. 'The life he gave Ron,' she continued. 'The poor man couldn't do anything right by Jasper,' and her face was smudged with more tears.

'Don't cry. Have some wine.' Mortified, Eve filled Sue's glass from the carafe beside her.

Sue looked around the crowded restaurant. 'I'm making a fool of myself, aren't I?'

'You're all right,' Eve said, smiling to hide her discomfort. She was beginning to think that this meeting hadn't been such a good idea.

Sue was smiling again, distracted now by the two men who had just sat down at the next table. She became a caricature of herself, smiling coquettishly, flirting openly with them. 'Isn't the one on the right divine?' she lisped, excitement soaking through her voice.

It struck Eve, as she cast a sidelong glance at the ordinary-looking man, that Sue's new-found freedom was going to her head – as was the wine. She had consumed the whole carafe.

Sue noticed Eve's expression, and said, 'It's the booze, pay no attention. You know men and me. It means nothing.'

You're right, Eve thought sourly. You stole my daddy and thought nothing of it.

'You know Ron had an affair?' Sue said.

'Oh!'

Sue nodded vigorously. 'It didn't last long. I was seething when I discovered it. I thought, You'll pay for this, I'll get my own back, and I did. He never looked at another woman all the years he was with me except for that one incident and I put a stop to it. I bet you're shocked?' Sue looked at her defiantly.

'Why should I be? He had an affair with you, didn't he? They say if you do it once you'll do it again. And he always had an eye for the ladies, you knew that,' Eve said. 'What did you do?'

Sue leaned towards Eve and said, with an idiotic grin, 'Killed him.'

'*What!*' Eve almost jumped out of her seat as faces blurred and the room spun.

'Not literally, silly.' Sue put her hand on Eve's arm. 'Listen, instead of taking up with another man, I decided to woo him back. I went off to New York for a couple of weeks, had a makeover, bought some new clothes, made a pass at him when I got back. He couldn't resist me. In fact, we spent so much time in bed that it weakened his heart. Of course, I wasn't aware of that at the time.' She tilted her head. 'I'll let you in on a little secret. He died on the job.'

'Oh!' was all Eve managed.

'Yeah. He died screwing me. What a way to go. You better believe it.'

Eve froze at a mental picture of the two of them naked in bed, Ron's head lolling, his eyes staring blankly, Sue phoning for help.

Sue saw her friend's face and dropped her knife and fork. 'I suppose I shouldn't have told you,' she said.

Silence built between them and Sue shifted uncomfortably, her face and ears flaming red. The voices of the other diners buzzed around them.

'You know what you are, don't you?' Eve said. 'You're the slut of all sluts. The poor man didn't stand a chance with you.'

'I made him happy,' Sue whined.

'You tart. You took him away from us and you killed him.'

Sue said, 'I'd better be going.' She stood up, turned away from the table and wobbled off, the men at the next table gazing after her.

Eve vowed that she would never forgive Sue Hope for this. She never wanted to see her again. She had the same heavy feeling she'd had the day her father left home. As she sat there, she realised that she had never forgiven her father for deserting her and she never would.

Chapter Twenty-Two

Mrs Browne was cleaning the bar, her coat still on to keep out the November chill, her hat on her head, a cigarette stuck to her lips, when Pauline came in.

'Did Madge phone?' Pauline asked.

'No,' Mrs Browne replied. 'The post's on the hall table.'

There was an envelope with Madge's familiar handwriting on it. Pauline slit it open: 'I'm going into hospital for tests. Dr Strong doesn't want to leave anything to chance.' She visualised Madge propped up in bed, writing slowly, careful to keep the letter cheerful, thinking that a hospital stay in Wexford would be less trouble for Pauline. Ten years ago, when Seamus had disappeared, Madge had been everything to Pauline. She had looked after Seamie when Pauline had gone to Belfast to find his father, and when she had returned, in despair, Madge had urged her to go to Montauk, had promised to visit her there. She'd kept her word. Pauline recalled Madge's holiday, the picnics in the Hamptons, Madge perched on a grassy dune, eating fresh clams from a nearby seafood bar. Later they'd bought copper pots and trinkets on the South Shore. Before Madge left they took the train to Manhattan, leaving Seamie with Aunt Mary, and went shopping. Madge, still robust then had been thrilled with her new coat, an extravagance she would never have permitted herself in the past.

Madge had written constantly after that, offering to pay Pauline's fare home for a visit, which Pauline had refused, claiming she was too busy. Now she was sorry. She found Madge's cousin Sadie's phone number and dialled. Eventually Sadie answered.

'She's not so good,' she said in response to Pauline's enquiry. 'But I'll be visiting her later on today and I'll know more.'

Pauline's heart lurched. 'What if it's really serious?'

'We'll just have to wait and see, but sure they can do wonderful things nowadays, only she'd have to go up to the Mater hospital for surgery if the worst comes to the worst.'

'Tell her I'll be down to see her tomorrow.'

'Tomorrow?' Mrs Browne echoed, coming down the hall trailing her vacuum cleaner. 'Is she bad?'

'No,' Pauline said, knowing that Madge wouldn't want her business broadcast and that Mrs Browne was an old gossip, who skimped on her time and took Madge for a fool.

Early next morning the knock on the front door shook the foundations of the pub. Pauline waited for Mrs Browne to answer it. Eventually the Hoover was switched off and Pauline could hear Mrs Browne's voice calling, 'What do you think I am, a bloody robot?' Then she trundled up the stairs and popped her head round the door. 'A gentleman to see you,' she said. 'A foreigner. I showed him into the bar.'

'Thanks.'

Pauline forced herself to her feet and went downstairs, Mrs Browne trailing behind her. She walked into the bar and found a Crombie-clad, dapper man with a beard, who doffed his Robin Hood hat, and smiled at her. 'You may not remember me.' He spoke with an accent, tugging his beard between thumb and forefinger. Pauline waited at the edge of panic. 'My name is Pierre Duval. I hope I didn't disturb you.'

'How do you do?' Pauline said, thinking what a nice man he was when the worry as to what he wanted rose up again.

'I was going to telephone you but I thought perhaps it would be more appropriate, in the circumstances, to call and see you myself. If you are free, that is. Otherwise I shall leave now and make an appointment to see you later, perhaps.'

'What can I do for you?' Pauline asked, puzzled.

Mr Duval lowered his voice. 'It is about our mutual friend, John Scully.'

Pauline froze.

'When I got involved in a business transaction with Mr Scully I did not feel that anything dishonest was happening.' Mr Duval looked at her as if she would be doing him a great favour just by listening. 'You see, I'm in the business of money transactions for clients,' he explained. 'In this instance Mr Scully was making a payment to me for a client. Straightforward dealing on my part, you understand, a small percentage for me.'

'Yes,' Pauline prompted.

'I did wonder why the money was in your possession.' He coughed, his face contorting with the effort. 'Mind you,' he said, with a flash of a smile, 'I knew you to be an honest woman by your face.'

'Mr Duval, you'll forgive me if I tell you that I can't recall meeting you before,' Pauline said, mortified.

'It is understandable, I suppose. You were both in such a hurry that day you came to my apartment in Zürich. Our business transaction couldn't have taken more than a few minutes. I took the money-belts. You left.' He caught the flash of recognition in her eyes. 'The problem is that the money Mr Scully gave me, the money you had on your person . . .' he hesitated '. . . was counterfeit.'

'What?'

They stared at one another, both trapped in the knowledge that somehow Scully had hoodwinked them both. 'Nothing like this has ever happened before,' Mr Duval continued. 'The members of Mr Scully's organisation do not seem to know his whereabouts.' His eyes bored into hers. 'He seems to have disappeared without trace.'

Pauline felt her stomach slide downward with the sickening certainty that this little man who had come all the way from Zürich and meant business was also a crook in the guise of a gentleman. She watched him as he looked around assessing everything, and wondered if he were about to take the lot.

'What will you have to drink?' she asked, biding her time, yet poised to move, pick up the phone.

'Nothing, thank you. I just wondered if you could tell me where I could find Mr Scully.'

'I've no idea,' Pauline said. 'I haven't seen him since I was in Zürich.'

'Ah, I thought so.' Mr Duval rose. 'He's fooled us both. But I'll find him. Of that you can be sure. My client is getting very anxious.'

Pauline led the way to the hall, glad that Mrs Browne was nearby should this man try to pull a fast one on her.

At the hall door he turned to her. 'I've been a fool, Miss Quirk,' he said, 'I trusted Mr Scully. Made a friend of him. Didn't check the money properly. Broke the rules – against my better judgement too, I might add. What a mistake.' From the expression in his eyes she could see that he was outraged by Scully's betrayal. 'Let's hope he turns up soon before it's too late.'

'He's crazy,' Pauline said, more to herself than Mr Duval. 'I must have been a lunatic to let myself get into this.'

'I will keep you informed,' he said, almost comfortingly.

With a wave of his hand Mr Duval was gone, walking briskly up the road. Pauline had the impulse to shout after him to stay away. Instead, she found herself going after him, begging him to spare her a moment. 'Please, Mr Duval,' she said, in a savage whisper, 'don't do anything rash. I expect to hear from Scully soon. I have a son and I don't know what I would do if anything were to happen to him.' She was unable to stop herself babbling.

'Miss Quirk, I don't wish to harm you or take anything from you,' Mr Duval said, affronted at the very idea. 'I want the money that's owed to me, that's all. Naturally if I don't get it . . .' He stopped and let his eyes slide over the façade of the pub. '. . . I shall be forced to seek compensation in some other way.' Then he was striding off down the street without a backward glance.

Chapter Twenty-Three

Eve picked out a light blue woollen dress and jacket to match, smart but not too formal. She loved the new, *haute couture* styles that were emerging: loose-fitting stylish clothes, proving that efficiency and elegance could go hand in hand. She had a dinner date with her husband in Dublin and she was happy that she had been home in time to take his call inviting her to meet Howey Swartz, his new business associate. Now that David was home their reawakened love made her feel that it would last for ever. This was what she told herself as she parked her car in Stephen's Green.

She was early, walking through the park, which was stark in its mantle of snow, the evening frost hardening the slush into ice. Instead of going into the hotel she wandered around the shops, admiring the lighted windows. The season of goodwill was evident in the pyramids of Christmas trees and coils of holly and mistletoe piled high at street corners.

David's antennae were for business, Eve reflected, as she walked slowly back towards the hotel. He lived for hidden deals beneath the surface of polite conversation. Clinching them was his emotional currency. It made him happy and that happiness sustained him in the other areas of his life. She had no objection to his work because she also needed the activity of business to stimulate her. It gave them a shared interest and a buffer against the humdrum of daily life. Tonight they were about to celebrate another coup, judging by what David had said on the phone.

He was seated at a table near the window engrossed in conversation with another man when Eve walked into the elegant dining room.

'Hello, darling,' he said, standing up and coming to meet her. With his arm around her shoulders he drew her towards the table. 'This is Howey Swartz. Howey, meet my wife, Eve.'

'How do you do?' Eve smiled.

Howey stood up, shook hands then glanced at his watch. 'Hell, what a bitch, I've a plane to catch,' he said, and downed the rest of his drink.

'Oh!' Eve said, disappointed.

David shrugged. 'Can't be helped. We'll meet again soon.'

After Howey had gone they sat down, David smiling and happy.

'That must have gone well,' Eve said.

'It did. I'm sorry he had to go. He's an interesting guy.' He beckoned to a waiter. 'We've something to celebrate. I was going to let it keep but, hell, here goes.' Shunting his chair closer to hers, he said, 'Do you remember that Wall Street business I told you about? The one where I was being considered in the takeover?'

Eve nodded.

'Well, Sam Harvey, the old boy who owns it, had a heart-attack and when Howey met the family last week they told him they want our company to take over, within the next month. Can you believe it?'

Eve felt the blood rush to her head.

'How about it, Mrs Furlong? An apartment in Manhattan? Or would you prefer something further out?' He kissed her cheek, squeezed her hand.

The waiter was standing beside them and David ordered

whiskey for himself and mineral water for Eve. Then he went on, 'I know you're happy here and it's your life too. But the hotel's on its feet and if we put in a manager I think you could be persuaded to come with me.' She said nothing, and he added hastily, 'Of course, if you're dead against it I'll cancel the whole thing and we won't go.'

'What does Jasper say?'

'He thinks it's a chance of a lifetime for me.' He paused, looked at her. 'He says I'm never going to make an impact here until I have a lot more experience abroad. And he knows.'

'How do you feel about it?'

'I agree with Dad. I think it's time I had a place to run.' He looked shy suddenly. 'With Dad's approval and backing it'll be a dream come true.'

Eve knew that he was right. It was his chance to make it into the big time, leap over his father, whom he always perceived as a stumbling block. She would have to say yes, go to New York and make it work. He sat waiting, his eyes searching hers, unsure. 'I need you with me, otherwise it's no use,' he said, taking her hand.

'It's the hotel. I'm just getting it off the ground.'

'Dad will find you a good manager.'

Eve looked at him. This was Jasper's work. Behind the scenes he was reorganising their lives. About to protest, she changed her mind and said, 'When do we leave?'

'As soon as the house is sold.'

It wasn't until they were driving home that what David had told her began to sink in. She and Katie would be alone all day long in an apartment in New York until he came home in the evening. New York streets teemed with junkies and weirdos brandishing knives, drugs, guns; doors were forced open with credit cards. She thought of all the things she heard and read about the city. She glanced at David's calm profile as he drove along. He looked so self-satisfied that she wanted to scream.

In her bathroom she prepared slowly for bed, carefully removing her makeup, putting on her nightdress. When she finally slipped under the covers David took her in his arms, warming her cold body with his own. In the light of the bedside lamp she saw his face, his eyes pleading. They held each other, made love silently and briefly. Afterwards she lay awake for hours, already packing in her mind.

Pierre's salon was shimmering, fluorescent bright, its elegance and space-age equipment hinting at prohibitive prices. Pauline nudged Eve, who led the way to Reception and the obsequious girl who stood tall in spiky heels and tapped her fingernails on the appointments book.

'Pierre is running late,' she said, glancing towards him. He was absorbed in a consultation with a girl who looked like a model. 'You don't mind waiting about ten minutes?'

Light beamed from the ceiling and bulbs around the mirror, reflecting on the shiny surfaces and the wash-basins. Seated in a black vinyl chair, sipping coffee, a pile of glossy magazines stacked before her, Pauline had her nails manicured while Eve's hair was washed.

'What style do you have in mind?' Pierre was running competent fingers through Pauline's hair when she was seated in front of his mirror.

'What do you suggest?'

'Take some of it away. It's too heavy,' he said, gazing with her into the mirror, scrutinising her face from every angle.

As he sectioned off her hair and began to snip Pauline kept her eyes down, watching clumps of hair fall. Silently, he cut, combed, razored, stopping often to measure the strands against her face. He continued until he had achieved the curve he was aiming for. Finally he blow-dried it.

'Now,' he said, whipping off her cloak, as if unveiling a statue, 'voilà.'

Pauline moved her head, the new shape framing her face, softening her expression, making her eyes bigger.

'Great.' She smiled. 'Terrific. I love it.'

Pierre smiled a professional smile and marched her to the desk, where Eve was waiting, her own hair cut into a style that swung when she moved her head.

In Alfredo's wine bar in Wicklow Street Eve told Pauline about the move, feeling her friend's distress. Pauline kept her eyes on the tablecloth as she slowly absorbed the shock of Eve's news. 'This is his big break,' Eve finished quietly. 'I can't let him down.'

'I suppose not,' Pauline agreed.

'Anyway,' Eve concluded, with false brightness, 'Katie will have her father around all the time. It's nice being a proper family.'

Pauline nodded.

Suddenly Eve said, 'I don't want to go, Pauline. I don't want to live in New York. I've put so much into building up the business. Fixing our home. David didn't even discuss it with me until it was too late. All the arrangements were made behind my back.'

'Men!' Pauline threw up her hands in despair.

Eve looked at her. 'I should be glad to help my husband with his career. Like a good wife would. Oh, God!' Covering her face with her hands she wept.

'It's not the end of the world,' Pauline said. 'It's not like emigration in the old days. Those poor unfortunates never came back. You can get a flight to and from New York any day of the week now and, let's face it, you can afford it.'

'I suppose.' Eve sniffed.

'Listen,' Pauline said, catching hold of her friend's wrist, 'I've got an idea. After a month or so, long enough to get yourselves settled in, come home on some pretext. You'll find plenty of excuses. Then keep coming back regularly. Think of

New York as a sort of holiday. That way, it won't be such a wrench and you won't feel the time passing.'

'Yeah. I'd be keeping an eye on the hotel at the same time.'

'That's it. Meanwhile, I'll watch things at this end, phone you and tell you when there's a crisis.' Pauline winked at her.

'You're a star, Pauline. What would I do without you?'

'I'd rather have you here, of course, but I think you should give it a go, for David's sake.'

They paid the bill then, and marched out, clinging together, giggling as they blundered along the street dodging the traffic. Arm in arm they strolled through Stephen's Green, Eve repeating Pauline's idea like a speech she had to memorise. She clutched at this small glimmer of hope and felt better. Looking up at the beautiful façades of the buildings all around her, their stonework shelved in snow, she knew she could never leave Dublin for long.

The early commuter train was crowded. Eve stared out at the city and the suburbs, Pauline's coat warm against her shoulder. As the train pulled into Sandymount station, Pauline jolted Eve out of her reverie. 'Look,' she said, in a racked whisper. 'Over there,' Pauline persisted.

It was Geoff, with a young girl hanging on his arm. She was small, slight, her long hair streaming in the wind. Unaware of their stares she smiled and said something to Geoff, who leaned towards her, his face creasing with laughter. He didn't see Pauline, missing the look of contempt she flung at him.

'Didn't take him long,' Pauline said bitterly. 'Where did he meet her?'

'I've no idea,' Eve said, absent-mindedly.

When they got off the train and were walking home, Eve said, 'Are you sure I shouldn't tell David I don't want to go?'

'No, don't. Remember the plan.' Pauline stood still. 'Should I call Geoff and tell him I saw him with someone else?'

'No. Can't you see he's getting his own back on you for going off with Scully?'

'But I didn't go off with Scully. I never had an affair with him, Eve.'

'I believe you but Geoff obviously doesn't.'

'Look, for the past ten years I haven't as much as looked at a man. When I think of the opportunities I passed up. Sorry, I shouldn't be mouthing off like this, you have your own troubles.'

Eve started to laugh.

'Why are you laughing? This is serious. How can I persuade him I'm not having an affair with Scully?'

'Don't bother.' They were both giggling, then laughing uproariously, holding on to each other, staggering on the towpath. It was like all those years ago when they were children, when everything became so hilarious that they couldn't stop themselves from getting hysterical.

'Life was much less complicated when we were kids,' Eve pronounced.

'And much more dreary,' Pauline added.

Liberated by the laughter Eve said, 'I'll tell you what! Let's take another day off next week.'

'Good idea. We'll go on another shopping spree. Have another hairdo.' They took off again, laughing all the way up the street.

'There was a phone call for you,' Tommy said, when Pauline returned. 'A man.'

'Did he give his name?'

Tommy squinted, thinking. 'I can't rightly remember. We were busy. Said he'd be staying in Dublin.'

'Did he say anything else?'

Tommy scratched his head. 'Asked a few questions, that's

all.' He saw the scared look on her face and shifted his gaze. 'Where you'd gone, what time you'd be back, that kind of thing. Said he'd be in touch, I think.'

Pauline climbed the stairs wondering if this man, whoever he was, was a collaborator of Scully's, or another smooth crook from some rival gang. Then she retraced her steps and went behind the bar.

'Listen, Tommy,' she said. 'Don't send anyone up to the flat unless you OK it with me first.'

'Right, Miss,' he said, shaking his head as if she had finally flipped.

Chapter Twenty-Four

On Christmas Eve the town was packed with last-minute shoppers, anxious to get Christmas trees, wrapping paper, cards, decorations, even turkeys at knockdown prices. Main Street was garish with fairy-lights. Pauline, on her way to Lynam's to collect a bike for Seamie, edged her way past children staring at toys, lagging behind their mothers. In Lynam's Bing Crosby was crooning 'I'm dreaming of a white Christmas,' his calm voice doing nothing to ease the frenzy. This year Pauline's gift list had extended to include Dinny and his wife Mary because Seamie and she would be spending Christmas on the farm. It was their first Christmas in Ireland for so many years and she was determined to splash out.

Midnight Mass at Saint Patrick's church in Ballingarret was full. Aunt Bea sat entranced, her hands folded in her lap, gazing at Seamie. He was one of the choristers, standing tall in cassock and white surplice singing 'Silent Night', his young, pure voice soaring effortlessly, his shining, solemn face reflecting the wonder of it all. Pauline, pride bursting out of her, watched the intent faces of the congregation. She gazed at the crib, ready for the baby Jesus, at the solid pillars, carved angels clinging to them, and their stone eyes uplifted to the magnificently crafted Gothic arches. Above them was a painting of the Blessed Virgin, her face rapturous, her blonde hair luxuriantly long beneath her blue veil, the golden sash of her robe glittering in the spotlight.

The congregation rose to join in with the choir and Father Byrne carried the baby Jesus to the crib, the choir following him in procession. Watching her son Pauline could tell that his faith was assured. It was confirmed in his strong voice and earnest composure. She doubted if God's love would reach out to include her. At that moment it seemed beyond her. She felt like a spectator at the feast.

Outside the south door Pauline shook hands with Father Byrne and wished him a happy Christmas. He said, 'Your boy has a great voice, Pauline.'

Before they ate their Christmas dinner, Aunt Bea, flanked by Dinny and Mary, Seamie next to Mary, gave thanks to God for 'full and plenty': the home He had provided for her and the certainty of three square meals a day. Pauline, catching Seamie's eye, cautioned him, with a nod, not to giggle.

Over the holidays Seamie caught the flu. Too sick to take much interest in anything he scrunched down into the old sofa, grumbling and watching television with what Aunt Bea called 'his doomsday face'. Anxiety about him made the old lady cross. 'The trouble with kids nowadays,' she said, 'is that they have it soft.' She cast an adoring glance at Seamie. 'Born with a silver spoon in your mouth, me lad, for stirrin' trouble.' She was sitting in her rocking-chair, looking old in her grey jumper and the slacks she had avoided wearing for years because her friend, Father Murtagh, had told her it was a sin for women to wear men's clothes. The wreckage of the newspaper was sprawled at her feet, a glass of whiskey in her hand. 'This bloody country is gone to the dogs,' she announced. 'It's supposed to be a democracy yet jobs are being lost, the emigration rate's rising, the coalition's falling apart and Haughey's making cutbacks on health, education and social welfare. What next?'

'Stop complainin'. It could be worse,' Dinny said.

'What did this country ever do for me? God help us all, but what does Ireland mean to a poor farmer like me? Only hard work, bad weather, unyielding soil, blighted crops.'

The sudden fall of snow had kept Aunt Bea indoors. When she wasn't preparing meals she sat in her rocking-chair reading the newspaper, her glasses perched on her nose, her cup of tea on the little table beside her, her sharp eyes on the world beyond her new kitchen curtains. Since the forming of the coalition government she had taken to airing her opinions on politicians, the economy, ready to rejoice at the least hint of scandal.

'You make a good livin',' Dinny said, at the end of her monologue.

'Any job in the world is easier than farming.'

'You could be stuck in the city with its smog and pollution,' Dinny countered.

'The sun can set on the whole bloody lot for all I care.' Aunt Bea rose from her chair and went off to her bedroom.

'She doesn't mean a word of it,' Dinny said to Seamie. 'She loves the land.'

Pauline was watching an old film starring James Cagney, thinking of a previous Christmas, wishing that it were Seamus she was expecting to return, not Scully. She could visualise Seamus. The Seamus who would stay in her mind for ever. He used to call out to her, as he put his key in the lock, 'I'm back. Are you there?' and her heart would jump for joy. First they would make love, then prepare a meal together, telling each other jokes as they cooked, choking with laughter or singing at the top of their voices.

When she had gone to Belfast to search for him, leaving her baby with Madge, she had been planning to announce their forthcoming marriage. She hadn't bargained on finding Martin

Dolan and his sordid world. Now she tried to imagine how they would have fared had Seamus not disappeared. All she could see, in hindsight, were their lives stretching ahead of them, a blank canvas.

Chapter Twenty-Five

On New Year's Eve, the sign of the Glencove Hotel was lit, and twinkling fairy-lights studded the avenue and the trees outside the entrance. Eve, in a long black backless dress, stood at the entrance to the new ballroom greeting her guests. Jasper was beside her, booming, 'Happy New Year,' to everyone. Irene, gracious in a crimson velvet gown, welcomed their friends with sweet, fluttery kisses. Eve noticed how tired Jasper looked, saw his forced eagerness in his role as expansive host in David's absence, and had no sympathy for him.

Taking a glass of orange juice from one of the waiters, she drank some quickly then went along the soft-carpeted corridor to join the guests already in the ballroom, their raised voices lifting her heart. Samantha and Ian, David's niece and nephew, were there in their new party clothes but Katie, who was too young to join in the celebrations, was in bed asleep. She had started packing for New York the previous week, thinking of it as a great adventure, had carefully placed the big doll she had got for Christmas in the packing case. 'Will she be safe?' she asked Eve.

'Perfectly,' Eve said. To own this doll had been Katie's dearest wish, ever since she had first laid eyes on it in Switzer's window. To part with it, even for a short while, was almost more than she could bear. 'I could carry her,' she had said, hopefully.

'She's too heavy,' Eve had said. 'We'll make a bed for her so that she's comfortable in there while she's travelling.'

'Happy New Year!' Myrtle Thompson called, dramatic in purple satin, her shrivelled husband already making haste to the bar.

Small groups of women in colourful ballgowns, their men dark-suited and clean-shaven, stood chatting, drinking punch.

'We were afraid we wouldn't make it,' a fat man in a tuxedo said. 'The roads are deplorable.'

Pauline was beside Eve. 'So far so good. I've checked with Chef. Food will be served around eleven.'

'Thanks,' Eve said. 'I don't know what I'd do without you.'

'Come and meet Linda and Garry McShane, friends of Jasper's from Scotland.' Irene was taking Eve's arm possessively.

Eve greeted them warmly. Then Henry Joyce, newly returned from the University of Connecticut, where he had delivered a paper on the elderly and their environment, claimed her. Giving her a big hug he said, 'You look wonderful.' With no wife in tow, due to her extended holiday in the States with her parents, he felt free to lavish all his attention on Eve's exposed back and the convoluted twists of her hair. 'Dance with me,' he said, sliding his arm through hers.

Before she realised it, he was leading her to the centre of the floor, past Jasper's watchful eye and Manus Corrigan's careful one.

'You've done a tremendous job on this place,' he said, circling his arm around her waist. Their eyes met and Eve's flickered away.

'It's going well,' she said modestly.

'I hear you're off to New York.'

Eve nodded. 'David's gone ahead to get everything ready for us.'

'You don't look too happy about it.'

'I'll survive,' she said lightly.

Henry drew her close to him, as Jasper wandered around, chatting, replenishing drinks, keeping an eye on everyone.

At eleven o'clock he sounded the dinner gong. The buffet table was laden with fresh salmon, garnished with lemon, slices of pink roast beef, ham, salads, rolls, cheese, fruit, heavy silver cutlery, a stack of Arklow Pottery plates to one side, and trays of red and white wine.

'Great party,' Henry Joyce said. 'You're a terrific girl, Eve. You certainly know how to entertain.'

'Thank you. I'm glad you're enjoying it,' Eve said, as they joined the end of the queue.

Jasper, reaching her side, said quietly and coldly, 'You seem to be full of the party spirit.'

They gazed at one another, their mutual dislike barely concealed.

Jasper turned to Henry, 'Well, Dr Joyce, you seem to be enjoying yourself too,' he said, humorously.

To Eve's surprise, Henry laughed heartily and clapped the other man on the back. 'Wonderful party. Happy New Year.'

Jasper nodded and moved on. Eve sat down with her plate, trying to join in with the banter and jokes going on around her but her heart wasn't in it. When he saw her struggling with her food, Henry asked, 'Are you all right?'

'It's very warm in here.'

'Let's get a breath of fresh air.'

Outside, the grass crunched beneath their feet as they walked down the garden and a silver moon sailed through the racing clouds. Eve felt glad to be away from the artificial smiles of the Thompsons, the Lawlors, the Gregorys and the Lynams, the fresh strawberries flown in from the Canaries, the pots of steaming Freeman's coffee, and the ever-decreasing space in the ballroom where the air was thick with the smoke from Jasper's Havana cigars.

Henry took off his jacket and draped it over her shoulders. 'You're going through a bad patch?'

'Yes.' She felt stomach muscles tighten.

'Is there anything I can do to help?'

'It'll sort itself out once we get away.'

'So you're really off to New York,' Henry said, as if he couldn't believe it.

'Yes,' Eve said, watching the trees stir in the wind. 'David's sorting out his new job.'

'And you?' Henry asked. 'What about Eve, the career woman?'

'No plans yet. I'll have to wait and see. Get Katie settled in first. What about you?'

Henry shrugged. 'I'm coping well on my own. It's amazing how used to it one gets.'

A surge of loneliness caught Eve unawares, forcing her to turn away. 'I'll miss Glencove,' she said, inclining her head towards the sea, the sharply defined black outline of ridge above the cove that she had walked over so often.

'I'll miss you.'

Puzzled, she looked at him.

'I suppose it's arrogant of me to say it but that's what I feel. I wish I could say more. Something like I'll visit you sometime.'

'Why not? I might be very glad to see a friendly face.'

They gazed at one another.

'There's a fireworks display at midnight,' Eve said, moving towards the path. 'We'd better get back.'

Henry caught hold of her, and kissed her lips. 'You're far too beautiful to have to worry about that lot in there,' he said, his face full of longing.

'Don't,' she said, and turned towards the hotel.

'Hello there,' Jasper drawled as they slipped back into the ballroom, antagonism obvious in his face. 'Can I have a word with you, Eve?'

Hearing the rebuke in his voice, she followed him into the lounge.

'What were you thinking of, going out there with Henry Joyce like that? It's enough to start the whispers,' he said. 'I would have thought a woman in your position would place a higher value on her reputation.'

'I've done nothing wrong.'

'You know what it's like around here.' Flushed with anger he went to pour himself a drink from the decanter on the sideboard. 'Your business will suffer if you're seen to be less than circumspect.'

Eve could imagine the speculative ripples of gossip spreading throughout the bridge club, the tennis club.

'Not half as much as it'll suffer while I'm away,' she retorted.

'I'll be here to look after everything.'

'I'll bet you will,' she rejoined.

'Now let's show a united front before our guests,' he said, and stretched out his hand.

'No thanks.' Eve turned on her heel and walked back into the ballroom.

Chapter Twenty-Six

Seamie was better, back in the flat with Pauline, eating his boiled egg and toast. When he heard the clatter of the letter-box he dived downstairs and came back with an airmail envelope. Hunched over the table, he opened it with a knife and read it behind his cup and saucer.

Pauline knew it was from Patty Huntly, Aunt Mary's next-door neighbour's child, who had been writing to him once a month since his return to Ireland. He always wrote back, sitting for a long time at the kitchen table, a wistful look in his face. Pauline suspected that he was homesick for Montauk, Aunt Mary's sprawling house and the activities of the neighbourhood. Mostly, he was probably lonely for Patty, his friend and playmate.

When Seamie went to boarding-school their correspondence became more frequent judging by the amount of stamps Pauline had to provide. The letters were kept in a drawer in his room, held neatly together with a rubber band.

'How are things in Montauk?' Pauline asked.

'They've had the worst fall of snow in years. Everyone was out on their sleighs.'

The longing in his voice made Pauline wince. She pictured the happy images Patty's letter evoked: children wrapped up warm, plummeting on their toboggans down the long sloping street where Aunt Mary's house was, the drives, boulevards, crescents, shopping centres, stretching endlessly ahead of them, covered with snow.

'We'd better get cracking,' Pauline said, rising from the table. 'I'll finish your shirts.'

'I wish I didn't have to go back to school,' Seamie said.

'You'll settle down quickly.' Pauline plugged in the iron.

When she took the pile of folded shirts to his room he was polishing his shoes. The tilt of his head, the flick of the chamois, and his curious concentration struck her sharply. It could have been Seamus standing there but with the softness of youth. Her eyes swept over her son in a concerned, protective way: it was painful to watch him packing, going out of the door, tall, brave, his shoulders squared, his mind gone from her already.

They were to visit Madge before she left him at school, and Pauline was at the wheel of her car, her eyes darting occasionally to her son's unhappy face, his graceful hands resting on his lap. 'I feel guilty about Madge,' she confided. 'I should have looked after her better, insisted on getting Dr Gregory to call when she began to get lethargic.'

'You did your best, Mom. Anyway, Madge does what suits her. If she'd wanted to see Dr Gregory she'd have gone to his surgery,' Seamie said.

Pauline smiled at him; he had always been able to cheer her, even when he was a little boy. When Madge had asked her to return to Glencove, Pauline knew she would never have come without Seamie's approval, regardless of what Aunt Mary or her son Tommy thought. That was the way it had always been.

She parked outside the Mater with a pang of pity for Madge, stranded in this strange place. A nurse marched them down a wide polished corridor to a small room off the coronary-care unit where Madge was dozing, her pale face tinged with grey,

her thinning hair combed back. Pauline, finger on lips, signalled
to Seamie not to speak and sat in the black vinyl chair beside
the bed, glad that Madge couldn't see the shock that must have
registered in her face at her friend's deterioration. Pauline looked
out at the city's rooftops, the chimney stacks squashed together
against the darkening sky.

Suddenly Madge's eyes opened. 'Well, well,' she said,
pleasure in her smile. 'Pauline! Seamie! What a lovely surprise!
I was taking forty winks,' she added, as she tried to sit up.

'How are you?' Pauline hugged her. Dr Strong's news that
Madge was improving had made her hopeful but now, seeing
her friend so weak, she had her doubts.

'I'm fine.' Madge smiled. 'I'm doing everything the nurses
tell me. Sure I'll be right as rain in no time. Come here, Seamie.
Give us a hug.'

Gingerly, Seamie put his arms around her. 'Hello, Aunt
Madge. We've brought you some presents,' he said.

A nurse in a blue uniform popped her head around the door
and asked if they'd like a cup of tea. 'Of course they would,'
Madge told her, and lay back against her pillows.

'She's coming on great, isn't she?' The nurse spoke with
high-pitched enthusiasm as if Madge weren't present. 'No more
draining tubes. She takes her meals. A little at a time, isn't that
right, Madge? Sure you'll be home before you know it.'

'I'll go to Sadie for a while,' Madge said to Pauline. 'It's
quiet there.'

When the nurse returned with the tray she gave Madge a
glass of orange juice.

'I'm thirsty all the time,' Madge said.

'It's the drugs,' the nurse said.

'Everything is the drugs,' Madge said, drifting into that
half-light between sleeping and waking, her mind confused
with half-remembered conversations, phrases, arguments, memories. Slowly, she began telling Seamie about her childhood in

Glencove and Seamie, settling into his chair beside her, listened enthralled.

The Glencove of Madge's youth had been smaller, a village in those days set snug into the Wicklow hills, its church and houses facing the sea. When the herrings were in, she would sit on the low garden wall of their farm and watch the fishing boats sail home, heavy and slow with the weight of their catch. As the harbour lights twinkled in the gathering dusk she would run down to meet her father off the *Grainne Maol* and help him with the gutting, her fingers deft. In the gathering darkness they would walk home, hand in hand, a gleaming dead eye peeping from the reed bag under her father's arm, the air strong with the fishy smell. Her mother would fry the herring in butter, or stuff it with oatmeal and bake it in the oven. Jars of pickled herring lined the pantry.

Pauline walked briskly through the hospital gates with the silent Seamie, her sadness hastening her steps, the bracing air on her face making her eyes smart. She stood gulping in the air, anaesthetising herself against the shock of having seen Madge so ill. Somehow she had always assumed that Madge was indestructible. Seamie, too, loved her, and out in the clear, open space he made no attempt to hide his tears.

It was a cold, blustery afternoon as Eve walked along the ridge. The sky was leaden, and a bitter wind blew in from the sea. She stopped to gaze over the dark waters, and the grey clouds on the horizon. Head down, she walked on, the collar of her coat turned up against the stiff wind, her scarf tight around her neck. The crunch of footsteps behind her made her turn round.

'Hello,' Henry said. 'Having a last look at the cove?'

'How did you guess?'

'I saw you pass by and thought I'd catch up with you.' He gave her a piercing look. 'Mind if I join you?'

Eve felt the awkwardness between them. They had never spent much time in each other's company, had never been alone together. When Henry started talking about New York, telling her about the hotel he stayed in and the places he had visited, she listened and the camaraderie of their youth returned as they trudged along. 'I'll be going over in the spring. To study Alzheimer's disease. Maybe we could have dinner together.' Though his voice was casual, his eyes were earnest.

'That'd be lovely.' A small shock of pleasure coursed through Eve at the thought. Then, guiltily, she said, 'Maybe you'd come and have dinner with us.' But it was too late. She knew, by the way he leaned closer to her, looked into her face, that he'd seen her eagerness.

There was no word from Scully. Pauline felt that the longer he stayed away the less of a threat he would be. There was no word from Geoff Ryan either but he was constantly on her mind: the way he kicked pebbles out of his way as he walked along, the slap of his hand on the counter when he was making a point. Thinking of his hands made her burn with longing. Those large, work-roughened hands, agile at the wheel of a crane, sinewy with a trowel piling brick upon brick. Strong, capable hands that had stroked her so gently.

Eve and she had talked about Geoff's defection. Pauline's feelings fluctuated between pride, bitterness, and self-pity. Eve thought that he had come to realise what he might be committing himself to if he took on a woman like Pauline. A woman who would never be dictated to, and who would never be content as a full-time wife. She'd always want a job of her own. But Geoff, the respectable contractor, would need to prove to himself and his neighbours that he could maintain a wife on his salary and at a decent standard, Eve contended. That was a side of him that at first Pauline had liked. She saw his values as solid and comforting. 'Perhaps my mistake was that I thought he was there for the taking on my terms,' she admitted. 'That I could continue to live my life as I pleased.'

One cold Saturday afternoon, at the end of January, Pauline stood in the playing-fields with a small group of spectators watching Seamie play in a Gaelic football match. Head thrust forward, lithe body curved, he leaped into the air and headed the ball into the net. The thud as he fell to the ground, the fields ringing with cheers, assured her that she had done the right thing in sending him away to school. He had settled down. Was 'fitting in', as Father Raphael had said, his shrewd, perceptive eyes on Pauline. Still she watched over him, terrified that he would float away from her in his new-found independence. Although he tried to act grown-up, he was still only a child and needed her to watch over him. These days, though, she seemed to be watching him all the time.

Driving home, the pale green fields blurring into dark mysterious shapes she was thinking about Geoff again. Often, in the dark, she lay suspended between sleep and wakefulness imagining his face beside her on the pillow, hollow cheeks carved like stone, mouth rigid in sleep, jaw arrogant. With the soft light of dawn he was lost to her.

Back at the pub she showered, put on her makeup, dressed for work. Her white blouse was creased and needed a lick of the iron so she tackled her makeup first. When she heard footsteps on the stairs she checked her watch, expecting it to be Tommy, reporting for work. How many times had she told him not to come upstairs but to phone through?

'Is that you, Tommy?' She went out onto the landing, taking her blouse with her to iron it in the kitchen.

Downstairs, facing her, his back to the range, hat in hand, was Mr Duval.

Pauline, in her bra and skirt, stood clutching her blouse to her bosom. 'Mr Duval!' she said, turning away hurriedly to put on her creased blouse.

'Forgive me if I frightened you,' he said.

'I didn't know you were in town.' Pauline buttoned her blouse, her eyes on his highly polished shoes.

'Scully is coming back,' he said, rocking back and forth on his heels.

'Who told you?'

'I have reliable sources.' His steely eyes didn't invite any more questions. 'Make sure to meet him when he contacts you. I am relying on you to get my money back.'

'When does he intend getting in touch with me?'

'Very soon.'

Pauline shivered.

Mr Duval noticed. 'Do whatever you have to do to get it. Otherwise there'll be trouble.' The warning flash in his eyes and the threat in his voice emphasised his words.

Pauline felt the room shift. For a split second she stood stock still, breathing fast, trembling.

'Now I mustn't keep you from your work. I'll see myself out.' With a nod, he was gone.

The next evening Father McCarthy came into the bar as soon as it opened. 'I hear Madge is getting on well,' he said to Pauline.

'She's making a great recovery. Going to her cousin Sadie's to convalesce,' Pauline told him.

'Good, good,' he said, looking around. Then he said, in a low voice, 'I hear you're in a spot of bother, Pauline.'

'Me, Father?' Pauline's face flamed.

He picked up the glass of whiskey she'd put in front of him, held it up to the light and twirled it before taking a sip. Pauline watched his throat as he swallowed.

'This is a serious matter. You may not know it but you're being watched,' he said. 'There are ruthless people walking around with no thought of God or their fellow man, Pauline. Be careful.'

'How do you mean, Father?'

'You must ensure that you don't get caught up in offences against the law of God or the laws of the state, for that matter. I don't mean to frighten you but I thought, perhaps, that it might be wise if you should talk to somebody. I have a great friend in the Pro Cathedral who is very sympathetic. Go to confession to him. Rid yourself of all the things that have been troubling you and let him advise you.'

'But I haven't been to confession for years, Father.'

'Go and ask God to grant you the courage to resist evil, overcome your weaknesses, turn away from all that endangers your immortal soul. Meantime, I will pray to our divine merciful Father to grant you the grace of a good confession and peace of soul.' He raised his eyes heavenward. 'Forgive them, Father, for they know not what they do,' he prayed, under his breath.

'Right, Father. I'll go. Maybe I'll feel better afterwards.'

'Of course you will.' Father McCarthy looked pleased as he finished his drink and made for the back door.

Pauline followed the priest out into the moonlight. He looked cold, unreal, like a statue, as he said, 'My friend, Father Gilhooley, will be there tomorrow evening at six o'clock. Second confessional on the left aisle. You'll see his name up over it. I'll tell him to expect you.'

'Thank you, Father.'

He was walking away, turning quickly under the branches of the tall trees. Pauline stared helplessly after him. Then she went through the side gate and stood in the weed-filled yard, haunting in its silence, the feeling of impending doom all pervasive. That same feeling she'd had before that someone was watching her.

The next evening she took the bus into the city, not wanting to drive home in rush-hour traffic. Fumbling in her purse for change she caught sight of her reflection in the window, flitting past the convent where she had met Geoff.

A group of girls with school-bags and hockey-sticks got on the bus at Bray, devilment in their flushed faces as they rushed forward to grab seats, chattering in excited voices. A big girl slid in beside Pauline, who moved closer to the window.

'Thanks,' the girl said, continuing her conversation with her pal in front, and Pauline turned back to her reflection. The reflection of a murderer, which reminded her always of that haunting night. The night she relived every time someone knocked at her door, or a stranger stopped her in the street. The night she paid for every day she lived.

The squeal of brakes as the bus stopped at the terminal in O'Connell Street jolted her back to the present. It was five to six. In another ten minutes she would have reached her destination. Frost hung in the air and the thin cries of the newspaper boys echoed at street corners. Buses rumbled over the bridge in the evening dusk where grim-faced, ragged children, their small hands outstretched, begged for money.

In contrast to the lighted shop-fronts of the busy thorough-fare, Marlborough Street was in deep shadow. The drone of the city traffic receded as she mounted the steps of the cathedral. At the main door heavy-breathing men were carrying out a coffin, a priest following them, his face obscure. Behind him, women dressed in black held each other up, their silence broken only by the sound of muffled weeping.

The inside of the church was dark, lit only from the side altars and the candles that burned before the statues. Pauline moved down the aisle, slid into the confession box.

The priest was already seated there, the shape of his head framed in the grille. As soon as she knelt down he said, 'How long since your last confession?'

'About eleven years.'

'I see.' He nodded. 'Did you attend the sacrament of the Eucharist during this time?'

'Occasionally, Father.'

'You were not in a state of grace.'

'No Father.'

'Now, tell me, my child, what was the act that kept you out of the Divine Light?'

'I ...' Unable to form the words, Pauline looked at the downcast face, the bristles of the beard, the hard mouth. The pious priest behind the grille was no representative of God. It was Scully. She got to her feet, groping, staggering backwards. That minute God ceased to exist for Pauline Quirk as reality flared.

'Wait,' he hissed. Then in a whisper, 'Pauline, wait.'

She was walking away.

'Pauline!'

She wheeled around. Scully, in white surplice, caught her arm, led her to a side altar. She shook off his hand. 'Who the hell do you think you are, stalking me, demanding—'

Scully moved stiffly, pushing her ahead of him. 'I had to see you,' he said, through gritted teeth.

'Here! Of all places! Dressed up like that! You're despicable.' She was half walking, half running away from him, wanting only to be free of the long-repressed sorrow and guilt.

He caught up with her. 'Not advisable,' he said. His right hand jerked upwards and she saw that he was holding a gun. He was going to kill her. For an instant everywhere seemed stuffy and overbright as the blood rushed to her head. Her body falling against the cold, hard pew made Scully reach out and grab her. 'Steady,' he said, breathing sharply. Slowly, he lowered his arm and put away the gun.

For a minute neither of them spoke. Pauline was rooted to the ground, her eyes on Scully's face, transformed by the bristly beard.

'You'd be very foolish to run off,' he said. 'Be under no illusions. One careless move on your part ...' He smiled enigmatically. 'Come into the curate's house,' he said. 'We'll have a quiet drink.'

Dumbfounded, Pauline followed him. In the sitting room Scully went to the glass cabinet, took out a bottle of Cork Dry Gin and a bottle of tonic water. He poured drinks for them both.

'Sit down, have this,' he said, handing a glass to her.

She took it, with the feeling that she was going to need it. 'What are you doing here?' she asked, her hand trembling as she lifted the glass to her lips.

'I'm here for a funeral. Incognito, of course.'

'Where does Father Gilhooley come into it?' Pauline looked around.

'He got my message to Father McCarthy.'

'So, Father McCarthy's in this too?'

Scully hesitated. 'He knows I'm back, and, like the others, he's getting anxious about the money. Father Gilhooley asked him to make sure you got here.' Scully finished his drink and poured himself another. 'I didn't trust you after you ran out on me in Zürich. I hid in the confessional in case you took one look at me and ran off again.'

'You hardly expected me to hang around waiting for you to get arrested.'

Scully shrugged. 'I managed. I stayed well out of the way until the dust settled. But things went badly wrong. That's why I'm here. I need your help, Pauline.'

'What is it this time?' she asked, exasperated.

Scully sat back looking at her. 'I mind the first time I ever laid eyes on you. You were wearing a short blue dress and I couldn't take my eyes off you. I remember you were so nervous that you wouldn't sit down.'

'Would you blame me?'

'I said something that made you laugh. It was love at first sight for me. When we were alone we used to talk a lot, remember? I told you my life story, my plans. You listened. I knew nothing about you except that you were a girlfriend of Martin's.'

'Ex-girlfriend,' Pauline corrected.

'I knew he didn't stand a chance with you.' He was watching her intently.

She kept her head bowed, remained silent, listening.

'I found Martin the night I arrived back in Belfast after I'd been in London, on that difficult job, I might add. I remember waiting at the station for the train home, thinking I had enough money to get Martin and myself away from there for a while. I was elated about that because things were getting very tricky in Belfast, as you know. You were at that rally, remember?'

Pauline nodded.

'I'd been depressed about having to leave you behind to go on that assignment and was looking forward to seeing you again. It was a hot, sticky night, a night I'll never forget as long as I live. When I walked into the flat I was met by the devastation, Martin's body blasted to pieces. At first I thought it was the enemy and that you had been taken in for questioning. When I went into your bedroom, saw the open drawers, Martin's gun on the floor, I suspected you had killed him. I knew that if it *was* you I'd cover up for you. So I hid the gun.' Scully closed his eyes, sighed. 'I also knew that there was no hope of anything happening between us.' He lit a cigarette and continued. 'I phoned a few of the lads, had a bit of a send-off for Martin. While the others were getting drunk I sat out on the balcony in the moonlight, my head between my knees, sick, grieving for my friend, weeping for you. I thought my world had come to an end.' He looked at her, tears in his eyes. 'You see, I loved you, Pauline.'

Pauline stared disbelievingly at him. He had stopped talking, and in the silence that followed he sat with his eyes downcast, his mouth sagging.

'I had no idea,' she said, feebly. How, in God's name, she wondered, did he ever get the impression that she could have fancied him?

'It's true. I was even beginning to resent Martin. I wanted you all to myself, knowing that you were the worst possible choice for me. I couldn't help it.'

It was all coming back to Pauline. Snatches of conversation they'd had about love, she telling him that Seamus had never suspected that Scully was in love with her. She had never loved him, never would – and he was about to make her pay for it, she suspected.

He laughed again, a laugh full of the memories of past enjoyment. Then his expression changed to annoyance. 'There are women like you, Pauline, who specialise in making men fall in love with them. It's the way they function.'

Pauline thought of all the boys and men who smiled at her, opened doors for her, let her have their seat on a bus or train. It had never occurred to her that it was because of her looks. As far as she was concerned she was too tall and gangly, her nose too prominent. And she remembered a weak moment in Switzerland, in Berne, when she had confided in Scully her feelings for Geoff.

Scully poured himself another gin and tonic and sat fiddling with his glass. 'All the time you were in the States I waited for you. I knew from Agnes Dolan that you were back. I called to the pub a couple of times. Watched you. Saw you coming out of the convent one day. I could have told you there and then who I was, but I wanted to watch you for a while longer, make sure that I wasn't still in love with you.' He stopped, looked her straight in the eye. 'Far from loving you, I loathed you. Loathed your beauty and your weaknesses.'

As he was making his strange confession, pouring out his soul, Pauline thought that love had little to do with his feelings. She was afraid to say this to him.

'I suppose I knew then that it was a love that could never be fulfilled.' He was getting drunk, his speech garbled yet he was telling the truth.

It was frightening to be loved by someone you did not love in return. What if Scully were to go to Geoff and convince him that there had been something between himself and Pauline?

She looked at him again. Now there was no hatred in his face, just detached reflection and withdrawal: his mind was still focused on the past. Pauline, reluctant to start him off again, kept quiet.

When he finally came out of his reverie he said, 'I need your help,' in a quiet, controlled voice. 'There's a lot at stake.'

'That's your problem,' she replied.

Scully got up and stood over her. 'You listen to me. This is important. The situation is dangerous.'

'To whom?'

'To both of us. I mean business, Pauline. That money we exchanged in Zürich was counterfeit.'

'I know. Your friend, Mr Duval told me. He's been looking for you.'

'Don't worry about him. Now, the real money is hidden in one of the rooms at the Glencove, and I want you to get it for me.'

'Which?'

'Twenty-one.'

'But that's not in use. It's kept for Eve and the family.'

'I managed to get a duplicate key to it when I was working there – for your boyfriend – after we finished at the convent. All you have to do is get in and get the money for me. Obviously I can't do it myself.'

'What about Mr Duval? What if he's watching me?'

'As far as he's concerned I'm not due home for another couple of days. If you get to the hotel first thing in the morning we'll have given him the slip.'

'You're good at this.'

'I've no intention of letting anything go wrong this time.

I've just got to get to tomorrow morning and then I'm off. They won't catch up with me this time.'

Pauline buried her face in her hands. 'Do you know,' she said when she looked up, 'before you came on the scene I had a perfectly good life. You've made a complete mess of it.'

'No, Pauline,' he contradicted her. 'You're carrying far too much guilt for life ever to be perfect for you.'

Furious, Pauline said, 'Let's stay on our best behaviour until this is all over and done with. What about the masked men who were looking for you? They said they'd be back too.'

'I suppose they will,' Scully said, his voice tightening. 'But I'll be away. Now,' he said. 'This is the plan. You'll go to the hotel early tomorrow morning, before anyone is up. Park out of sight. Speak to no one. If anyone stops you, act normal, say hello, but don't say you're looking for me. Keep going. There's a small brown briefcase hidden in a panel behind the pipes. Get it, drive it to Rosslare. Take your time, don't rush. I don't want you to draw attention to yourself. Meet me at the Old Tree pub there at around eleven o'clock. We're getting the six o'clock ferry. You'll carry the money the way you did before.'

'Rosslare! The ferry!'

'You don't think I'd risk Customs at Dun Laoghaire, or the airport? This is the last time, I promise. After this you'll never have to see me again.' He stood up. 'I'll be waiting for you. One more journey and you'll be as free as a bird.'

'And if I don't do it?'

He tapped the revolver in the belt of his trousers. 'Any funny tricks from you and I'll give you what you gave Martin.' He laughed humourlessly. 'That is a promise.'

She stood up to go. He patted her shoulder and said, 'You get a good rest tonight. You'll need it.'

She walked briskly to the bus stop, the wind whistling around her. The moon rode high, wrapping the city in an icy glow. She cupped her hands to her mouth and blew out her breath to warm them.

Chapter Twenty-Seven

'You're off early this morning,' Eve said to David, endeavouring to sound cheerful, already hating New York.

'New business. More than we can handle,' he said, draining his coffee cup, putting files into his briefcase.

'Don't work too hard,' she said sarcastically, clearing away the breakfast dishes and calling to Katie to hurry up or she'd be late for school.

'Try to have a nice day,' he said, equally sarcastic. 'Find something to do.'

Eve swung around from the kitchen sink. 'I'm trying. I really am trying,' she said. 'Give me a little more time. Let's go out somewhere together soon, on our own, no clients.'

'I can't this week. I'm flying to Miami tomorrow. Next week? We'll do something then, I promise,' he said, and kissed the top of her head.

Eve turned away.

'Come on,' he said, coaxingly, putting his arms around her. 'I'll make it up to you when I get back.'

'It's all right,' she said.

'Look, I've got to go now. We'll talk later.'

'What about?'

'This tension, strain, whatever it is you're going through.'

'What I'm going through,' Eve blazed, 'is to do with this place, your job, our marriage.'

'Calm down,' he said. 'You're overreacting to everything.'

'And you're working too hard.'

'I love my job.'

'That's part of the problem and until you recognise it there's no point in us talking about anything. Anyway, don't worry about me. I've got plenty of things to do,' she lied, turning off the radio, making for the cloakroom, getting out the coats.

'Wrap up warm. It's cold out there,' David said, and planted a kiss on Katie's cheek when she appeared.

'I know,' Eve said.

They hunched into their jackets, the wind whipping around them as they opened the front door.

'I'll phone you later to see how you are,' David called as he got into his cab.

It snowed as they walked through the Upper West Side to Katie's school. Although it was only a block away the bitter cold made the walk unpleasant. Since coming here both David and she had lost their spontaneity. Perhaps it was the treacherous weather, which made everything seem such an effort, or perhaps it was the unsafe neighbourhoods. Whatever the reason, she had lost faith in their marriage. On the way home, she thought of her dead baby, then of how Katie must be missing her grandparents, and Tabby. She thought of the hotel, her abandoned career ... Henry, his open face, his passion. At that moment she would have done anything to feel his strong arms around her.

Since her arrival in New York she had made friends at her A.A. meetings but she had been unable to shake off her loneliness and isolation, which was slowly turning into a depression that worried David. She was tired of his endless questions: their late-night conversations always ended in rows, his anger with her for not snapping out of her misery barely contained. She winced when she thought of their mechanical love-making. It was driven by David's own desires without a thought for hers. Or so it seemed.

Back in the apartment she made a cup of coffee and sat by the radiator, staring out at the snow. It was turning into a blizzard. In the beginning David had taken her to dinner with some of his Wall Street friends, and had urged her to go out shopping. He had even suggested she join a tennis club or a gym. Now she wondered if his shuttered expression in the evenings when he returned from work, his deliberate tolerance, would drive her mad.

The phone rang. 'Eve. It's Henry. I'm in New York. Can we meet?'

'Henry! I was just thinking about you.'

'How are you? Settling down?'

'Trying to.' Eve made an effort to sound cheerful.

'Let's have dinner tomorrow night?'

'I'd love to. But David'll be away and—'

'Great. Meet me at Grand Central Station, eight o'clock.'

He hung up before she had a chance to argue.

What harm would it do to have dinner with Henry? she thought the next evening as she rummaged through her wardrobe and picked out a turquoise Frank Usher sheath dress she'd bought before she left Ireland. That afternoon Estelle, her hairdresser, had done her hair, pinning it back in a chignon. In the cab she felt guilty about what she was doing – and David had an instinct for hidden emotions: he would know if she were suffering from guilt.

At Grand Central Station she waited outside walking up and down, wrapped against the icy wind. 'Eve.' Henry was loping towards her in clothes too gaudy to wear in Glencove. Her heart leaped as he kissed her hard on the lips in full view of the throng heading for various destinations.

'Not here,' she said, pulling away, glancing around to see if anyone was watching them.

The restaurant he took her to was busy, and over dinner they talked. Henry sat opposite her and told her all the news from home. Then he asked her about her new life in New York.

'There's not much to tell,' she said, thinking of her misery. 'I take Katie to school, walk through the park, make sure everything at home is running smoothly while David works himself to death.'

'It won't last for ever.'

'David thinks we might stay on indefinitely. He's anxious to build up a strong link here, and he doesn't approve of me going home soon either. He thinks I should make more of an effort to settle down.' Eve said.

'New York's not such a bad place when you get used to it.'

'It's all right for a visit, I agree. I bet you're having a ball.'

'I'm enjoying myself now,' he said, taking her hand. 'I'm in an exciting city with a beautiful woman.'

They ate their meal, while Henry talked about his new ventures but his eyes signalled that he couldn't bear to sit there much longer. That he'd die if he didn't have her soon. At last he called for the check, saying, 'Let's get out of here,' and took her hand to lead her out with boyish exuberance.

'Where are we going?' she asked, as he walked into the middle of the street to flag down a cab.

'My hotel,' he said, taking her hand, ushering her into the cab. 'It'll be all right,' he assured her, seeing her hesitate. He gave the cab driver the address. 'I'll have you home before dawn,' he said, as they set off.

'No,' Eve shouted, so loud that the cab driver screeched to a halt and gazed into his rear-view mirror.

'Make up your mind, ma'am! Going to his place or not?' he asked.

'Sorry,' Eve said, and stumbled out.

Henry followed. 'What's up?' he asked, leaning against the window, his brows knitted.

'Henry, I'm sorry. I can't do it,' she said. 'It's not that I don't . . .' She faltered. 'I'd better go home.'

'Home!' Henry said, puzzled. 'But it's only eleven thirty. I thought you . . . we . . . What's the matter?'

'I've changed my mind.'

'Hey, you can't do this, Eve.' His hands manacled her wrists. 'We've got a thing for each other. You know we have.'

'There's too much at stake. Let me go. Please, Henry,' she said.

'You heard the lady,' the cab driver bellowed. 'She's changed her mind. She wants to go home.'

Henry let go of her wrists, jumped back into the cab and slammed the door. She hailed a cab for herself, and sat staring out of the window all the way home. She was relieved that he was gone, yet sad that she'd destroyed their evening.

'Here you are, ma'am,' the cab driver said.

Avoiding his eyes, Eve opened her handbag and paid him.

'You OK, ma'am?' he asked, his eyes concerned beneath the peak of his cap.

'Yes, thank you,' she said, fumbling for her key.

'You sure you're all right?' the man asked again.

'Fine,' she said.

She escaped to the other side of the street, leaving him looking after her, and blundered up the steps of the apartment block, opened the hall door noisily, amazed to see the light in the window of David's study. He was in the hall, on his way to greet her. 'I had to cancel Miami,' he said, and waited for her to say something. When she did not, he asked, 'Had a good evening?'

'Yes, thank you,' she said, stiffly.

'It doesn't have to be like this, Eve.'

'There's nothing I seem able to do about it.'

'There's nothing you're willing to do about it,' David corrected.

When she woke up the next morning and saw David sleeping quietly beside her, she was overcome by sorrow. What was happening to them? They were so distant, like strangers.

Chapter Twenty-Eight

In her bedroom Pauline shut the door tight, opened the window and breathed in the night air. The moon was behind a bank of cloud, its light faint and scattered. If only it would snow, she thought, gazing at the pale, cold sky. Snow so heavily that everything would come to a halt and she would be incarcerated in Glencove, unable to travel with Scully.

When the faint light of dawn peeped through the curtains, she woke from a fitful sleep. She got out of bed, pulled back the curtains and peered out, inwardly railing at Scully and the next atrocity he was planning – and at herself for becoming his victim. She picked up the money-belts and her big sweater, then thought suddenly of Scully, sleeping soundly, his face composed, and how that composure would change if he discovered that she had sneaked off again. It strengthened her resolve to do his bidding.

Hands shaking she picked up her makeup from the dressing table and began to put it on. When she was ready, she went downstairs, opened the hall door, hesitated, then shut it behind her. Outside, there was no one in sight. As she walked to her car the last vestiges of defiance rose in her and she took a step back towards the house, her anger rising. Why should she do anything for Scully? Because she'd be dead if she didn't. She unlocked her car and slipped in behind the wheel, then drove down the dark road.

As she went past the river, silver in the early-morning light, she saw the milk float moving stealthily from house to house, its jingling bottles stark white. She wondered if she was destined to sneak around for the rest of her life. As she turned left she noticed a blue car following her. Automatically she pressed her foot on the accelerator and drove on. She turned into the Sea Road and the blue car came too. A White Heather laundry van, coming from the opposite direction, nipped in behind her, blocking her view. She whipped into the rear entrance of the Glencove Hotel, her brakes protesting at her sudden stop outside the back door.

Once inside she took the stairs two at a time and went along the corridor to Room 21. She opened the door, not making a sound, located the cupboard, climbed up on a chair, reached and removed the panel in front of the pipes. The briefcase was exactly where Scully had told her it would be. She opened it, emptied out the money, put it in neat bundles then transferred it to the money-belts. She strapped two around her waist, another across her chest. Finally she put on the big sweater again to cover the bulges. It took longer than she'd thought. When she'd finished she put the briefcase back in its hiding place, replaced the panel and shut the cupboard door.

She locked the room behind her, and went downstairs. The night porter greeted her as she walked through the lobby, and Greta, bleary-eyed, asked what she was doing there so early in the morning. Pauline greeted her with a smile, said she was running an errand for Eve, and went out of the door. She got into her car and drove out of the gates, frantically avoiding Jasper's black Jaguar, which was coming towards her.

When she reached the crossroads she took the road for Wicklow, her eyes darting to the rear-view mirror to see if she was being followed. The road stretched before her, a curved line cutting through the dark woods. She turned on the radio, tried to concentrate on the weather forecast, but her thoughts returned to Scully. She would deliver the money and go home. After that he would leave her alone.

She had come from being a lonely, desperate girl to a respected landlady in the Glencove community but Scully had brought back all the negative feelings she had thought were gone: the false starts, failures, contradictions. She was vulnerable again.

The sky cleared as she drove past Wicklow; dull in the grey morning. On the winding road she passed a herd of cows, heavy with milk, swaying from side to side. The smell of fresh dung was strong in the air. Further on, the landscape widened to encompass silent fields as the day brightened. Farmhouses dotted here and there rose out of the morning mist. Suddenly, she was a child again, no more than six years old, running wild, legs scratched, dress torn. Later, as a member of the gang she had roamed through the woods on summer evenings. Later still, she had tantalised the boys with thigh-hugging mini-skirts, too much makeup, and tottering high heels.

Her mother had made all her clothes until she became ill when Pauline was seven. She remembered the sewing machine on the wooden table in the sunny kitchen, and had a vague recollection of her mother's tired smile as Pauline stood to have a dress fitted. She could still remember her father's quick step at the back door, his cheerful smile, her mother clearing away her sewing to make space for the preparation of the evening meal.

Now Art Garfunkel was singing 'Bright Eyes', Seamie's favourite song. She had hardly recognised Seamie that first Sunday she visited him in his new school. He had come into the recreation hall, tall and gangly in his black school blazer and grey flannel trousers, awkward and diffident with her. Though their relationship was occasionally volatile, especially when he contradicted her, or swore at her under his breath, Pauline prided herself that it was close and happy. They were often physical with one another, sometimes wrestling or jostling, often embracing in a kind of rough and tumble. On his first visit home for Hallowe'en he'd been reticent about school life but during the Christmas holidays he had stretched out on the spare bed in her room at Aunt Bea's and talked about his routine at St Benedict's. He told her about the gym, the library, his teachers, the other lads, the games.

She passed tall hedgerows, trees, bushes. Scully had been so infuriatingly certain that he could keep her under his control. She was in deep trouble this time and she knew it. A soft target was what she was.

And then she remembered Geoff, the bitter expression on his face when he had said she knew nothing about love. What did *he* know about love that he should hold her in such contempt? He hadn't even given her a chance to explain herself. But was he right? As she passed through Gorey she thought of Martin, then Seamus: the sex, the fights, the lack of effort to control their basic needs, their youth, their final harrowing end. Had she made an effort with either of them? She had to admit that she hadn't. She had gone from one situation to another, letting her impulses take over most of the time.

She hadn't tried very hard with Madge either. Madge, standing at the cooker, humming along with the radio, the smell of rashers cooking under the grill. Madge pouring drinks, her blouse dipping into the beer, her skirt stretched over hips and buttocks, her garish lipstick making her mouth bigger as she argued about politics. Now Madge's life comprised long silences and inertia as she slept her life away.

The Old Tree pub in Rosslare was quiet. Only one customer, a man in a Frank Sinatra hat, slouched in a corner as if he'd been in that spot all his life. There was no sign of Scully. Pauline waited, sipping Coke, checking her watch every five minutes. By midday, when Scully hadn't appeared, she decided to return to Glencove. She paid for her drink walked slowly to the door, tired of her life, tired of all the pain. She'd go back to her flat and wait. As soon as she could get rid of Scully and his money she would have a long, badly needed sleep, then make a fresh start.

'Miss Quirk!' A voice cut through the air as she reached her car. Standing before her was the man in the hat whom she'd seen in the pub. 'Thought you'd got away with it?'

'Where's Scully?' she gasped.

'Mr Scully can't make it but, if you step this way with me, I'll relieve you of your burden.' He laughed at her shock.

'Who are you?'

'Never mind that, just hand over the money.'

She stood trapped in the small space. To her left a narrow path ran down by the side of the pub, secluded by a wall on one side and a hedge on the other. There was a queer feeling in her stomach. This was not an adventure. This was a matter of life and death. There was no hope that the man would give up and go. She wouldn't be that lucky. Numb with the enormity of her plight she willed herself to think, and think quickly. At that moment her only concern was her son.

The tall man led her down the path, over loose gravel, and in through a gate to a thicket. He stopped her as they approached a clump of trees. He stood, his gun poised, his mouth turned down at the corners. 'Scully thought he'd outwit us,' he said, 'but he was wrong. Now, where's the money?'

'I'm wearing it.'

Pauline saw the snake tattoo on his outstretched arm and recognised him as one of the masked men who'd invaded her flat – an enemy of Scully.

'Strip off in broad daylight?' she said, in a desperate bid to gain a little time to think.

'Shouldn't be any trouble to a girl like you.' His hand shook as he moved closer, the barrel of his gun inches away from her.

She tried to calm herself. This was not the end. If she could get out into the woods beyond the thicket and the trees, she might have a chance to escape him. 'Can I go behind that tree?' she asked, pointing to the nearest one in the field beside them.

Snakeman looked at it. 'Two minutes, and I'll be watching you all the time. I'll shoot if you try to escape.'

She opened the gate, and let it swing back as she made for the tree and hid behind it. She imagined Snakeman standing there, his chest heaving as he listened for sounds of her undressing. What was she to do? Scully would kill her if she didn't have the money for him. And where was he anyhow?

'Are you ready?' Snakeman's voice was rough.

'Not quite,' she called back, keeping her voice light.

She edged past the trees, and went further into the thicket, until she got to the path that led into the woods, still shrouded in morning mist. Everywhere was quiet. Bracken and twigs brushed her legs and tore at her jeans and she had to watch her footing. Further into the woods the mist thickened and she heard a faint rustling sound to her left. She stopped and listened. All was still, save for the twittering of sparrows. She continued, terrified that the snapping twigs would draw attention to her. The bottoms of her jeans were wet and clung to her ankles.

Encouraged by the distance she was putting between Snakeman and herself, she quickened her pace, her fear diminishing. Deeper into the woods she felt enclosed in her own little world, everything else far away. Suddenly, the sun broke through the clouds, glittering on dewdrops, dispersing the mist. The air grew warm and thick, the money-belts heavier.

When eventually she came to a gap in the trees, she saw a clearing, and beyond that a wide, open field and a line of houses that led back to the town and safety.

Standing still, the leaves of the trees moving around her, dappled green in the light, she rested, proud of herself. Pigeons cooed and birds sang as she took a narrow path to the clearing, ducking among low branches, climbing over brambles and thorny bushes, bending with great difficulty, the houses in the distance becoming more distinct. She heard a sound, and turned rapidly to her left. Moving back into the shelter of the woods, she crouched, waiting, praying that it was an animal.

The snapping of twigs, and parting branches made her jump. Snakeman stood there, his gun pointed at her.

'Thought you'd give me the slip, did you?' he said. 'I know these woods like the back of my hand.'

She stood up shivering.

'You're wanted by the police,' he said.

'How do you know?'

Her stomach churned as he came closer.

'You made a mistake in taking up with Scully. He's a bad lot. The best way to exonerate yourself is to hand over the money and get out of here as fast as you can. Now come here.'

She moved a bit closer, sinking to the ground and starting to remove her jumper as she groped for a stick or a big stone.

'Hurry up, or I'll have to undress you myself,' he said.

She could see the sweat trickling down his forehead. Another couple of steps and he was beside her. Panic-stricken she picked up a stump of wood, jagged at one end.

'OK,' she said, rising, her hand behind her back, pretending to fiddle with her bra strap. The instant he relaxed she sprang, aiming the stick at his skull, but only delivering a glancing blow that knocked him sideways.

As he regained his balance she flailed out again, bringing it down on his head, but this time he dropped the gun from his hand as he fell. Panting, he scrabbled for it and she lunged forward with new strength, hitting him as hard as she could. Hitting, hitting, hitting.

'Ha!' he cried, his hands covering his head. 'You won't get away with this. You're done for—'

A black car came tearing up the far side of the field, siren blaring, gardai jumping out, running ahead, skipping over stones and clumps of bushes to get to her. She leaned against the tree, waiting, the sweat trickling down her back, her big woollen jumper off, the money-belts around her waist exposed.

'Hello, officer,' she said, to the burly guard who approached her.

He stopped, stared at her and the groaning man who, by now, had risen and was holding his hat to the side of his blood-splattered face. 'She deliberately attacked me,' he complained, before the guard had a chance to say anything.

Another car came tearing up the road.

'Miss Quirk,' the guard said. 'I'm from the Special Branch Division. I'm arresting you on suspicion of transporting money for illegal purposes and on suspicion of membership of the IRA.'

With a great sense of relief Pauline removed the money-belts and handed them to him.

Chapter Twenty-Nine

'I'm going home,' Eve said to David, when he returned from work late one evening.

'Home?' David said, looking at her searchingly. 'But we've only been here a couple of months.'

'Mummy phoned. Pauline's in trouble. She's been arrested. I'm not sure what for,' Eve said.

'Why am I not surprised?' David said, ironically.

'You don't know anything about it.'

'I always knew Pauline Quirk had unsavoury connections. What does surprise me is you rushing back to be with her, leaving me here in our new home.' He stopped to gaze around at the sparsely furnished hall, the bare walls, bare floor. 'This move won't work if you're not prepared to give it a go.'

'I told you, there's a crisis.'

'I don't want you to go. I don't want you mixed up with Pauline Quirk.' His voice had an edge to it.

'She's stood by me all these years. And she's my friend.'

'Look, Eve.' David came close to her. 'I'm asking you not to go. If you run home every time there's a spot of trouble we'll never settle down, be a real family. I'd like us to have another baby. Wouldn't it be lovely for Katie to have a sister or brother?'

'I don't want more kids yet. Certainly not in New York.'

The thoughts of pushing a trolley up and down the aisles of the supermarket, a slobbering baby in front, appalled her. Up until now she had made David use contraceptives, which he hated. A new baby would bring post-natal depression and sleepless nights. She had begun to make excuses not to make love. She was tired, her period was overdue, she had a headache.

'You're frigid,' David had said resentfully one night. 'Or else you don't fancy me any more.'

'I'm going to bed now,' she said, wishing he'd stop talking and let her.

He smiled unpleasantly as he allowed her to pass. 'Anything to avoid a confrontation.'

She began to climb the staircase.

'We've got to talk, Eve.' David's voice was insistent. 'Running back home isn't going to solve your problems.'

She pretended not to hear him, went into the bedroom, shut the door and locked it. Much later she heard him knock. 'Eve,' he called, 'could you open the door, please?'

'Sleep somewhere else,' she retorted.

For the first time in their marriage she was sending him away from their marital bed.

When she apologised the next morning she made the situation worse: David thought she had decided not to go home. When he found her packing that evening, he said, 'I thought you'd changed your mind!'

'I haven't.'

'Eve, I'm trying hard to make things work,' he said.

'And I'm not?'

'Not since we came out here. In fact, you seem to have disconnected yourself from me altogether.'

'And you're so tied up with your business that you've no time for me,' she said, flinging clothes into her suitcase.

Next morning Katie woke him in the spare room, jumping

all over him, telling him they were leaving soon, asking him to come with them.

'I'll take you to the airport,' David said to Eve, when he got downstairs.

They drove through the busy streets, Katie chattering excitedly about seeing her grandpa again. 'Why are you not coming with us, Daddy?' she asked fretfully.

'I have to work, darling. But you'll be back soon.'

'I'll call you when I get there,' Eve said, holding his arm, scared of what the anger between them might do to them if it continued.

He nodded. 'Be good for Mummy,' he said to Katie and kissed her.

'I will,' she said, and waved as he pulled away from the kerb.

Throughout the flight, Eve decided that if she could find something useful to do in New York, everything would be all right. But perhaps it was more complicated than that. A coldness had developed between David and herself that had never been there before: maybe their love for one another had gone. And what about Henry? In him she had seen the chance of escape from the tedium that had come into her life since she stopped working. She thought about their last meeting and felt guilty again: she had wanted him. Of that there was no doubt. She had wanted the passion and tenderness he had offered so openly.

Henry was an exciting man, but Eve doubted that he would bother speaking to her again after the way she had treated him in New York. And now she knew all about love. She knew that it was sentimental, inconsistent and capricious. A cold comfort most of the time.

Pauline was delivered to the small dark interview room in Glencove Gardai Station, where she sat waiting, eyes puffy, head in her hands. Suddenly the door opened and the room was flooded with light. Getting to her feet she found herself facing a tall guard who said, 'Hello, Miss Quirk, I'm Superintendent Treacy. You have not been formally charged but I'll be taking your statement. First there's someone to here to see you.'

Sergeant Enright came into the room. Pauline steeled herself for his wrath. It didn't come. 'Pauline,' he said, facing her, his uniform ill-fitting, a pinched look on his face.

They sat down opposite one another, awkward in the glaring silence.

'I'll leave you to it,' Superintendent Treacy said, and left.

'Well,' Sergeant Enright said, clearing his throat as if to try to loosen his tongue, 'this is a bad state of affairs. Under Section four of the Criminal Justice Act you can be interviewed for up to six hours. You'd better have a good reason for being in the possession of all that money.'

'How did the guards know where to find me?' Pauline asked.

'They were tailing Scully. Knew he was back in the country for a funeral.'

He went on to explain that John Scully had been arrested that morning. 'He was on his way to meet you but the guards were waiting for him at the Old Tree pub. They tied him up and locked him in an outhouse, then waited to make contact with you. Luckily, someone saw them and alerted Johnny Timmons, the proprietor. He phoned the station. You led us straight to them.'

'I did!' Pauline scarcely recognised her own voice.

'You've been under surveillance for a while now, with suspicious characters like Duval calling to you at all hours of the night. God alone knows how you got mixed up in all of this.'

'How do you know about Duval?'

'He was arrested earlier too. Between them they're filling in the missing gaps. Scully's an evil piece of work. How you got in with him is beyond me. There's so much evidence stacked against him that he'll probably get life – and good enough for him.'

Pauline concentrated on her hands so that she would not cry as she listened to Sergeant Enright repeat the word 'life'. Their eyes met, his sad. He said, 'Once he's out of the way things will be easier for you.'

Pauline could no longer hold back the tears. 'It's much worse than you think, Sergeant. I don't know what to do,' she said. 'I can't cope.'

Sergeant Enright's eyes widened, as he searched her pale raised face. He whispered, 'Off the record, admit to nothing. And get yourself a good lawyer.'

Superintendent Treacy returned with another guard and a tape-recorder, which he switched on. 'This is my colleague Detective Sergeant Plunkett and this interview is being tape-recorded. You are not obliged to say anything, but anything you say may be taken down and given in evidence. You are entitled to legal representation at this point.'

'I'll leave you to it,' Sergeant Enright said to Pauline, giving her an encouraging pat on the back.

Superintendent Treacy said, 'Name and address please?'

'Pauline Quirk.'

'Speak up.'

'Pauline Quirk, Kinsella's Select Bar.'

'When were you born?'

'The twenty-fifth of March, nineteen forty-eight.'

'You do know why you are being arrested?'

'I'd like to talk to my solicitor, please.' Pauline choked on every word as tears streamed down her face.

'You can contact him or her at any time,' Superintendent Treacy said. 'You are here for questioning about transporting money for illegal purposes.'

Pauline met the Superintendent's eyes.

'When did you first meet John Scully?' he asked.

'In nineteen sixty eight, in Belfast,' she said, 'during my search for my boyfriend, Seamus Gilfoyle. During my enforced stay in Belfast.'

'Why did he choose you as a courier's aide?'

'He knew that if he threatened Seamie I'd do it.'

'Did you know the reason for the trip?'

'No.'

'Did you know what the money was for?'

'No.'

'Did you ask?'

'He wouldn't tell me.'

'The trip was not successful. You aborted the mission.'

'When I discovered that the money was for arms I left.'

'When did Scully contact you again?'

'Last week when he asked me to deliver money to him in Wexford.'

'You had no contact with him until then?'

'None.'

'Why did you agree to do that?'

'To get him out of my life, once and for all. I was sick of him and the people who were looking for him.'

'You are discharged for now due to lack of evidence, Miss Quirk. But we may need your help with further enquiries on this case. I would ask you not to leave the vicinity of Glencove, and to surrender your passport.'

Back at the flat, Pauline sipped a cup of strong tea, then lay on her bed, sleepless, crying. Overwhelmed with tiredness she finally fell asleep and dreamed that she was travelling on a train. All the other passengers were dressed in black and stared ahead. Suddenly she was catapulted out of her seat and flung against the steel bar of the door. Blood pumping from her head, she stumbled towards the other passengers. They didn't move, just stared ahead with sightless eyes. She yelled at them but they didn't seem to hear her. Her shrieks woke her up.

It was in all the newspapers. The front-page headline screamed: 'Glencove Woman Questioned about Transporting Money for Illegal Purposes.'

This kind of thing didn't happen in Glencove. People would ask themselves about her political affiliations. They would wonder why she had become embroiled in something so dangerous and if money had drawn her into it? She put down the newspaper, humiliated. There was no end to the damage that this would do. The limelight wouldn't last, but the memory and shame would stay in the minds and hearts of people long after the details were forgotten. Isn't that Pauline Quirk who was involved in selling arms? they would ask.

'Pauline?' Eve approached her friend and sat cautiously on the edge of her bed. 'It's me.'

Pauline's head lolled sideways as she stared vacantly at Eve. 'Eve! How did you get here?'

'I flew in this morning. Tommy told me to come up. You look ill. Shall I send for a doctor?'

'No,' Pauline whispered hoarsely, 'I'm not ill. I'm in deep trouble.'

'I know. I came home to help you,' Eve said, taking her hand and holding it tight.

'Oh, Eve!' Pauline said, breaking down. 'There's nothing you can do. No one can help me now. You heard what happened?'

'I only know what it says in the newspapers,' Eve said, stroking her friend's forehead. 'I don't believe a word of it.'

'It's true,' Pauline said. 'I was caught with money belonging to Scully. He forced me into it, Eve, and now that he's been arrested God knows what he'll tell them to save his own skin.' She shuddered.

Eve gripped her hand. 'Pauline, it can't be that bad.'

'It's worse than you think, Eve. Worse than anything you can possibly imagine.'

'I'll get you a good lawyer. Manus Corrigan will help me. He has all the right legal connections. He can arrange it.'

'It'll cost a fortune.'

'I'll go to see Harry Wise. Sell some of the hotel shares if I have to. We'll have you out of this in no time.'

But Pauline was in despair. 'Thanks, Eve, but as I said before it's worse than you know,' she said.

'It couldn't be so bad that you can't tell me.'

'Something terrible happened a long time ago,' Pauline muttered. 'Sergeant Enright said not to say anything.'

'I might be able to help.'

Pauline brought her clenched fists up to her face. 'I can't talk about it.'

Eve stared disbelievingly at her friend, who lay like a sick child, no fight left in her.

Pauline continued, 'Anyway you wouldn't want to know.' Her voice shook. 'And I don't care any more.'

'Rubbish,' Eve said. 'It's not like you to give up, Pauline. I'll be back later.'

When she came back, she left her engine running and dashed up to the flat. 'We've got to get the money for the criminal defence lawyer. According to Manus he'll cost a bomb. I'll go to Harry Wise or Mr Cummins. We'll give the hotel as collateral.'

'No,' Pauline said. 'I can't let you do that. This is my problem, Eve. I can't involve you in such a mess. I'll go to Aunt Bea first. She'll help me.' She looked at Eve. 'I think I'll die of shame,' she said.

'Nonsense,' Eve said. 'We'll talk this through. Come on, you're coming home with me.'

Everything happened so fast that all Pauline could remember afterwards was being led by Eve out of the pub and driving to Eve's house, stopping on the way to pick up fish and chips.

'I'm not very hungry,' Pauline said, when they got in.

'Try some anyway,' Eve coaxed, unwrapping the chips. 'It's a long time since we've eaten fish and chips like this,' she said, and poured wine for Pauline, mineral water for herself.

Slowly, sitting in the empty kitchen, Pauline told her story, sparing none of the details from the time she first met Martin, then Seamus, and the nightmare of Seamus's disappearance. She told Eve how she had been trapped in Belfast with Martin, how Martin's attempts to possess and control her had failed, but she did not confide her involvement in Martin's death. Eve's brow was knitted with concern for her friend. Pauline went on, 'You see, Martin was naïve enough to think that what we had once shared could be made new. But it was impossible. After that, I couldn't look at a man, couldn't bear to be touched by one, all the time I was living in the States, until I met Geoff. It was like a miracle. I began to live again. I'd given up hope of ever being able to have those feelings again. But with him I was able to let myself go. Then Scully turned up and spoiled everything.' Pauline hung her head.

'I had no idea,' Eve said.

'There were so many times when I wanted to talk to you. Spill it all out. But I was so ashamed.'

'What happened wasn't your fault. With crazy nuts like Martin Dolan messing up your life, how could you be blamed? You're a good woman, Pauline. You're a responsible mother, with a well-cared-for child.'

'Thank you,' Pauline said, grateful to have someone so positive on her side. 'What I dread most is having to explain it all to Seamie. I'm supposed to be collecting him from school tomorrow ... I don't know how I'm going to face him.'

'I'll bring him home for you,' Eve said. 'Then you can have a good talk before things go any further.'

When Seamie got home he was subdued. 'Joe Breen in my class showed me the newspaper article,' he said.

Pauline said, 'I'm so sorry you had to find out like this. I never dreamed—' She stopped, unable to continue.

'Mom, did you really transport arms?' Seamie asked, matter-of-factly.

She took a deep breath, then said, 'I accompanied Scully. I had no choice. It's done, it can't be undone. The sad thing is that it's what I'll always be remembered for.' She was unable to say the comforting things she wanted to say.

Seamie took a deep breath. 'I'll remember you for a lot more than that. I'll remember us together in Montauk and here in Glencove, the laughs and the jokes. I'll always remember how much I missed you when you came back to Ireland and when I went away to boarding-school.' Then he wiped his eyes with the back of his hand. 'I'm going to the cove. I'll see you later.'

'Seamie, you can't. It's pitch black out there.'

'I'll be all right,' he said, striding off.

Chapter Thirty

'Hello, Jasper,' Eve said, the last vestiges of confidence draining from her as she surveyed the foyer of the hotel. It was ablaze with light. Strains of music drifted from the lounge. Gone was the beige carpet she had had fitted before she went to New York. In its place was the finest marble floor that led to the new wing and gave an open, palatial feeling.

Jasper Furlong smiled at her. 'I've been expecting you. Come on,' he said, taking her arm. 'Let me show you around.'

Tightening his grip he guided her down the foyer, through the double door, along the corridor to the new dining room. Paintings from Jasper's house in Glencove lined the walls, and flower arrangements were placed here and there. When she saw elegant ladies in lavish gowns seated on gilt chairs next to men in evening dress, she gasped in shock. To one side was an enormous grand piano. A man in a dinner-jacket was playing a classical medley. This wasn't her hotel any more. She had stepped into another world, the world of the politically powerful, the socially prominent, the wealthy.

'Jasper, what have you done?' she said, feeling the curious glances in her direction.

'Nothing like opulence to attract the competition,' he said

with a maddening smile. 'This evening I'm hosting a dinner for the Industrial Development Association. You may join me if you like. And by the way, Eve, this mess your friend, Pauline Quirk, is in—'

'What about it?' Eve broke in.

'Well,' Jasper smiled at her benevolently, 'I'd appreciate it if you kept well out of it. It's a nasty business. Who knows what the outcome might be?'

'Who indeed?' Eve agreed. 'But Pauline needs me and I intend to be there for her.'

'Won't do your reputation any good. And you have a certain standing in the community.'

'That's the first time you've ever acknowledged it,' Eve said, defying him to caution her further, but Jasper was gazing around the room his smile fixed. He glimpsed someone he knew and waved as he said to Eve, 'Some of the country's foremost financial brains are here tonight. I must introduce you to them.'

Though outwardly calm, Eve's ears were ringing with tension and her mouth was dry. Beside her, Jasper surveyed the room, a satisfied look on his face. He was closing in on her business, determined not to let the hotel escape his grasp this time. Eve decided that now was not the time to tackle him and moved away to stand near the piano. But she was not going to relinquish the hotel to him without a fight, or stand by and let him snatch it.

'Waiting for someone?'

It was Henry Joyce, towering above her in a dinner-jacket. 'You look lost,' he said.

She bristled. 'I was just about to leave,' she said. 'I feel like an impostor in my own hotel.'

'Wait.' Henry's hand was on her arm. 'I let you go in New York,' he said, 'a mistake I'm not sure I want to repeat.'

They stared at one another, neither of them able to look away.

He said, 'I didn't know you were home.'

'It's a good job I am,' Eve replied. 'Not a minute too soon.'

Under Jasper's gaze she moved away from Henry, and went through the lounge to the foyer. Henry followed. 'Let's go somewhere quiet,' he said. 'You're obviously upset.'

'What about this dinner you're meant to be attending?'

'I don't think I'll be missing much,' he said, steering her towards the entrance.

'Why did you come back so soon?' he asked as they drove towards Wicklow.

'To be with Pauline,' she said.

He raised an eyebrow. 'What exalted circles you move in.'

Eve could feel her temper rising. 'Pauline's a good friend of mine.'

'Then you'll be here for a while,' he said, with a smile.

'Looks like it – and with Jasper Furlong up to his tricks again. He's got the worst mean streak of anyone I know. Look what he's done! He's changed the décor, taken away the old-world atmosphere. The place is unrecognisable.'

'He's spent a lot of money on it.'

'Without my permission. He took my grandfather's business and now he wants mine.'

'He's working very hard,' Henry said. 'He's there day and night. Why, I don't know. He can't envisage making a profit. It's too soon.'

'He's a shark. Financial gain is not his priority this time. He wants to enhance his standing and reputation in the town. Build up his clientele. The big man wants control.'

'Well, you'd better watch him then. When it comes to business there's no sentiment in Jasper. Not that he doesn't stick to the letter of the law. A man who knows as much as he does about private investment and trading has to be watched. And being married to his son won't influence him either.'

'I realise that. And I also know that it's impossible to run a business from the other side of the world.'

'Jasper knows that too.' Henry was thoughtful for a few minutes. 'If you were thinking of selling, Eve, I might be interested.'

Eve was amazed.

'The way it's done up now it would be ideal for a luxury leisure club.'

'Are you serious?'

'Never more serious in my life. Think about it. Meantime, I want to make love to you.'

'Henry!'

He laughed. 'There's no one listening,' he said.

For a moment she felt torn, the tension between them fuelled by her growing desire for him, thoughts of David, the child she'd had with him, and the one she'd lost. 'I can't,' she said finally.

Henry laughed. 'Relax, darling. Don't look so tragic. Perhaps we could meet in the city next week. See a play, go to a movie. Anything to get your mind off Jasper.'

'I promised Pauline I'd stay with her,' Eve said. 'I think she might be in for a tough time.'

'She could be, but you watch your own health. You have your own problems.'

'I'm all right. As long as I don't take a drink I'll cope.'

Pauline walked down Main Street in Glencove, past the bank and the craft shop next door to Eve's coffee-shop, where Bewley's coffee was advertised in gold letters on a red sign. The square outside the church was busy with Saturday-morning shoppers, some of whom stared at her. Walking past the church she felt people's eyes on her yet although she was frightened she felt removed from the scene, a spectator at someone else's tragedy. From then on she was afraid to venture out. At the front door each morning she put on the sunglasses she'd bought in Montauk but as soon as she stepped out on to the street she turned back and slammed the door behind her.

One night she ventured to the supermarket, but when she reached the checkout, Myrtle Thompson was behind her, her brows raised quizzically, deliberately avoiding Pauline's eyes. Pauline left her basket of groceries, pushed her way out and ran home, people staring after her. She felt like shouting at them, 'Ask me, go on ask me! Say what's on your mind!' But she didn't have the courage.

Eve saved her by forcing her out for walks, cooking meals for her, calling to the flat saying, 'Come on. Get up,' and hauling her out of bed, reminding her that she'd have to keep going for Seamie's sake.

Each night they walked for miles together in the dark, and slowly Pauline began to function again. She hung out the washing each morning, did the ironing while the radio blared hit tunes to keep her from thinking. She found it difficult to remember what day of the week it was and sank deeper and deeper into a world of isolation and fear: fear of the luminous dial on the clock announcing the coming of morning, fear of the knock on the door. As she lay in her bed, her arm over her head, the world around her was falling apart. Everything she had built up was crumbling: in the town, where rumours blew through the streets like the wind; in Ballingarret where Aunt Bea's thin lips were pressed together in an aggrieved silence; in Bray, where Geoff must be baffled by the revelations; and in Wexford, where Seamie was dreaming of the States and his little friend Patty – and where a silent Madge was harnessing her strength to return to her business.

Mr William Forde, of Forde and Son Solicitors, the foremost

firm dealing exclusively in criminal law, who retained the services of Lawrence Peterson-Smyth, a top criminal Junior Counsel in the Four Courts, approached Pauline. He led her across an expanse of carpet to his office in a Georgian house in Fitzwilliam Square. He was a short, robust man, with horn-rimmed spectacles, which gave an owlish appearance to his pleasant, if unreadable face. When he took both her hands in his, she was surprised at his gentleness. In his office he seated himself behind an enormous desk and consulted his papers. 'Let's get down to business,' he said. 'It's clear from what you've said that there are several issues here but we need to establish how exactly you got involved in all of this.' He looked expectantly at her. 'I'm afraid I'll have a lot of questions to ask you. I must prepare a case for Counsel, Mr Peterson-Smyth, before I arrange a consultation in the Law Library in due course.'

'Yes.'

He began by asking her what she did for a living, went on to her first meeting with John Scully and her relationship with him during her time in Belfast. Frowning slightly, he made notes while she talked. He asked her how long altogether she had known Scully and how many months she had spent in Belfast. How she had spent her time. When he looked up, he said, 'Sorry about all the questions but the facts are crucial to the case.'

His kindly, avuncular air struck Pauline. It was as though she were doing him a great service by answering his questions. She could hear the shake in her own voice as she spoke. Yet she was clear and precise, determined to tell the truth.

Mr Forde leaned back in his chair. 'Let's go forward a bit. You met Scully again in June of last year. When did he start giving you orders?'

'At the carnival in August.'

'What did he say?'

'He told me I had to take a trip to Paris. He didn't tell me that it was to buy arms.'

'Were you concerned about going?'

'I didn't want to go. Because of my past connections I felt I had no choice. Scully threatened to kill my son and I knew he meant business. I was afraid of what might happen to Seamie if I refused.'

Mr Forde looked at her. 'Aha! You were under severe duress. If this case comes to trial, duress will be a good defence. Leave this with me. I'll work on the details. Scully's the man they're really after. Meanwhile, I think you should see Dr Deasey, a psychiatrist, as a precautionary measure if the State proceeds against you. It could strengthen your case. I'll get you an appointment.' He shuffled his papers. 'I should know by the end of the week if a trial is to take place, and if so I'll push for a date. Get it over and done with.'

'Thank you,' Pauline said.

Mr Forde walked with her along the corridor, shook hands with her at the top of the stairs. Outside, she went quickly to her car, paying no attention to the hawkers selling clusters of early daffodils, or the traffic coming at her from all directions. Then she sat locked in her own silent world, breathing deeply. Struggling to calm herself she wondered how she'd get through the next few weeks. If she were charged, and that was still a possibility, she'd need money for legal fees. She hated going cap in hand again to Aunt Bea. But she'd have to. It was the only solution.

Chapter Thirty-One

Pauline drove through the woods of Ballingarret. The bog to the left was a dark brown curve of rutted landscape with occasional glimpses of the lake through the pale trees. The road to Aunt Bea's farm was potholed and waterlogged after the recent rain. Outside the farmhouse, the air was fresh and a pale sun shimmered on the lake, lightening its metallic surface to a silvery haze. Its salty smell mingled with the odour of the turf smoke from Aunt Bea's chimney and Pauline felt lonely for her childhood.

She found Aunt Bea resting, Brute at the foot of her bed. Pauline stood in the doorway watching her scraggy chest rising and falling. Aunt Bea stirred, opened her eyes, gazed blankly at Pauline. 'Oh! It's you,' she said. Shifting herself sideways she slid off the bed. 'I was taking forty winks,' she said, straightening herself laboriously, smoothing down her overall. 'I wasn't expecting anybody,'

'It's just a quick visit,' Pauline said.

'What is the time?'

'Four o'clock. I came to tell you how it went with the lawyer.'

'I was praying to St Anthony for you.' Aunt Bea sighed.

While she helped her aunt prepare the evening meal, Pauline

told her about Mr Forde, keeping her mood expansive and her answers to Aunt Bea's questions relaxed. Aunt Bea had money, but Pauline knew from experience that she liked Pauline to ask for her help. It tightened her grip on her niece and gave her an excuse to have her say.

'What does this Mr Forde think your chances are?' Aunt Bea asked.

'He thinks I have a good chance of getting off.' Pauline looked at her, noticing that her hair was now almost white.

'He does!' Aunt Bea turned to Pauline, her sharp eyes on her.

'He's expensive, though, and I can't afford to pay him. You're my only hope until I sell my shares in the hotel.'

Aunt Bea was standing near the table, her head tilted to one side. She sighed. 'You don't have to concern yourself about the money,' she said, and puffed out her chest as she spoke. 'After all, Pauline, what have I worked for all these years if it isn't to help out one of me own at a time like this? Your father helped me out when I was stuck for a bit of grazing. Never asked anything in return only that I kept you on the straight and narrow. God knows, I didn't do such a good job.'

'You did your best.'

'I was too hard on you, I realise that now. But sure what would a spinster like me know about rearin' youngsters? Now, this is what I'll do,' she said, 'I'll sell off some of the farm if I have to. Sure I'm getting too old to manage it all.' She was looking out of the window, over the fields, her bony fingers knotted together.

'But you love the farm,' Pauline protested.

Aunt Bea's joints creaked as she moved around, setting the table, filling the milk jug. 'I do and I don't,' she said. 'Times were hard in this place. All our lives there was nothing but talk of land, how much we had, how much more the neighbours had. Land was top priority, no time for anything else. Your poor mother knew all about it. She had to do her share, too, even though she was delicate.'

'I still miss her,' Pauline said.

'Me, too.' Aunt Bea sighed. 'It's a hard oul' life, especially here in the country where the heart is dragged out of you. To get labourers these days is impossible and I get tired easily too now. Maybe I'll take a trip away to the sun, warm me old bones before it's too late,' she said, more to herself. 'Before the land soaks up everything that's left in me.'

Pauline made no comment, knowing from past experience that Aunt Bea's decisions were always accepted without comment. To question them might upset her. The last thing she wanted was a release of Aunt Bea's sad memories, and confidences about her lack of a family.

Aunt Bea went outside for turf. Pauline followed, watching her as she gazed out over the bog, her face implacable.

'I'll pay you back,' Pauline said, 'every penny, as soon as I can sell my share in the hotel.'

'No need. I've made up my mind. That's enough on the matter. I don't boil my cabbage twice.' Aunt Bea was looking at her hands, the nails thick and broken, as she said, 'When I inherited this place I inherited a load of debts along with it. Not a soul to turn to for help. So I worked as hard as any man. You think I don't know much about men. You wouldn't believe how handsome Manus Corrigan's uncle was. I thought at the time that I'd die if I didn't get him. Well, I didn't get him and, of course, I didn't die. Mind you, I had no idea about life and no one to tell me that he was out of my league. With an aged father and responsibilities, I didn't stand a chance. Oh, I lost many an opportunity and when I got on my feet I felt cheated of my chance of happiness. This farm dictated my life, brought me nothing but hard work.'

'I didn't know all that,' Pauline said, looking at her aunt with admiration. Aunt Bea had achieved, if not happiness, status in being a farmer. She could hold her own with any other in the county, always improving her land, modernising her machinery, increasing her stock. Her eccentric passion for the farm and her fierce independence had always been the main focus of her life.

'Ah! Sure there's no use grumbling,' Aunt Bea continued. 'It never solved anything. I'll keep the house. Maybe a field or two to grow beet for the cattle and a few vegetables. That'll be enough to keep me going.' She was thoughtful for a moment, gazing all around her. 'I'll go to the bank in the morning, arrange everything.'

Pauline couldn't bear to let her see the tears that came with a sudden, unexpected rush. She walked down the path away from the kindness she couldn't bear. 'We won't go short.' Aunt Bea came after her. She sounded stern, like a parent.

Somewhere a dog barked. Rooks rummaged in the trees. A pig grunted. Everything was still. Pauline watched her aunt go in at the back door, her turf basket in her arms, the sunlight on her pale erect head, and loved her for the woman that she was.

Eve flipped through the pages of the file marked Confidential Breakdown of Investments and Securities of Freeman's Enterprises, hardly believing her eyes. 'Where did you get this?' she said, running her finger along the rows of figures, individual investments, dividends, company stock.

'Never mind where I got it,' Harry Wise said. 'Take a good look at what's happening. Jasper's selling off his shares.'

'But why?'

Harry shrugged. 'Could be any number of reasons. He may need cash. A little bird tells me he's very keen to get his hands on your hotel. By the look of these figures, Freeman Enterprises is an encumbrance he could do without.'

'He was adamant that it was not for sale.'

'That was before his venture into the property market. I

think you'll find that if you offer him the hotel in exchange for Freeman's, lock, stock and barrel, before he can sell off any more of his stock, he'll agree.'

'Do you really think so?'

'He's very committed to this coastline development scheme. Property is cheap at the moment, all over the city, across the country. Some people can't meet their mortgage repayments and the banks are repossessing left, right and centre in an effort to cut their losses. So it's haymaking time for the likes of Jasper. He's built the apartment block and now he wants to expand.' Harry was thoughtful for a moment. 'You get your grandfather's business back, Eve. It's a much more lucrative business now. And you could develop it from New York. I could take care of things here.'

Eve sat back in her chair trying to imagine herself perched in an office on the fortieth floor of a skyscraper, overlooking Central Park, in the heart of the financial district of New York. When she had seen David's office for the first time she had felt a soaring, magical quality at being so high up, away from the ordinariness of her everyday life, and the people on the ground, all rushing past. She had imagined that she could reach out and touch the surrounding buildings, and wondered what it would be like to look out over the world every day from such a vantage-point. The thought of building an empire of her own in the business community, dining with like-minded people who would appreciate her and her talents, the occasional lunch with David, time permitting, made her want to reach for the phone and call him.

'I always wanted to buy that business back,' she said, coming out of her reverie.

'Now's your chance. You're entitled to a lucky break. After all, Jasper all but robbed the business from your grandfather.'

'I'll go and talk to him. See what he has to say.'

'Whatever you do, don't say you saw these files.'

'I certainly won't,' she said.

There was a message for her to phone Tommy Reilly when she got back to the hotel.

'I was wondering if you've seen Pauline?' Tommy asked her when she rang him.

'Isn't she at her aunt Bea's?'

'She left there hours ago.' Tommy's voice was rising.

'Is something the matter?'

'It's Seamie. He's gone missing. The guards are here. But no one seems to know where Pauline is. We're very worried.'

'I'm on my way over.'

Pauline slipped in the back door. Kinsella's was eerily quiet for the time of evening, Tommy nowhere to be seen. 'Tommy,' she called into the bar, 'I'm back,' and continued on upstairs.

The first person she saw coming towards her was Eve. 'Hello,' Pauline said, 'what are you doing here?'

Eve put her arms around her. Mrs Browne was standing in the kitchen doorway, her hands held out in front of her in a gesture of hopelessness. 'Thank God you're home!' she exclaimed. 'Where were you?'

'What's going on?' Pauline asked, in surprise. It was then that she noticed the man standing in the sitting room, and Sergeant Enright coming up the stairs to meet her. Awkwardly he said, 'Evening, Pauline. This is Inspector McKnight. We have a couple of questions for you.'

Pauline went white. Eve was beside her, gripping her arm. 'Here, sit down. Take the weight off your feet,' she said, pulling out a chair.

Eve held Pauline's hand while the middle-aged, well-dressed Inspector, in an impeccable dark suit, white shirt and a tie with a gold crest, told her that Seamie had disappeared.

Pauline looked at him levelly. 'That's absurd,' she said. 'He's in boarding-school.' Inspector McKnight explained to her that Seamie had gone to a football match in Wexford town with the rest of his class the previous afternoon and when he hadn't returned the headmaster became anxious and had phoned home. When he could get no answer all evening he had called the police.

Confused, all three of them looked at the Inspector.

'Have you any idea where he might have gone?'

Pauline shook her head. What had happened? Was Seamie lost somewhere, frightened or panicking? She saw him flattened under the wheels of cars, crushed by a train.

'Get her a glass of water,' the Inspector said.

'Here, move back. Don't crowd her,' Mrs Browne rasped. 'We were trying to find you for hours.' She pressed the glass to Pauline's lips. 'Sip this.'

'When did you leave the pub, Miss Quirk?' the Inspector asked.

Pauline took a deep breath. 'This morning. Early.'

'Where exactly did you go?'

'To see my aunt Bea.'

Seamie was missing.

'Miss Quirk, have you seen your boy recently?'

'Not for a couple of weeks. He's due home this weekend.' Her voice broke.

'Why all these questions?' Mrs Browne waved her hands agitatedly. 'Can't you see she's in a state? Maybe the boy is off somewhere having a good time.'

Pauline tried to visualise Seamie at the cinema with a group of friends, but failed.

Sergeant Enright scratched his head thoughtfully.

Detective Inspector McKnight said, 'We think the boy may have been abducted and we're trying to establish a motive.'

'What?' Pauline quavered.

She saw him swathed in bandages, his eyes closed, lost in unconsciousness, or in the darkened room of a killer, who would stop at nothing to get at Pauline. She saw her son bleeding from his head, gagged and bound. She saw his killer swoop down on him.

'Seamie was last seen talking to a man during the match. We're now trying to locate that man, and we're making all sorts of other enquiries. There's a countrywide search under way but we have to proceed cautiously. We don't know who or what we're dealing with. Young Seamie could be in danger so that's why we're keeping the lid on it. With your impending trial we want no media involvement, no public appeals. So far we haven't got a lead on the case, so there is nothing to do but wait,' the Inspector said.

'We'll need photographs of him,' Sergeant Enright added. 'Do you have any?'

'We're bound to hear something soon,' Eve said. 'Wexford's not all that far away and he was seen yesterday, alive and well.' She kept hold of Pauline's hands while she spoke.

But Pauline was thinking of the vast tracts of land between Glencove and Wexford: mountains, rivers and sea. What about the sand dunes of Brittas Bay that Seamie loved so much? Supposing he'd been kidnapped and dumped there? She closed her eyes, a clear vision of Seamie alone in the sand dunes, lost, life going on normally all around him. Tears dripped off her nose and chin. She didn't even attempt to wipe them away. Mrs Browne, Eve, Sergeant Enright swam above her, advancing, retreating, like puppets, their hands waving, their eyes peering down at her, their voices floating over her head.

'Get her into bed, she's fainting.'

'No,' Pauline said, sounding desperate. 'I want to wait for—'

'You're a sensible girl, Pauline,' Sergeant Enright said. 'You need rest. We'll call you the minute there's—'

'Listen,' Pauline interrupted, 'I can't bear to think of us all sitting here and Seamie out there lost. I want to go and look for him.' A nerve throbbed in her temple as she tried to remember the last thing Seamie had said to her. Eve and Mrs Browne came either side of her, and Pauline allowed herself to be led upstairs. Head swirling she lay down on her bed. Seamie couldn't be dead. That thought was too much to bear. She tried to pray. 'Lord, bring back my child. He's all I have.'

Eve covered her with the duvet and left Mrs Browne to sit with her.

'Do you think I've been bad to him? Sending him off to boarding-school when he didn't really want to go,' Pauline asked Mrs Browne.

'How can we ever tell?' Mrs Browne said, too crushed by Seamie's disappearance to comfort her.

'Why did I let him out of my sight? Why do I always get everything wrong?' Pauline wailed.

Dr Gregory came and gave her a sedative, advising Mrs Browne to stay with her until she fell asleep.

'Can you think of a motive?' Inspector McKnight asked Eve, when she returned to the kitchen.

She shook her head. 'Pauline was very protective of Seamie, to the point of paranoia sometimes. That's why I was so amazed when she sent him to boarding-school. She hated to let him out of her sight and she had him primed never to talk to strangers. He's a sensible boy, you know.'

McKnight stared ahead. 'She probably thought it safer,' he said.

Father McCarthy came blustering up the stairs, his thinning hair windswept, face red with anxiety and exertion.

'Father,' Eve greeted him, 'I'm glad to see you.'

'Well, well, I just heard the news from Father Raphael,' he said, perching uncomfortably on the edge of a chair. 'A right how-do-you-do.' His sharp blue eyes darted from Inspector McKnight to Sergeant Enright, and it was evident that he considered them dangerous meddlers in other people's lives. 'I don't like it. Not one bit.'

'You know Miss Quirk well, Father?' Inspector McKnight asked.

'Of course. Pauline is one of my parishioners.'

'And her son?'

'A fine boy.'

'Can you give us any information that might help us with our enquiries, Father?' McKnight asked politely.

Father McCarthy said, 'It's not Pauline's fault. She reared that child without a father.'

'We are aware of that,' McKnight said curtly. 'We're wondering if you know of anyone in the organisation who might want to harm Seamie.' His shrewd eyes were trained on the priest, who was outraged. 'There's nobody in the wide world would want to harm that young boy,' he roared. 'And sure Seamie's not here long enough to know anyone.'

'You're acquainted with John Scully?' McKnight persisted.

Father McCarthy's eyes shifted towards the window. 'I know him reasonably well.'

'He's involved in this whole mess,' Inspector McKnight said.

'He had nothing to do with Pauline's son. Sure isn't he behind bars?'

'He's a member of the IRA,' Sergeant Enright supplied.

Father McCarthy didn't reply.

'This could be a political situation,' McKnight persisted.

'It isn't a political situation,' Father McCarthy protested. 'I told you, Pauline might have been a little misguided in the past but nobody would harm her son.'

Aunt Bea arrived, tall and austere in her good tweed costume and pork-pie hat. 'I came as soon as I got Sergeant Enright's message. I decided there was nothing for it but to come into

Glencove to see for myself. Dinny brought me.' Her face was chalk white. 'Any word?'

'Not yet.' Eve put an arm around her shoulders.

'The poor boy.' Aunt Bea clenched and unclenched her hands. 'What's to be done? Where's Pauline?'

'Resting.'

'Would you like to go into the sitting room? It's more comfortable in there,' Mrs Browne said to her.

'No. I'll wait here, thank you.'

'I'll make a pot of tea,' Mrs Browne said.

'I'll do it.' Aunt Bea pushed past her to grab the kettle.

Mrs Browne, her lips pursed, took the good tea-set down from the dresser, and put cups and saucers on the table.

'Why doesn't someone do something?' Aunt Bea asked, when it was obvious that she could stick the silence no longer.

'We're doing all we can, Miss Connelly,' Inspector McKnight said, tightly.

For a moment it seemed as if Aunt Bea would turn on him but instead she moved to the window with a look of bewilderment in her eyes.

The phone rang. Sergeant Enright picked it up, spoke for a minute, then put it down. 'A word in private, Inspector,' he said, heading for the landing.

Pauline woke in the darkened room to the sound of policemen's voices. Reality dawned and, with it, the dull ache of recollection, making her cry out in anguish. She got up and went downstairs.

As she walked into the kitchen Eve came to her.

'Have you found him?' Pauline asked.

'No,' Detective Inspector McKnight said, 'but we've got a lead. A boy fitting his description was seen boarding the *Enterprise* for Belfast.'

251

'Belfast!' Pauline choked.

'He may have gone to find his father's family.'

'*What?*'

'Oh, my God.' Aunt Bea's voice was laced with doom.

'Take it easy,' Sergeant Enright said. 'It's only a theory. What with the trial and all.'

'Does he know where the Gilfoyles live?'

'Yes. Madge told him all about his grandmother. She felt he should know.'

'Well, he's taken the bull by the horns,' Aunt Bea said. 'Gone off by himself, the poor lamb.'

'Let's go, then,' Inspector McKnight said to Sergeant Enright.

'I'll come with you,' Eve said, and to Pauline, 'We'll be back before you know it.'

Mrs Browne went home to get some sleep but Aunt Bea insisted on staying with Pauline.

Alone in her bedroom, Pauline was overcome with desperation as she stared out at the darkness. What if she were never to see Seamie again? Never to gaze into his eyes, or touch his silky hair? What if Mrs Gilfoyle didn't believe that Seamie was their grandson and turned him out into the savage streets to be killed or maimed before Eve got to him? Supposing he was already dead. Seamie's birth had given her life real significance, and a new hope.

She finally slept and dreamed that she was walking along the beach with Seamie in the middle of the night. Quickly he removed his jacket and sneakers and ran off down the strand, jumping over small rocks, reckless, running towards the sea, his long skinny legs flying.

Gathering himself up he smashed into the rolling waves, his arms wide, and swam away from the shore with strong slow strokes. Pauline was running after him calling, 'Seamie, come back in. Get out of there, you stupid kid.' Winded, she fell on her hands and knees in the sand, crying uncontrollably, begging him to come back. Just when she thought that he was gone for good, that she would never see him again, he came lumbering out of the sea, shaking off the water, laughing, telling her it was only a bit of fun.

Chapter Thirty-Two

Pauline was at the pub door, Aunt Bea beside her, the skin taut across her face. Mrs Browne was blinking in delight at the spectacle of Seamie alighting from the police car with Eve, Sergeant Enright plodding after him, saying, 'We've found him.'

'I can see that,' Aunt Bea said wryly.

'Seamie?' Pauline ran to him, cupped her hands around his face. 'Are you all right?' she asked looking into his eyes.

'Mom.'

'Oh, Seamie!' Her throat constricted. She was thrilled and furious all at once. 'I was so worried about you.' Pauline hugged him, then stood back from him to inspect him.

'I'm all right,' he said, suddenly shy and awkward.

The last vestiges of baby softness had dissolved from his face. He looked thinner, wirier, and there was a new watchfulness in his eyes.

'Don't I get a kiss?'

'I didn't mean to upset you, Mom,' he said, holding her, his voice breaking.

'I know that,' she said.

'Put him to bed,' Eve urged. 'He's exhausted. You can

question him all you like after he's had a sleep. I'm going home to bed myself.'

'I'll never be able to repay you, Eve,' Pauline choked out.

'Don't worry about it. I'll see you tomorrow.'

That evening, when Seamie woke up, he said, 'Mom, I went to find my dad's family.'

Suddenly she was not in the least surprised that he had gone to them: she had always known that one day he would. 'Why didn't you tell me you wanted to go?' she said.

'Because you wouldn't have let me. Anyway, I wanted to find them for myself.'

Pauline went to bed early and lay listening to him playing his music, sad to think how changed they already were with each other, Seamie from guilt for running off to Belfast, she from worry over her impending trial.

The next evening they walked together along the beach, watching the waves glinting silver in the twilight, curling towards the shore. Seamie stood gazing out to sea, lost in contemplation, the pockets of his jacket bulging with stones.

'Do you really hate school?' Pauline asked him.

'It's a madhouse,' he said, flinging a stone into the water. 'I'll get used to it, I guess.'

'I thought you were settling down.'

'I was. In a way.'

'Before all this hullabaloo about the trial?'

'Yeah.'

'Have you got a favourite teacher?'

'I like Tubby O'Reilly. That's his nickname because he's so enormous. He stinks of cigarettes and beer, but he makes the maths class interesting.'

'That's what counts,' Pauline said. 'Tell me why you ran away.'

'I figured there'd got to be more to my father than this

character whose name pops up every now and again. I wanted to know what it was. What really happened to him.' Seamie was silent for a moment. 'It's a strange feeling not having a dad. Only knowing him from what you told me as a child. I always thought he was a powerful, clever man. I looked for a photograph of him to see what he looked like. When we came back to Ireland I used to look at men in the street wondering if my dad had been like any of them. I often imagined meeting him.'

'Why didn't you ask me?'

'You only ever talked about him as some kind of patriotic hero. I wanted to know him as an ordinary dad, and the stories you told me about him were like the legends we used to read about.' He faced Pauline, his hair blowing into his eyes.

'The stories I told you about your father were based on facts. I had to make them interesting for you to get to know and love him. I found it so hard to tell you the whole truth.' Pauline put her hands to her face. 'Most of the secrets I've kept all these years will be out in the open soon.' She faltered, took a deep breath and continued. 'You'll see for yourself what kind of people we really were and you'll have to make your own judgements. I just hope you won't blame me too much.'

Seamie walked on ahead of her, his feet sinking into the sand. He turned suddenly and said, 'At least I know now for sure that he's dead and I'm never going to meet him. That dream is over and I'll just have to accept it.'

'I'm sorry.' Pauline wanted to hug him but he seemed too remote.

'No. It's better this way. Honest,' he said. 'Before, I didn't know where I belonged. I thought that if I met my dad's people my life would be different. But Granny Gilfoyle didn't know me. She sat down on a chair, put her fist to her forehead, and said, "Seamie, Seamie," trying to remember.'

'She never knew you,' Pauline said, her arms encircling Seamie's waist, comforting him.

'Why?'

'You were only a baby and I couldn't bring you to Belfast with me. I didn't think I'd be away long and it might have been dangerous.'

'Why didn't you just go with Dad when he was leaving?'

'I wanted to but he wouldn't hear of it. One minute we were at the carnival, the next he was rushing back to the flat, telling me to stay and enjoy myself. I knew something was up. I followed him home but he was packing, slipping off without a word. He told me he'd send for me soon and that we'd be married in Belfast. He was looking forward to being a father.'

'What happened?'

'Things went badly wrong. He'd been tricked. Caught up in something he knew nothing about.'

She was silent for a few seconds, willing herself to hold steady, wanting to protect Seamie from the harsher side of the story. 'I don't know any more. I'm still confused by it all,' she said.

Seamie gripped her tighter. 'At least we're together. That's all that matters. If anyone says anything bad to you, I'll punch them.' He bunched a fist.

'No, you won't.' Pauline sniffed.

'And I have a granny, too. I promised I'd go visit with her in the summer.' Seamie stopped. 'Listen, Mom, no matter what happens I'm on your side.'

They walked back along the beach, holding on to each other, their feet sinking into the sand, slowing them down.

That night, when Seamie had fallen asleep, Pauline lay awake and thought of all the mothers in the world. Mothers who would kill for their children. Only, she had already killed and her child was suffering for it.

✶   ✶   ✶

They were seated in Jasper's study at Rathmore. The rest of the family had long since departed for a walk on the beach, Irene the last to go.

'I must say you've chosen a most inconvenient time,' Jasper said, glancing at his watch. 'I've a tennis match in half an hour.'

'I won't keep you. It's nearly Katie's bedtime and I promised I'd read her a story.'

'Right, then, what is it?' Jasper's shrewd eyes were wary.

'I'll get straight to the point,' Eve said, seating herself opposite him, steeling herself. 'I'm not interested in your office handling my affairs any longer,' she said. 'I'll do it personally.'

'How can you run your hotel from New York?'

'I have one or two options,' Eve said. 'I know I'm new to the business, but I've been prudent and the hotel is now beginning to show a profit.'

'So?'

'Because you've put a lot of money into it, I'm willing to let you have it, with all its facilities, and its potential, as a straight swap for Freeman's Enterprises.'

'*What?*' Jasper exploded.

'I'm not sure about the minimum amount of investment capital your company would require for Freeman's Enterprises, but—'

'Freeman's is worth far more than the Glencove.' Jasper was indignant. 'And it's not for sale.'

Eve permitted herself a smile. 'Neither was the hotel until Henry Joyce made an offer for it and I realised I could multiply my money.'

Jasper was astonished. 'Henry Joyce?' he asked.

'Henry Joyce wants to turn it into a health and leisure club.'

Jasper threw back his head and laughed. 'He's as conceited in business as he is in his personal life,' he said. 'It's inconceivable.'

'Why?'

'It's too big a risk. I invest money for people, Eve. Given the present economic climate, and the government's performance, few of our citizens can afford to join an exclusive health and leisure club, either now or in the future.'

'Henry has a certain type of client in mind, mainly his wealthy patients. I don't see why he shouldn't make a go of it. On the other hand it would scupper your expansion plans for the coastline.'

Jasper's eyes narrowed. 'Stop playing games with me.'

'Either you swap the hotel for Freeman's or I sell to Henry, and sue you for damages to my property.'

'Damages? I've spent a fortune on the place.'

'And spoilt its character.'

'So you think this blackmail stunt of yours will make me change my mind?'

'If I were in your shoes, that's what I'd do. Admit it, it's what you want.'

Jasper grunted. 'I'll have my accountant look into the matter. That's as far as I'm prepared to go.'

'I'd prefer it if we used an independent accountant, from a top firm. Someone like Tom Price from Price and Gamble.'

Jasper sighed. 'As you wish. You do like having your own way. Mind you, you always were a little madam. Ever since I can remember.'

'If we're to enjoy a proper business relationship, I suggest we treat one another with civility.' And with that Eve stood up and left him.

'Mum,' Katie hollered, as soon as she saw Eve, and ran up the beach ahead of Irene to throw herself into her mother's arms.

'Hey! What is it?' Laughing, Eve lifted her up and twirled her round.

'I was waiting for you,' she said. 'You were ages.'

'No, I wasn't,' Eve said, taking her hand.

'We've been as far as the point and she's tired out,' Irene explained.

'Come on,' Eve coaxed. 'I'll read that story I promised you.'

'Are we staying here all day tomorrow, Mum?'

'Yes, but the day after that we're going shopping.' Eve was eyeing Katie's long white legs, noticing how tall she was getting. 'Everything you have is too small.'

In their bedroom Eve got out a book and sat with her on the bed.

'Oh, good, I like *Jemima Puddle Duck*,' Katie said sleepily. When Eve had finished the story, she asked, 'When are we going to see Daddy again?'

Eve bent to kiss her. 'Soon,' she said, and switched off the bedside lamp.

'I'd like to see him tomorrow.'

Chapter Thirty-Three

Tommy was waiting for Pauline when she returned from Seamie's school, signalling to her over the customers' heads that he wanted to speak to her. 'There was a phone call for you,' he said, with the confident smile of someone imparting good news. 'From Geoff Ryan.'

Pauline's heart pounded. 'Did he leave a message?'

'Said he'd call over later on.'

When she answered the door to Geoff that evening, his eyes were dark and fathomless against the lilac sky. Shadowed in the twilight his face looked young, vulnerable. 'Geoff!' was all she said.

'I heard you were in trouble,' he said. 'Is there anything I can do to help? Would you like to come out for a while?'

They drove to the Roundwood Inn where Geoff had booked a table. His eagerness to talk and listen relaxed her.

'Why didn't you tell me all this before?' he said.

'How could I! I'd buried that whole episode of my life. Or so I thought, until Scully turned up.'

She talked on and on, grateful for the effort Geoff was making in trying to understand it all. When they returned to the pub he stretched out his arms and encircled her. 'I'll do anything I can to help you, Pauline,' he said, and kissed her. Her body arched against him, his ardour reawakening her passion, but her mind was distant from what was happening. She was fearful of letting him get close to her again. He looked at her questioningly. 'Do you want more time?' he asked. 'It might help.'

He was watching her in that calculating way of his, trying to assess what was really going on in her mind.

'I'm scared, Geoff.'

'I know, darling, I know,' he said. 'But I can wait.'

The following week he took her to the Guinea Pig in Dalkey for a meal. Afterwards, they walked along Killiney strand, passing a few solitary strollers on the way. Another day they went to Brittas Bay. Pauline brought a picnic. Although the weather was cold they wrapped up warm and sat in the shelter of the dunes, high above the sea, sipping tea from a flask, eating sandwiches, listening to the waves crashing against the shore. The sea stretched to meet the horizon where banks of clouds shaped and reshaped themselves as a thunderstorm threatened over the dark woods to the left.

As the days passed and the trial drew nearer, Pauline was filled with a mixture of relief and dread. Intimacy with Geoff was unthinkable: the thought of being locked up occupied her mind totally. He called in regularly at the pub, but although she was pleased to see him, she would watch him leave with a perverse relief at being alone.

Preparing for bed each night, she would look out over the dark outline of rooftops merging with the trees. She was lonely and afraid, and resolute in her acceptance that there could never be anything between Geoff and herself now. The penalty of her crime was being exacted; the consequences of her actions had to be faced. She would be shunned and she would have to accept it just as she had accepted that she wasn't entitled to love. She would tell Geoff soon. Get it over with.

'It's not going to work out between us,' she told Geoff, over a drink in a pub in Wicklow. 'I can't pretend any longer. I just can't see further than the trouble I'm in. It's consuming me.'

'It'll be over soon. They can't have been able to pin anything on you or you'd have been in for more questioning.'

'No.' Pauline pondered. 'It'll never be over for me. And I mustn't drag you into it.'

'So that means there's nothing left between us?' he asked.

Pauline nodded.

'I don't believe that,' he said.

'I'm sorry, but that's the way it is.' The words struck hollow in her ears.

Geoff shrugged. 'If that's the way you want it, we'd better not prolong the agony,' he said, standing up to go.

She was grateful for his composure, astonished at herself for having the courage to stick to her decision, relieved that she had.

The next day, laden with parcels, footsore from chasing bargains in the spring sales, Eve sank into a chair opposite Pauline in the coffee-shop and placed her parcels under the table. It was late morning and other shoppers were filing in for a reviving cup of coffee.

'I told Geoff I couldn't see him any more,' Pauline said.

Eve stopped pouring coffee to look up at her. 'A bit drastic, I would have thought.'

'I'd only lose him again,' Pauline said, shrinking back in her seat. She wanted to explain how she felt but instead she gazed over the heads of the women around her, glad that their presence prevented Eve from quizzing her too much. It would keep for another time.

'It's not the right time to make big decisions,' Eve said.

'It was so perfect in the beginning. I was happy to be with him. Just the two of us together.' She was thinking of their lovemaking before everything went wrong, the joy in their coming together, and she knew it would never be like that again.

'I'm sure Geoff understands.'

'I don't know,' Pauline said, shaking her head. 'I'm not prepared to risk it.'

Dr Deasey, the psychiatrist, was a quiet-spoken man with thick eyebrows and a neatly trimmed beard. He sat still in his chair, with bright, expectant eyes. His smile was friendly and he exuded infinite patience as he waited for Pauline to speak.

'Where would you like to begin?' he asked.

'I've no idea.' Pauline blushed.

'Why don't you tell me about your childhood? Was it much the same as everyone else's?'

'Yes, until my mother died.'

'Life was different after that?'

Pauline thought for a minute. 'I was different. I felt different from all the other children I knew.'

'In what way?'

'Every way. I stayed in more, played on my own. I knew everyone was watching me, seeing how I was coping.' She talked about her loneliness, her parents and her special childhood. Special because she was the only child of a shy, sad mother, and a quiet, nervous father, both too inhibited as parents to give real definition to her life. That had been left to Aunt Bea, who viewed the world with a jaundiced eye.

Dr Deasey listened, his voice gentle as he coaxed her to expand here and there. 'What was your relationship with your father like?'

'We got on well enough.'

'Good. Let me explain to you, Pauline, that this is the warming up, the getting to know you. I want to build a picture slowly, piece by piece, that will bring me to the Pauline of today.'

Pauline continued unravelling the past, surprising herself at her sudden, blunt arrival at the present. Several times Dr Deasey intervened, often turning her narrative to Scully, noting, through her reticence and fear, the impact he had had on her.

'I thought I'd seen the last of him,' she explained, 'but as soon as I came back from the States he appeared. He started by calling into the pub. When he heard about Seamie he seemed to take over my life, ordering me around, telling me when to come and go, popping up everywhere.'

'Did you try explaining to him what your feelings about him were?'

'Several times. He took no notice.'

Scully had intimidated her with bully-boy tactics threatening the thing she held most precious, her Seamie.

'You have suffered severe mental anguish and fear, and you would make a credible witness, if it comes to that,' Dr Deasey said.

After she had left his office, Pauline felt elated at his final words, but on the way home, she sank back into depression, wondering if she would be behind bars for the rest of her life. She would never see wide open fields again, or the sea, or the town she loved. Never take Seamie to a football match, or Disneyland, or go camping with him. She would never wear nice clothes, or make love, or drink her favourite wine with a meal.

Geoff said, 'I'm going away, Pauline. I think it's for the best.' They were walking along the riverbank in Bray. Then he told her about the job he'd been offered in Los Angeles, in charge of the construction work at the airport there.

'It's so sudden.' Her words seemed to come from a distance as her brain registered bafflement, comprehension and, finally, acceptance in the short space of time between his phone call asking her to meet him and this news. She cleared her throat, her eyes on the fresh green foliage of the trees, washed clean with the rain. The clouds racing overhead and the cold air pressing against her cheek made her dizzy. 'I mean, there's no reason why you shouldn't go or anything, but it's . . .' She didn't know what to say next.

'It's too good an opportunity to let slip.'

'Yes, I suppose so.'

'Luckily, my passport's up to date so I can go right away.'

'Thanks for letting me know. I wouldn't have liked to hear it from someone else,' she said. If they had still been together, he would have talked it over with her, asked her opinion.

'It's a once-in-a-lifetime offer,' he said, as they strolled along. 'If I turn it down I'll wonder about it for the rest of my life.' He reached into his jacket pocket, took out his cigarettes and tapped one against the box before lighting it.

'I'm delighted for you,' she said, appraising the sparkle in his eyes and the smile that hovered on his lips.

Her mouth was dry and her hands shook as they turned towards the sea, leaving behind the houses and shops, walking along the path under the poplar trees, their steps slow as if they had all the time in the world. They came across children at the corner shooting marbles, their eyes on the extravagant glass rainbows rolling along the pavement, their heads bobbing with excitement. Each specimen was scrutinised for its brilliance and texture, the winner greeted with excitement.

Afterwards Pauline couldn't recall everything she'd said to him, or what he'd said to her. All she remembered was that she'd stayed cheerful, determined to be happy for him. Maybe she'd said something about wishing she could go back to Montauk.

It was dark when they returned to the pub. She made a brave effort not to cry when he took her in his arms to say goodbye, his lips touching her bowed head. He took her cold hands, chafed them. She kept her eyes on his shoulders, wondering what was going on in his mind.

'Goodbye,' he said, holding her lightly, his eyes begging for understanding, something.

'Goodbye.' She pulled away and walked towards the door of the pub. It was as if she were travelling a great distance alone. At the door she turned and said, 'Good luck.'

He smiled, waiting for her to say more but she didn't.

'I'll see you when I get back,' he called, as she went inside.

'Who knows?' she said, and slowly shut the door.

She packed quickly, filling her bag with a pile of clothes she plucked indiscriminately from her wardrobe. Breathing rapidly to prevent herself crying she brushed her teeth to relieve the dryness of her mouth. Her cheeks burned as she glanced in the bathroom mirror. She stumbled into the bedroom, reached out for things she might need, her Ladyshave, perfume, hairbrush. Zipping her bag she left it on the landing while she checked that all the windows were shut. Then she closed all the doors, took the key off the hook and locked up behind her. She glanced around once before she got into her car and drove off to Ballingarret.

Chapter Thirty-Four

'I can't believe I said all those things to Jasper. I certainly can't believe he took me seriously.'

Henry laughed. 'You *were* serious.'

'I suppose I was. And now I'm ravenous,' Eve said, picking up her soup spoon. 'If it wasn't for you, Henry, I wouldn't have had the nerve. Once I mentioned your offer for the hotel everything went so quickly.'

Henry roared with laughter. 'I knew it would goad him into action.'

Eve gazed at him gratefully. 'You were right. Thank you,' she said.

He nodded. 'Least I could do, seeing as you won't let me make love to you.'

A silence fell between them. He was watching her, and she knew that he was aware of her sudden awkwardness, and the burden of expectation this statement put on her. What was she was doing eating a candlelight dinner with this man? Her eyes fell to his hands as he lifted his knife and fork: delicate hands with long, slender fingers. She wondered if she would tell David about Henry's part in the deal with Jasper? Or about this intimate dinner.

'Eve?' Henry's voice was gentle, bringing her back.

'Sorry, I was miles away.'

'No, you weren't. You were wondering what the hell you were doing here.'

Embarrassed, Eve said, 'Let's not complicate things,' and told him that she had come to celebrate Jasper's agreement. 'It seemed a good idea at the time.'

It was obviously not what Henry had wanted to hear. 'Let's just enjoy ourselves and be happy,' he said. 'Forget about Jasper and the business. Pretend it's just you and me, now, this minute. That nothing else matters.'

'I wish it were so,' Eve said, regretfully.

Henry looked at her. 'What did ... David say about the swap?'

'I haven't told him yet,' Eve said, amazed to discover that she neither knew nor cared what David thought. 'He's busy with his own work. In fact, he's so busy lately, he seems to have slipped away into another world.'

Henry sighed. 'It's strange how we change, isn't it?'

'Yes, I suppose it is.'

'Lucy and I don't love one another any more,' he said. 'At least it's something we're agreed on.'

'I'm sorry,' Eve said, not knowing what else to say.

'Between my consultancy work and the practice I just worked and worked and somewhere along the way we lost each other. Haven't you found marriage difficult too?'

'At times,' Eve said, deciding not to elaborate.

Henry said, 'You're a beautiful woman, Eve. You could have choices.'

'I'm a married woman.'

'So am I married. But why should that stop us from enjoying one another's company now? And I am enjoying myself.'

'Me too,' Eve found herself saying.

'Let's go mad and have some dessert?'

'Why not? It's not often we get the chance to go mad.'

They both laughed.

*　　*　　*

Eve came to Ballingarret to spend the night with Pauline. 'Well,' she said, when they were finally alone in the kitchen, the door closed, the light from the dim bulb casting shadows on the wall, 'how are you bearing up?'

'Not too bad.' Pauline stoked the range.

Outside, the wind swayed the dark branches, huge against the net curtains. The kitchen was warm and cosy, the smell of turf mingling pleasantly with that of the roast of lamb they'd had for dinner. Down the passage Brute snored peacefully.

Pauline put the kettle on, removed the lid of the tea-caddy. Suddenly there was nothing to say.

'How are you, really?' Eve's eyes were sympathetic as they sat facing each other across the table.

'I'm fine, honestly.' Her nonchalance camouflaged her anxiety. 'Glad you're here.'

Eve's presence gave Pauline a temporary amnesty from her troubles because Eve had a natural propensity towards kindness and gave it unstintingly. She understood other people's pain because she had been through so much herself. Her support had made Aunt Bea more tranquil too.

As if reading her thoughts, Eve said, 'Aunt Bea seems to be coping well?'

'Oh! She doesn't say much. Acts as if she's taking it in her stride. Says she doesn't care that people are talking. But, of course, she does. She's stopped buying the newspaper.'

'She'll come through it. Wait and see.'

'I hope so.' Pauline knew that Aunt Bea was upset by recent events. She was unused to having attention focused on her family, and, to use her own term, she was 'wound up' by it all.

'I think she's wary of me,' Eve said. 'The way she looks at me sometimes. I suppose she never really trusted me after my youthful escapades.'

Pauline smiled, recalling a younger, fickle Eve, who had shocked the people of Glencove with her elopement and later her divorce. She had been a disgrace to her family, in the eyes of a great many people including Aunt Bea. 'That was a long time ago,' Pauline consoled her. 'She knows what a good friend you are to me.'

'Aunt Bea would say a leopard never changes his spots.' Eve laughed. 'And maybe she's right.'

'You settled down. Look at you! Respectable, happily married, a good businesswoman.'

There was a brief silence. Then Eve said, 'I not so sure about the happily married bit. I've been seeing Henry since I came home.'

'Oh!' Pauline was amazed when Eve told her about her date in New York and the subsequent meetings in Glencove. She wondered if she was being prepared for more surprising revelations. 'You obviously like him,' she said, knowing that was inadequate but not wishing to interfere.

'Is it really that obvious?'

'Your whole face lights up at the mention of his name.'

'I do like him. I don't deny it. He's nice, clever, attractive. But I'm not going to do anything that might compromise my marriage.'

'Then what *are* you going to do?' Pauline asked bluntly.

'Get back to New York as soon as you're sorted out.'

Pauline nodded. 'If you fancy him all that much I suppose you'd better get back to David quick,' Pauline said.

Eve nodded. 'I think so, and that's sort of what I came to talk to you about. I offered Jasper the hotel in return for Freeman's Enterprises. Straight swap. I think he'll take it.'

'You did *what?*' Pauline was poleaxed.

'I can't run the hotel from New York, Pauline, but I can expand Freeman's from there.'

As Pauline was about to protest, Eve said, 'Listen, you

needed to sell your shares to pay your legal fees. Now I'll be in a position to give you a good price for them. Freeman's will be worth far more than the hotel when I get it into the States. What I want you to do for me is look after my coffee-shops while I'm away. I spoke to David last night on the phone. He's getting very impatient.'

'I can't say I blame him. But how can I look after the coffee-shops and the pub?'

'I'll take you on as an overall manager. You just make sure everything's running smoothly. Pop in regularly, keep an eye on things. In return I'll put you on a retainer of, say—'

'Wait!' Pauline interrupted. 'You're jumping the gun a bit. My name hasn't been cleared yet. They could still charge me.'

'We'll worry about that if it happens. Meantime, I need your help. You're the only one I trust.'

'Thanks,' Pauline said shyly. 'But don't name a figure yet. Let's see how I get on.'

Finally they slept, side by side in the narrow twin beds with matching white candlewick bedspreads, Eve almost as soon as she lay down, Pauline much later.

She woke next morning to the comforting sound of Eve talking to Aunt Bea. In the kitchen they were having breakfast, Aunt Bea presiding, Eve smart in a well-tailored navy suit, a white striped shirt, and her hair sleek – she looked ready for anything.

'I wish you could stay longer,' Pauline said.

'I've got to get back to the hotel.' Eve looked at her watch. 'We're picking up after the winter now, thinking of weekend specials for the summer – you know, "summertime in the Garden of Ireland", that sort of thing to promote the hotel. I'm off to see our advertising man this morning.'

'Watch your health,' Aunt Bea cautioned. 'All that respon- sibility will tell on you, if you're not careful. You don't want to end up skin and bone like Pauline,' she said, placing a blue willow-patterned plate of bacon, egg, sausage, tomato, black and white pudding, and fried bread in front of her niece.

'I can't eat all this,' Pauline protested.

'It'll do you good,' Aunt Bea said firmly. She looked at the clock. 'I might get you to drop me off at Dunphy's, Eve. It's the new place at the corner, on your way home. We're almost out of essentials. I don't need to remind you, Pauline, that Mary won't be here today. You'll have to feed the hens and collect the eggs. Oh, and make sure Dinny cleans out the pigsty. I might call in to see Mrs McNamara for a few minutes. She's had her gall bladder removed. Will you be all right until I get back?'

'Take your time. I'll be fine,' Pauline said.

Eve was stunned by the old lady's energy. 'Does she ever give herself a break?' she whispered to Pauline as she left.

'Only when she's asleep,' Pauline said.

Eve drove through Glencove, past the mansions on the hill, the church, the cemetery, the new houses, the park, the swings and roundabouts on the green where she had often taken Katie to play. She parked her car near the woods and walked along a path of twisted roots, stopping to watch the tall grass shift and stir in the breeze, and listen to the birds.

Slowly she climbed, digging her heels into the slippery surface, emerging from a clump of trees to find Henry standing a few feet away from her, his back to her, looking out over the sea.

'Hello!' she called.

He turned. 'What kept you?'

'I was packing.'

'When are you off?' He looked defeated.

'The day after tomorrow.'

'*What?*'

'Katie's missing David and she's missing school.'

'And when were you going to let me know?'

'I'm waiting for Jasper to give me a written agreement, then I'll go. I don't want to leave anything to chance.'

'The least you could have done—'

'I don't want a row, Henry.' Eve could hear the tremor in her voice.

They stared at each other.

'Henry, I want to put my life back together. Get on with it. If it means going back to New York, trying again with David, then I'll do it.' Her eyes stung.

'Where do I come into the picture?'

'You don't. There's really no choice. Katie is fretting and I'm responsible.' They stared at each other.

'I could let you go and lose you altogether,' Henry mused, 'or I could wait, try to persuade you into letting me love you in another while. When Katie's a bit older and when you've really had enough of David.'

Eve didn't answer him.

'But what good would that do?' he continued, more to himself than her.

She could hear her own heartbeat.

'I could beg,' he added.

'Henry, don't!' In the silence that followed she kept her eyes averted, wishing he would go.

'So, I count for nothing in your life. That's what it boils down to.'

'You're a good friend.'

He laughed bitterly. 'That's what we pretended to be,' he said, shaking his head from side to side. 'And we got away with it. But we both know different.' His hair lifted in the breeze. 'It's not all my doing either. You have to take some responsibility in this too, Eve – be honest about your feelings for me.'

'I did everything I could not to let it happen. You know that.'

'But you couldn't prevent us falling in love, could you?' He grabbed her, pulled her towards him. 'You wanted me, didn't you?'

'Stop it! Please, Henry. You're hurting me.' Her voice rang out louder than she'd intended.

Henry dropped his hands to his sides in a gesture of hopelessness. 'Sorry,' he said. 'I'm going. But don't forget, I'll be waiting for you because I know you want me.' With tears in his eyes, he turned and made his way down the path.

For a long time after he'd gone she stood still, looking at the small trees that bordered the ridge and ran parallel to the sea, at the cliffs, the mountains beyond, purple against the indigo sky. She was drinking it all in, because she had to make it last for a long time. She had given up any idea of a relationship with Henry. They had come to the end. Whatever they might have had was gone. She would not be the one to whom he would turn in the night. Her name would not be the name he called out. They yearned for one another but they would never share the comfort of a daily life together. She was sad and she knew she would miss him. But she knew she had made the right decision.

She would phone David now, let him know the time of her arrival in New York. Everything would be all right when she saw him again.

Chapter Thirty-Five

Pauline ate a slice of bread and butter, sitting at the kitchen table, looking out of the window. The sky was grey, the clouds were dense and threatening. Wind blew through the new-leafed trees on the road and snapped at the cherry tree, scattering its blossoms. It whined around the farmhouse, rattled the window-panes, and tore at the corrugated roof on the pig shed, threatening to blow it off. Dinny had made a good job of painting the kitchen. The new white paint had lifted the dullness, but before long structural damage would have to be seen to. Winter storms had cracked a slate on the roof and the window-frames were scraped bare of paint. Spring sunshine glittered on the dirty panes and exposed the flaking eaves. Aunt Bea would have to get the whole thing done before next winter.

Everywhere was quiet. Seamie, home from school, was still asleep. The thought of her son filled Pauline with sadness: he was so young, so dependent on her. What she was about to do might destroy him. She had heard nothing from the police and because the suspense was killing her she had decided to go and see Sergeant Enright — to tell him everything before Scully did.

'Mom.'

'Seamie! You scared me. I didn't hear you get up.'

'You all right?' He was beside her, holding her tightly.

'I'm fine,' she said, forcing a cheerfulness she didn't feel.

He looked at her sharply. 'I'm starved. Shall I make breakfast?'

'I'll do it,' she said, pulling away.

'OK.' He shrugged, but looked hurt.

'You can set the table,' she said in a softer voice. 'What'll you have?'

Brightening, he said, 'Anything that's going.'

Pauline's heart clutched with love for the round, earnest face and the big gentle eyes. Dutifully he took out the place mats and put them on the table, began rummaging in the bread bin while Pauline put rashers and sausages under the grill, broke an egg into the hot frying pan. It crackled and hissed.

'I'm going to see Sergeant Enright,' Pauline said lightly. 'See if there's any news. All this waiting is getting me down.'

Seamie was cutting the bread, putting it in the toaster. 'It'll all be over soon. Stop worrying,' he said, as though Scully had been no more than an inconvenience that had to be dealt with.

The sun streamed through the kitchen window, dispersing the clouds. Across the table Pauline watched her son eat with his usual enthusiasm. As he put down his knife and fork, Aunt Bea came into the kitchen, with her hat and coat on. 'I'm coming to Glencove with you,' she said.

'I might be delayed,' Pauline said, not wanting to have to take her to the barracks.

'That's all right. I've got things to do and Dinny's taking Seamie to the market.'

'Great,' Seamie said, and wiped his plate with a hunk of bread.

Pauline wasn't fooled. She knew Aunt Bea didn't want her to be alone in case Sergeant Enright had bad news for her.

✢   ✢   ✢

Sergeant Enright was in his office at the barracks. 'I called into the pub but you weren't there,' he said.

'I haven't been able to get back to it,' Pauline said. 'I won't until all this is over. Have you heard anything?'

'You saved me a journey. I was going to go out to Ballingarret this afternoon to tell you that you needn't worry your head about Scully. An extradition warrant has been served on him.'

'Oh!'

'It'll be in all the papers tomorrow. He's wanted up North for the killing of an internment officer. There's so much substantial evidence against him for gun-running from other sources that you'll not be needed to testify.'

Sergeant Enright relaxed in his chair, a smile on his face.

Pauline studied the desk. Then she looked up. 'I came to see you about another matter too, Sergeant.' Her voice was barely above a whisper and the policeman had to lean forward to hear her.

'What is it?'

'I killed Martin Dolan.'

'You did *what?*' Sergeant Enright could hardly believe his ears.

Pauline took a deep breath and rushed on. 'I'd come to the conclusion that Seamus was dead and I was desperate to get away. I knew Martin must have had something to do with his murder. I wanted to find out what happened, hear it from his own lips. I knew, too, that I would antagonise him if I asked him straight out. So when he came in with a few drinks on him and started talking . . .' Pauline went on and on stopping only for breath.

Sergeant Enright listened.

'He'd never have told me had he not been drunk. I never dreamed that my reaction would result—' She swallowed back her tears. 'You see, I couldn't leave Belfast until I knew.' There was relief in the release of words that came tumbling out, and the tears that spilled from her eyes. She wiped them away with the back of her hand. 'Scully suspected that I did it. He's been blackmailing me since I came back. Now he'll tell the guards. I'm finished.'

Sergeant Enright was shaking his head. 'Stop, Pauline, stop,' he said. 'Hold it a minute.' He lifted his arms as if to embrace her. 'Calm down. Let's take this one step at a time.'

Pauline looked up at him. 'Where's the gun you shot him with?'

'Scully got rid of it. He was going to cover for me, he said, if I would be his girlfriend.'

Sergeant Enright breathed a sigh of relief. 'Well, then, Scully only suspects that it was you. He has no proof. My advice to you is to say nothing about this to anyone else. You've told me off the record, as a friend, so to speak. Now, leave it at that. It all happened a long time ago and you've suffered greatly with all this bullying that Scully went on with, and your conscience driving you demented.'

He stood up, paced the room. 'My God! This is awful. If only I'd listened to you in the beginning when you came to me that time Seamus Gilfoyle disappeared. I should have investigated it properly then. We'd have nipped things in the bud. But I thought you were exaggerating. Nothing like that ever happened in Glencove and I certainly didn't want any trouble. Life was nice and peaceful at the time. Crime was unheard of. Apart from a few fines here and there, that is.' He took a deep breath. 'When I first came to Glencove, Pauline, I found it a very strange place. Your father welcomed me with his friendship. Years later he asked me to keep an eye on you when you started work in Kinsella's.' Sergeant Enright's face was tight with emotion. 'I failed him by not listening to you, not taking you seriously. I didn't want any trouble, didn't want upstarts like Martin Dolan and Seamus Gilfoyle around. I thought they'd outgrow their patriot carry-on and clear off. I was wrong.' He looked at her, his voice full of urgency as he said, 'What I did was just as bad as what you did, Pauline. I committed the sin of failure to engage. I failed to engage myself in your life as a friend and protector and in my duties as a police officer. You were young, vulnerable, frightened, and I let you down. I abrogated my responsibilities so I, too, must carry some of the blame for Martin's death.' Forcefully he said, 'I make a pledge to you now, Pauline, I'll be here for you this time. I'll see you right.'

'How?'

'There is no evidence to convict you or anyone of Martin Dolan's death. No one saw it happen and the murder weapon was never found. It's clear to me, from what you have disclosed, that you were forced into a situation. Take my advice and sit tight. Say nothing about Martin Dolan's death. You've paid the price for that. I guarantee you that when all Scully's story comes out he won't be seen in a favourable light.' Rising from his chair, he said, 'Who's to say that Scully will say anything about you? He knows the law. Knows he'll be seen as a bullying thug. No one will be sympathetic towards him and with the trial being up North the whole sorry business will be over and done with and you won't have to know a thing about it.'

'Do you really think so?'

'Yes, I do.' Sergeant Enright rubbed his eyes. 'Your father was a decent man, Pauline. He worried about the company you were keeping but was helpless to do anything about it. I've been watching you from a distance ever since you took up with Martin Dolan. I knew you weren't involved directly in their goings-on so I wasn't too worried. I never had any inkling that it would become so serious. You're under suspicion of carrying monies for the illegal purchases of arms, but you were only doing a message for Scully. Further proof of his bullying. They haven't found enough evidence to substantiate that charge and Scully's word won't be worth a damn by the time he's convicted of all the things he's wanted up North for. Now, Pauline, trust me. This conversation will go no further. I'll take your secret to the grave and you do the same.'

He patted her arm in a comforting way, as Pauline sat, shoulders hunched. 'You should have come and told me all this sooner. I could have saved you a lot of heartache.'

Seagulls sailed through the blue sky, circling slowly, dropping one by one, on to the prow of a fishing boat, their harsh cries heralding the day's end as Pauline and Aunt Bea walked along by the harbour, Pauline relaying to her the news about Scully. Aunt Bea sighed with relief. 'Course I always believed that you did no harm and, with Scully out of the way, it'll all die down. It'll be forgotten as soon as the next bit of scandal hits town.' Pauline wasn't so sure that she agreed but she knew that now she would do what Sergeant Enright had said and get on with her life.

The sun glinted on the windows of distant houses. Cars moved slowly along the Sea Road, homeward bound. The full tide slapped sluggishly against the harbour wall. A noisy group of teenagers gathered, talking earnestly, passing cigarettes around. One of the girls laughed suddenly, jumped up and ran off towards the cove, her hair streaming in the wind, her laughter convulsing her as a tall, rangy lad loped after her. She stopped until he drew near, then ran off with him chasing her.

'The cut of her in the short dress,' Aunt Bea huffed disapprovingly. 'She'll catch her death.'

Pauline was feeling their childish freedom, that freedom of the long, harmonious summers of years ago, when, walking home from school, Clare, Eve and she would make plans to lure the boys. Bossy Clare, taking the lead in most of their games, running ahead to alert them that the boys were here or there. Drama unfolded at the beach or on picnics, wherever the boys might be. Pauline recalled Sneak Murphy falling off his bike at Eve's feet, Henry Joyce painstakingly removing the sticklebacks from Clare's clean white blouse after chasing her through a meadow, and Agnes Dolan's wrath at having to cut the same sticklebacks out of her daughter's mane of hair.

For the first time in eleven years, Pauline felt free. A shiver of pleasure coursed down her spine, as she went over every fragment of the information she had just been given, and repeated to herself, I am free, I am free. Now no one would ever have to find out about the circumstances of Martin's death and her involvement in it. Not Eve, not Aunt Bea. Not Agnes Dolan. She would go to confession. Properly this time. Not to Father McCarthy but to some strange priest, in a parish far away. She'd drive to Galway, maybe. Make a good confession, do penance.

'Young ones nowadays,' Aunt Bea said, her eyes on the giddy girls. 'They're uncouth. Dragged up.'

'I wore my skirts as short as that,' Pauline said, walking on, Aunt Bea following her.

'Don't I know it!' Aunt Bea said. 'But at least you had me to straighten you out. Parents nowadays don't care.'

'Summer's on its way,' Pauline remarked, looking at the exquisite gold-tipped wings of the seagulls. 'And I'm going back to the pub,' she announced as they moved off in the direction of the town.

'When?' Aunt Bea said.

'As soon as I leave Seamie back to school. I have to face it and, with Madge coming home, I'll have to air the place.'

'I'll give you a hand.'

'No, thanks. You've been away from the farm long enough. Dinny will be getting exasperated. I'll drop you back on my way to school with Seamie.'

'Do you think he'll settle down to some schoolwork now that this is all over?'

'I think so. He's not unhappy, you know. He loves the games and the choir.'

'Takes after me. I was in the local choir when I was a girl. Did I ever tell you that?'

'No,' and Pauline smiled as Aunt Bea started into one of her intricate stories as they set off for Ballingarret.

As soon as Pauline opened the door of the pub she burst into tears, ran upstairs, into the bathroom, and turned the shower on full. She tore off her clothes and stepped under the torrent, covered her head in shampoo and scrubbed her hair letting the full force of the water beat down on her upturned face, shoulders, her breasts. Tears blinded her as the foamy rivulets streamed down her legs, striking her sensitive skin until her thighs and hips were red. As the water poured down, a huge lump of grief dislodged itself and she cried out all her unarticulated anguish. Moments that she had not let herself think about – lifting the gun, holding it, firing the shot, Martin's splattered brains on the wall – were remembered and expressed in the pain that echoed through the flat and hailed the first notch in the healing process.

Abruptly she turned off the water, and dried herself roughly. Wrapped in her dressing-gown she made a pot of tea. Exhausted, still sniffing, she went to bed, where she snuggled under the duvet and thought about the past terrifying weeks, vowing that she would never again make the mistakes she had made in the past.

Her life was about to change, she thought. She would get a place of her own, as soon as Madge was well, and not continue to live in the flat over the pub, without a stick of furniture to call her own and Madge's family photographs on the walls. She wouldn't waste any more valuable time and energy dwelling on the past either. The old photographs and letters she kept in a shoebox under her bed would be torn up: photographs too faded for her to see what her mother had looked like, letters too inconclusive in their information to satisfy her curiosity, the neat handwriting leaving her wondering. The few possessions Pauline had of her mother's provided only flashes of memory: her wedding ring, her silver hairbrush, strands of her hair still in it. At that moment Pauline felt the loss of her mother more keenly than ever. If she had lived, her own life would have been so different.

But from now on she would take responsibility for her own life. Make decisions for herself. Nobody would ever again assault her mind as Martin Dolan and Scully had and get away with it.

She woke the next morning with a thumping headache and lay facing the window, staring at the soft light creeping under the curtains. This was the first day on which she would attempt to fall back into the pattern of life in Glencove.

After breakfast she lit the range in the cold kitchen, peeped into the shadowy sitting room on her way down to the bar. There she wiped clean the surfaces, washed and hung out the glass cloths to dry, and swept the floor – jobs she had delegated for too long, small, routine acts that gave order to her life and a pattern to her day. All the time she kept reminding herself that she was free to do as she liked: to come and go as she pleased, to marry if she wished, to have more children. She'd never been married. Hadn't given it any thought since Seamus's death. Maybe she *should* settle down. There'd been enough anarchy in her life. She was wiser now, having learned the hard way that love can cause a great deal of suffering. But she wasn't bitter. She just felt entitled to a measure of happiness.

Yes, she might get married, have another child. The thought frightened her as she remembered how terrified she'd been when she first held the fragile bundle that Mrs Muldoon, the midwife, had placed in her arms: the tight fists coiled like springs, her baby's trusting grip of her finger.

She'd missed a great precious part of Seamie's babyhood: his first tooth, its imprint still on the red plastic teething ring Aunt Bea had bought him, his squib of fine hair. Besotted Madge in letters to Pauline recorded his funny antics, letters she'd never received because Madge had no address for her. Madge had given them to her years later and she'd kept them in her shoebox along with his teething ring and his first pair of kid shoes. All testaments to the fact that she hadn't been there to guide his first steps, dry his tears, applaud his achievements.

Now Seamie was a twelve-year-old and his gangly body housed an awkward, sensitive, sometimes suspicious person, whose frequent mood swings fluctuated between elation and depression. Pauline would rack her brains to find release for his intense boredom, which seemed to be the preserve of teenagers. A shopping trip to Dublin, on a weekend break, to buy him jeans or she could take him to the latest movie at the Ambassador or the Carlton, for burgers and fries at McDonald's afterwards.

When she'd finished her chores she went back up to the flat. She washed her hands then gazed into the bathroom mirror, puzzling over her hair, checking her skin, wincing at the serious expression in her eyes, her thinness in the ill-fitting dress. 'Smile', she said to the mirror. 'Wake up and join the real world again, Pauline Quirk.'

Later she went out before the pub got busy. She walked down the Sea Road to the harbour, passing vehicles parked by the pier wall where fishermen in yellow oilskins stood talking, securing ropes to large iron rings, boxes of fish piled up beside them. Huddled into her windcheater she passed by swiftly and veered towards the stretch of green path that led over the ridge to the cove. The sharp wind made her eyes water as she drew near to the row of labourers' cottages crouched into the headland where Dermy McQuaid lived. It flattened the long, neglected grass on either side of the path. She marched along, undaunted by a sudden squall of rain. Dermy had been ill and she was on her way to visit him. Her first social call for ages. Suddenly, focusing on the heaving blue water, at once familiar and comforting, she wasn't afraid.

Chapter Thirty-Six

'I'm glad you're going back to David,' Dorothy said to Eve, over lunch at the hotel.

'You are?' Eve said, taken aback at her mother's decisive tone.

'He'll be getting restless,' Dorothy said, taking a sip of wine. 'You've been home since the end of January. He'll think you've forgotten all about him.'

'I suppose you're right,' Eve said reluctantly.

'Don't concern yourself about me,' Dorothy went on. 'I'll be fine.'

Eve was not in the least anxious about her mother's ability to cope. Over recent weeks she had noticed a growing of strength in her. There had been a shift in the balance of Dorothy's thinking: her loss of interest in her home and garden in favour of her appearance. Dorothy had recently begun wearing brightly coloured sports sweaters, patterned slacks and leisure suits. Her lipstick was bright and her hair neatly permed.

'As a matter of fact,' Dorothy said casually, and with a slight frown, 'Desmond has asked me to marry him.'

Eve felt her stomach hit the floor. She kept her eyes on the tumble of hothouse roses in the vase over the stone fireplace. She had never dreamed that another man would captivate Dorothy. Desmond Mackey had charmed her with his undivided attention, and his little terms of endearment.

'What did you tell him?' she asked, noting the light in Dorothy's eyes, the smile hovering on her lips.

'Naturally I said I would,' Dorothy said, with girlish pleasure.

Lost for words Eve looked at her.

'You seem surprised,' Dorothy said.

'It's a bit of a shock, that's all.'

'Desmond thinks we ought to sell up and buy a place of our own.'

'This *is* your own.'

'It's mine, not his and he'd like us to make a fresh start together. Perhaps Malahide, or Howth.'

'That's the far side!'

'Well, yes.' Dorothy hesitated. 'He's a member of Malahide golf club.'

'Don't you need some time to think about it all?' Eve asked.

'We don't have the luxury of time at our age,' Dorothy snapped.

'But you don't know him very well.'

'I know him well enough. He's a kind, thoughtful man.'

Dorothy had been happy enough living alone in her bijou house in the Dell, a corner of what had been originally Joyce's field, filling her life with flower-arranging on Tuesdays, bridge on Wednesdays, golf on Fridays. She'd met Desmond at a golf outing the previous August, and now she was about to settle down with him. A man Eve had met only a couple of times.

'I think June is a lovely month for a wedding,' Dorothy was saying. 'All those beautiful roses. Don't look so glum, Eve. It's something to look forward to. A good excuse for you to come home.'

'Yes.' Eve sank into her armchair, swamped with the burden of having to provide a suitable wedding for her highly strung pernickety mother and her beau.

'I'd better start making plans,' said the astute Dorothy. 'Of course, we'll be having the reception in the Glencove.'

Eve wished she could summon up congratulations and good wishes, but she was too stunned to think. And what about Agnes Dolan? What would happen to her?

Agnes lived alone, collected her pension, watered her plants, tended her garden, cleaned for Dorothy three times a week, and drank copious cups of tea while reading the daily newspaper. Her curtains still dazzled white in the sunshine and her linoleum was waxed and polished to a high gleam as was her glass-fronted china cabinet, which held Clare's music trophies, rows and rows of silver cups, polished and preserved to show off to the neighbours.

'So, what do you think of Mummy's news?' Eve asked as soon as Agnes answered the door.

'I can't believe it,' Agnes said. 'Not that she isn't perfectly entitled to remarry. After all, she's alone a long time now. And she's a widow too.'

'That's true,' Eve mused. 'Do you know, Agnes, I hardly know this man.'

'He's all right. A bit dull for my liking, but they get on well. He plays bridge and there's the golf, of course. She's healthy and strong, plenty of life in her.'

'Who am I to object?' Eve said.

'No, nor me either. I'm delighted for her,' Agnes said, without conviction. 'Not that I think she's all that sure herself. She needs to get away and think. That's what I told her. It's a big step, you know, Eve.' Agnes drummed her strong fingers on the kitchen table, her mouth squeezed tight. Eve, who knew her so well, saw the shock it had caused her in the crease of her brow and the grey pallor of her skin.

'What will you do if she goes to live in Malahide?'

'I'll go with her.'

'Just like that?'

Agnes nodded. 'I've promised her I would. We've been together all our lives.'

'Don't I know it!' Eve agreed.

'We're hardly going to let a man come between us at this stage,' Agnes said, with a twinkle in her eye.

Eve laughed. 'What about your home?'

Agnes shrugged. 'It'll be here when I come back.'

'Mother's getting married again,' she said to Pauline.

Pauline gaped at her.

'I know Daddy isn't dead very long but as far as she's concerned he's been dead for the last eleven years.'

'Good for her,' Pauline said. 'I'm delighted.'

'She tells me not to worry about her but I think she's doing it because she's lonely,' Eve said.

'She deserves a bit of happiness,' Pauline said. 'She's had a hard time of it.'

Eve agreed. Then she said, resignedly, 'I'm all packed.'

'I'll take you to the airport,' Pauline said.

'Thanks. That'd be great.'

'How do you feel about going?'

Eve looked around her bedroom, at the suitcase full of clothes, the open drawers, the empty wardrobe, and Katie's toys piled in a cardboard box in the corner waiting to be stowed in the loft.

'I suppose I'll get used to living out of a suitcase,' she said, lying back on her bed, her eyes on the ceiling, wishing she could take Katie and go anywhere but New York. She wondered what David was doing at that minute. Was he at home preparing for her return? Going to bed excited at the thought of having her back? She doubted it.

He was probably on the telephone, talking to an important client.

She had spoken to him regularly on the telephone, giving him the excuse of Pauline's trial for her prolonged stay. Also, there had been the rapid growth in business with the introduction of the summer specials, and her proposal to Jasper.

David had listened politely, but had been barely able to keep the bitterness out of his voice when he explained to her that without his family he felt lost. 'I need you,' he'd said, not in a grovelling way, but matter-of-factly. 'I need you here, breathing the same air as me, and I find it difficult to say this.'

Flattered but baffled, too, Eve wondered how such a tough businessman like David could have suddenly become so possessive. He seemed to want her with him now more than ever, but to run his home, applaud his victories. She wondered if she'd ever been truly in love with him. But now she felt she had no choice but to go back to David, knowing that she was hurting him too much by staying away. It didn't make the leaving any easier. She lay in bed for hours, thinking and thinking, and sometimes weeping quietly to herself. When she phoned him to give him the date and time of her arrival he said, 'I'm glad you're coming *home*. It's no fun being on my own.'

Each day Pauline took her meals, did her chores, read the newspaper, but still hadn't the courage to show her face in the bar. Instead, she sat answering letters and cards she'd received from well-wishers, while Mrs Browne thumped around preparing Madge's bedroom, airing the mattress, ironing sheets, sharing morsels of news whenever she thought of them. Madge was coming back and Pauline wondered how things would be.

The thought that dominated all others was of Geoff. Geoff was a cautious man. If he ever did return to her, he would come with the full knowledge of her past, and his acceptance of it. But she wanted him to know that her name had been cleared. How could she contact him? When Mrs Browne left, earlier than usual, one morning, she phoned Dwyer's Building Contractors, his previous employers, and asked for a forwarding address. The female voice at the other end said, 'I'm sorry, I'm afraid I can't give you that information. It's against the rules. If you'd like to leave a message we could pass it on.'

Pauline refused, thanked her and hung up. She'd get his phone number from somewhere. She'd tell him that everything was all right now, that maybe there was a chance for them. She was desperate to hear his voice.

What if he turned on her? Asked her what she wanted exactly, his voice cold, distant? That she couldn't bear. The best thing to do would be to write him a note. Just a few words on a page to let him know that he was on her mind. She sat at Madge's bureau, wrote the date on the top righthand corner of the pink notepaper then paused, wondering how to fill the blank page. She wrote 'Dear Geoff,' and stopped, picturing him standing on scaffolding, or sitting behind the wheel of a crane, his yellow hard-hat on his head, his beautiful eyes concentrated on a swinging pallet of bricks. As his image dissolved a new urgency took hold. Her hand shook as she wrote, 'I'm free, I love you.' She addressed the envelope to Dwyer's and posted it before she had a chance to change her mind.

Madge was frail. When she stood up to walk she felt light and hollow as if a gust of wind might blow her away. Only the clothes she wore had any substance. Having spent so long in a nightdress and dressing-gown, they were heavy and cumbersome.

'I don't want any fuss,' she told Pauline, baffled by the

quietness of the flat after the busy hospital ward that she had become used to. She lay in bed every morning gazing at the swaying creeper outside her bedroom window. She had always hoped that a day would come when she could take her ease. Now she had too much time on her hands. Time to watch the sun rise over the rooftops, to look at the colours of the sky, blue, lavender, violet, indigo, and its ever-changing patterns.

The rattle of milk bottles woke her at around six. From then on she measured her day against the bell for the ten o'clock mass, opening time, the Angelus bell, schoolchildren returning home, closing time. She had nothing to do but think and recover and, though she didn't complain, Pauline knew that she hated having to stay in bed.

Mrs Browne, perky-faced and bright-eyed, a heart-shaped brooch pinned to her bosom, appeared at her bedroom door each morning with a cup of coffee. 'I'm off to town with Mrs Rooney,' she said, one morning. 'Her horse came in at twenty to one and she's treating me to tea in the Savoy and that new film, *Ordinary People*, afterwards. Robert Redford's in it.'

'I wondered why you were all dressed up,' Madge said, feeling sorry for herself. 'Well for you, able to get out and about.'

'You'll be right as rain yourself in no time. Sure aren't you looking great? We'll be off to the pictures together in no time.'

Madge smiled at the flattery. Over the years she had learned to see through Mrs Browne and not to take everything she said at face value. 'To tell you the truth I'm more concerned about Pauline than I am about myself,' she confided.

'It's been a nightmare!' Mrs Browne agreed.

'All the trouble she brought on herself mixing with the likes of Seamus Gilfoyle. What she saw in him I'll never know. I told her so at the time.'

'Oh, a queer detail he was. No doubt about it.'

Madge nodded. 'She had to learn it the hard way, God love her. What a lesson.'

In Madge's recollections Pauline had been a rebellious girl, strutting and posing in the daytime, afraid of the dark at night. Not that she would ever admit to it. 'I'm praying to the Holy Spirit to guide her. I'd like to see her happy and settled with someone suitable.'

'You're looking for a miracle,' Mrs Browne said, under her breath.

With each day Madge improved. Before long death was losing its grip on her mind. Gradually Mrs Browne transformed herself into the role of nurse-companion, and spent most of her time perched at the end of Madge's bed, her knitting in her lap, her chores left to Pauline. She delivered newspapers, books from the library, endless cups of tea, and even read tit-bits out of the newspaper to her sometimes.

Soon Madge could walk as far as Dr Gregory's surgery. After a while she felt able to get to the harbour to feed the seagulls.

One day out of the blue she announced to Pauline, 'I'm thinking of going back behind the bar. I might as well be doing something. Dr Gregory thinks an hour or two a day wouldn't do me any harm. Might even be good for me.'

'I should be back there too,' Pauline said. 'It's not fair leaving it all to Tommy.'

'Nonsense,' Madge retorted. 'I appreciate having you up here with me. What a couple we make. A pair of crocks propping each other up.'

When Madge went back behind the bar, Pauline made sure she didn't stay too long, but noted the subtle change that took place in her once she started scratching at the surface of her old life. Her determination and courage, as she stepped forward each day with new strength, was amazing, and swept Pauline along with her. When her customers asked how she was coping, she'd reply, 'I'd feel much better if I were allowed to do a bit more. I can't stand sitting around!'

Chapter Thirty-Seven

Pauline drove Eve and Katie to the airport, promising Eve that she would think about joining her soon. She stayed with them until they went through the departure gates. Eve, who was not looking forward to the long journey in a cramped space, boarded the plane with trepidation. Katie sat beside her, over-excited and restless. Mercifully she slept until they were served their meal, and afterwards a colouring book and crayons were produced to ease the tedium of the flight for her.

While Katie coloured, Eve sat, hands pressed together. She was returning to David as to a refuge, knowing that if she wanted to hold her head high in Glencove, or anywhere for that matter, she would have to remain the wife of David Furlong. At her age, and with a young daughter, there were no choices left to her. She'd made her bed, and she must lie on it. From now on she would make a determined effort to avoid any more hurt between herself and David. She would adjust to life in New York. She would make plans for her new business, plans that would grow and, no doubt, spread into something useful.

Darkness came on gradually. Slowly they descended from the star-studded sky, Eve drowsy, Katie clasped tightly to her, fast asleep.

Katie woke to see the runway stretching out before her, its lights sheening the smooth surface. 'We're home,' Eve said as the aircraft stopped, and helped her on with her coat, fastening the buttons.

'Daddy will be here,' Katie said, taking her mother's outstretched hand. They made their way slowly down the aisle, went through Customs straggling behind the other passengers.

David was standing alone, head erect, shoulders squared, his eyes scanning the crowd until he saw them. Then he was lifting Katie up in his arms, embracing Eve, his fingers touching her face. 'You made it,' he said, with a smile.

Eve suddenly felt dizzy, but Katie, alert, wrapped round his neck was nearly choking him with love. Eve would have preferred to hail a cab and make her own way home, then greet him in private.

Their awkwardness with one another lasted through all the traffic.

Near home Katie cried, 'There's Amy's house,' recognising the familiar streets.

But when they went in, apart from the vase of flowers on the hall table, there was nothing familiar or homely to welcome them. Katie ran from room to room, shrieking and thumping on the wood-block floors, David trying to calm her with a promise of chocolate-chip ice-cream in her favourite downtown ice-cream parlour. Eve stared at the pristine white kitchen, wondering how she would ever make a life for them all here. How she would ever accept that New York was her home.

David made tea, put their mugs on the table, and poured milk into Katie's Toby mug, eager for news of his family. Eve told him that his parents were in good health, that nothing had changed, keeping her revelations about the hotel until later, when they could be told slowly, without interruption.

Later, in bed, they lay awake, talking. 'I've missed you, Eve,' David said, his arm around her shoulders. She knew it was true. How many times had she wished he wouldn't say it during their telephone conversations because it made her feel bad? Now, lying beside him, she was glad to hear it. 'Did you miss me?' he asked.

'Yes,' she said, merging into his arms, glad that it was the truth.

It was Madge who saw Geoff first, in the doorway, his eyes a startling blue as he surveyed the place.

Furtively she drew Pauline's attention by digging her elbow into her and whispering, 'Here's Geoff Ryan.'

'Oh!' was all Pauline said on coming out of the kitchenette and seeing him standing there.

'Hello, Pauline,' he said, his eyes crinkling at the corners, his jaw resolute.

'Hello.' She didn't ask him where he'd come from or what he was doing there. There was no need. She saw it in the sparkle of his eyes. They stood staring boldly at one another, unaware of the hunger in their eyes. She knew him by heart. Knew the way he smiled, the clothes he was wearing. A glow of warmth spread over her, softened her face, filled her eyes with tears, forced her to lower her head. 'I can't believe it,' she said, as she walked slowly towards him. Geoff held his arms out to her and she went into them like a child, pressing her face against the comforting tweed of his jacket.

Slowly, he led her out of the bar and they went up to the flat.

Geoff's face was soft in the mellow light. Her awareness of him was so strong that, thrilled yet terrified, she closed her eyes, waiting for the wild beatings of her heart to subside.

'Do you remember the first day you walked into the convent grounds?' he said.

She nodded.

'I took one look at you and everything went into a spin. I'd never laid eyes on you before and suddenly I wanted to take you to dinner, buy you beautiful clothes, spend every minute of the rest of my life with you. So let's get out of here now,' he whispered into her ear. 'While they're all too busy enjoying themselves to miss us.'

They drove to his flat in Bray, where they fell on to the bed, Pauline pressing herself against him, pulling him down on top of her. He broke away and went to stand by the window. She froze, thinking that he didn't want her until she saw he was undressing. She peeled off her stockings, slowly revealing her naked body. 'I can't stand this a minute longer,' he said as he came to her, and held her close, his body fitting hers perfectly. Kissing her neck, shoulders, the valley between her breasts, eventually he slid inside her to renew and restore. They moved together in a slow rhythm until suddenly the tempo changed. Their bodies convulsed, and she heard his strangled cry. Lying close together, the sweat of his body on hers, there was a sense of peace between them.

The following afternoon they walked along the path towards the cove, climbed up over the ridge way above the houses of Glencove.

'It's a long time since we were alone like this.' Geoff looked at her purposefully.

'Not that long.'

'It seems a lifetime. I kept away from you because you asked me to. It was hard but I knew it was for the best.'

Pauline continued walking beside him, not even raising her eyes to look at him.

'I didn't come back because I felt sorry for you, Pauline, or because I think you need someone to take care of you, but because I love you. I've been in love with you since I first laid eyes on you. I think you know that.'

They faced one another. 'I love you,' Geoff said.

The sun rose over the shining rocks on the beach below, new washed and slippery from the full tide. They walked on, the expanse of sea below them, the rocks to the right rising above them. Finally Geoff stopped. The wind had softened his face, giving him a boyish look. Pauline stared at him as he stood with his hands in his pockets, the sky beyond him the same blue as his eyes. 'I love you,' he said again.

She leaned against his shoulder, a cry of joy bursting from her heart. 'I love you too.'

They went quickly back the way they had come, displacing loose stones in their haste, holding each other to prevent themselves from slipping.

In the restaurant in Arklow Pauline traced the raised gold rim of the champagne glass she held in her hand, and watched the way the sunlight from the window fell on his shoulder, his face, his eyes, as he smiled at her and said, 'Here's to us.'

'To us,' she echoed, raising her glass.

He took her hand in his, and held it tight, his words of love coming to her slowly, making her world a place in which she was happy at last to be. Through the window she watched the swans trailing along the water on their way home, thinking of the miracle of it all, rejoicing.

'Well,' David said, from the bedroom door, 'is everything all right?'

'Everything's fine,' Eve said, replacing the receiver, keeping her hand on it, unwilling to lose the connection between herself and Nathan Sherman. He was a director of one of the largest banks in America, and he was prepared to give her credit to help her establish Freeman's in New York.

David sat down on the bed. 'What did he say?' he asked.

'I'm in business,' Eve said. 'Just think of all that's happened in a few short weeks. I can't believe it.'

David laughed. 'We still have to find you suitable premises.'

'Mr Sherman's going to help with that too. He's putting out feelers among his clients and he says—' She stopped to catch her breath, her plans unfolding like a great drama. Her joy caught David, too, her excitement captivating him. To David, the change in his wife was breathtaking. The boredom and depression had gone and Eve now looked forward to a bright future. Nothing was going to get in its way.

'I suppose life goes in cycles,' she said.

'Exactly what I was thinking,' he replied. 'A woman like you should never be bored. It shouldn't have happened. I was selfish to think that you'd be happy to spend all your time on Katie and me and the house. I suppose I convinced myself that I worked so hard I deserved it.'

'You do,' Eve assured him. 'Only I'm not a stay-at-home woman.'

'Let's celebrate tonight,' David said. 'Let's go out to dinner.'

That evening, Eve found she could talk to him properly at last, about her feelings of isolation in their sudden uprooting to New York, Jasper's hold over her hotel, Pauline's trouble. She refused to let herself dwell on the intricate patterns of the green fields and narrow dusty lanes of Ireland. Refused to let herself think about Henry. She owed it to Katie to make this marriage work.

That night they held each other in their bed. David's love for her, his patience, his gentleness and the nightmare of her loneliness made her reach out to him, and let her love him once more.

'Let's take ourselves off for a second honeymoon,' he said.

'What a terrific idea,' she said brightly, her new determination to be happy making her happier already.